Praise for *The Last Wolf*

ERTY OF
LIBRARY

"Wonde … enthralled!"

—Jea … selling author

"Raw, w … e final page."

—Amanda Bouchet, *USA Today* bestselling author of The Kingmaker Chronicles

"Pushes boundaries, and keeps you at the edge of your seat."

—Terry Spear, *USA Today* bestselling author of the Heart of the Wolf series

"[Vale's] outstanding worldbuilding makes this sensuous tale of life and love in the Pack—a werewolf society—well worth reading. Spellbound readers will watch for the next installment."

—*Booklist*, Starred Review

"A standout…a dense, gooey chocolate cake in page form. A wonderfully descriptive paranormal romance that breathes some much-needed life into the subgenre."

—*Kirkus Reviews*

"The unique, believable worldbuilding, flashes of humor, and Old Norse references make this exceptional debut of a promising series a solid choice for all paranormal readers."

—*Library Journal*

"The dark, rich world of Vale's debut novel is instantly engaging."

—*RT Book Reviews*

NO LONGER PROPERTY OF
SEATTLE PUBLIC LIBRARY

Also by Maria Vale

The Legend of All Wolves

The Last Wolf

A WOLF APART

MARIA VALE

Copyright © 2018 by Maria Vale
Cover and internal design © 2018 by Sourcebooks, Inc.
Cover design by Dawn Adams/Sourcebooks, Inc.
Cover art by Kris Keller

Sourcebooks and the colophon are registered trademarks of Sourcebooks, Inc.

All rights reserved. No part of this book may be reproduced in any form or by any electronic or mechanical means including information storage and retrieval systems—except in the case of brief quotations embodied in critical articles or reviews—without permission in writing from its publisher, Sourcebooks, Inc.

The characters and events portrayed in this book are fictitious or are used fictitiously. Any similarity to real persons, living or dead, is purely coincidental and not intended by the author.

Published by Sourcebooks Casablanca, an imprint of Sourcebooks, Inc.
P.O. Box 4410, Naperville, Illinois 60567-4410
(630) 961-3900
Fax: (630) 961-2168
sourcebooks.com

Printed and bound in the United States of America.
OPM 10 9 8 7 6 5 4 3 2 1

To M, H & G. My life and my loves.

Wulf is on iege, ic on oþerre.	*My wolf is on one island, I on another.*
Fæst is þaet eglond, fenne biworpen.	*Secure he is on that island, circled by fens.*
Sindon wælhreowe weras þaer on ige.	*They are bloodthirsty men on this island.*
Willað hy hine aþecgan gif he on þreat cymeð.	*They will oppress him if he comes to them.*
Ungelice is us.	*We are not alike.*
Wulf, min Wulf. Wena me þine	*Wolf, my wolf. My need for you*
Seoce gedydon, þine seldcymas	*Has made me sick. Your seldom-comings*
Murnende mod, nales meteliste.	*Disturb my mind, not the lack of prey.*
Ungelice is us.	*We are not alike.*
Þæt mon eaþe toslited þætte naefre gesomnad wæs:	*It breaks easily that which was never made one:*
Uncer giedd geador.	*Our song together.*
Ungelice is us.	*We are not alike.*

—From "Wolf and the Watcher,"
the tenth-century *Book of Exeter*

Chapter 1

I'VE DONE IT SO OFTEN, I DON'T HAVE TO THINK ABOUT IT anymore. My hands hardly seem to belong to me as they unfasten my cuff links. A quick twist to the left, then to the right. One after the other, they plink into the silver Tiffany tray beside the sink.

The tray is engraved in flowing eighteenth-century script, an absurdity for the plastics industry.

To Elijah Sorensson
with Gratitude from
Americans for Progressive Packaging

The platinum chain links with a bar in between were another gift. This from Aldrich Halvors to mark my first day at Halvors & Trianoff, nearly twenty-three years ago. Our Alpha, Nils, had just died. Shot along with his mate. And now another bullet has taken his successor, John.

Aldrich told me the cuff links were a reminder that no matter where we found ourselves, we were still crucial parts of the chain that bound the entire Pack.

Halvors. His real name, his Pack name, was Aldrich Halvorsson, but he gave that up. Just as he gave up any rank within the Pack hierarchy. When he died, he was the Omicron of his echelon even though he had once been so strong. Being Offland—being away from our Adirondack territory, being in skin for twenty-seven days at a stretch, being surrounded by humans—does that to you. Leaches your strength. Leaches your will. Leaches your soul.

Aldrich had already been Offland for years when I first met him in New York City, representing the Great North Pack's interests in a human-staffed firm founded with Pack money. Lori, who was Aldrich's assistant before she started to work for the surviving partner, now *my* partner, Maxim Trianoff, says that at the end, Aldrich had become increasingly withdrawn and would stare out the firm's huge plate-glass windows for days at a time.

He needed to go home.

An hour after he stared out that plate-glass window for the last time, Maxim got a call from the police. Aldrich had wrapped his car around a lamppost on the West Side Highway. He wasn't wearing a seat belt.

Wasn't wearing any clothes either.

It was a simple accident, but if the coroner had gotten involved, they'd have found that the corned beef hash in the driver's seat had been a man halfway to becoming a wolf.

He just couldn't wait another minute.

Almost makes me wonder if there's something in the HST offices. I gave two wolves who have been Offland as long as I have a ride down to the City this moon. Reena, who sits on the U.S. Second Circuit Court of Appeals, and her mate, Ingmar, who does something I couldn't quite figure out for the New York Department of State, only go home for the very rare holidays. And, of course, for the Iron Moon. For those three days out of thirty, when the moon is pregnant and full and her law is Iron and the Pack has no choice but to be wild.

Subordinate wolves in the 2nd Echelon, Reena and Ingmar seem unaffected by the tearing alienation of Offland. They yacked the whole way about lawyers and restaurants and real estate and *Hamilton*. It was like being trapped in an enclosed space with humans for five hours. Except without that horrible smell of carrion and steel humans always have.

I would've bitten them, but they're not in my echelon.

I toss my shirt (Turnbull) into the dry-cleaning bag and hang my suit (Brioni) before stepping into my marble-and-copper-tile shower stall.

My. Nothing in this apartment is *mine*. It was bought sight unseen from floor plans by Pack money managers who had determined that it was likely to appreciate, so when it came time for me to leave New York, the Great North would be able to net a tidy profit.

Remember that things Offland break easily, they said, as though I hadn't been warned repeatedly. As though the Pack hadn't already had to pay to replace various pixie-stick constructions that pass as furniture out here.

Don't do anything that will damage the resale value.

So I'm particularly careful when I scrub off the last remnants of my change, because I've already had to replace the showerhead once. The shower stall may be generously sized by human standards, but by Packish standards, it's a tight squeeze.

Then I carefully wipe out the drain strainer, scraping

out the fur and leaves and prickles of my home into the trash can.

In my bedroom, I hit the switch that changes the floor-to-ceiling windows from opaque to transparent. And when I stand here in skin, I have unobstructed views over the East River and can watch the moonrise and calculate how long it will be before I can go home again.

I am not like Aldrich. I did not give up my name—my Pack name—so now Halvors, Sorensson & Trianoff is acid-etched on the glass doors.

I did not give up my position either. Plenty have tried, but I am too strong and have fought too many wolves for too many years. Even the most powerful, most belligerent wolves of the Great North have begun to realize that there is no one powerful or belligerent enough to unseat me as Alpha of the 9th Echelon, the age group I have controlled since we made the transition to adulthood.

The Pack has been in turmoil since September when a badly injured Shifter came to us. All Packs hate and fear Shifters. Shifters can change, but unlike us, they don't *have* to, and that single difference has allowed them to become almost human, to become as corrupt and self-serving as humans.

The Iron Moon, those three days when we must be wild, is a sacred time for us, but like anything that is truly important, it comes with risks.

The risk that humans will come upon us by accident and, thinking that we are *ǽcewulfas*, real wolves, forever wolves, kill us. The risk that Shifters with their almost Packish senses will come upon us on purpose and, knowing exactly what we are, kill us.

If it had been up to me, I would have left Tiberius for

the coyotes that first night, but he was half Pack, and our Alpha, John, was soft. Soft on him, soft on Quicksilver, the runt who is now the Shifter's mate.

It turned out he was a lie. He had been sent to infiltrate us, find our weaknesses, by the godfather of all the Shifters, August Leveraux, his father. The fact that Tiberius changed allegiances from Shifter to Pack is in his nature. In the Old Tongue, Shifters are called *Hwerflic*. Changeable.

He killed many of the Shifters and humans who descended on us during the Iron Moon. I killed one. But the Great North Pack lost the Great Hall, our main gathering place. We almost lost our pups, our future. We lost four wolves, all of them highly placed, because the true meaning of leadership is sacrifice.

At the end of this Iron Moon, we laid the stones for the wolves we'd lost at the *Gemyndstow*, the memory place: Solveig Kerensdottir, Alpha of the 14th Echelon. Orion Tyldesson, Alpha of the 5th. Paula Carlsdottir, Beta of the 8th. And John Sigeburgsson, Alpha of the Great North, the Alpha of Alphas.

But John's stone, like all the others, is marked only with his name and the date of his last hunt. The Pack is a thing of hierarchies, but there is no hierarchy in death.

The ritual was silent, as our most important rituals always are. A nod to all those times we are wild and speechless. At the very center of the widening circle of stones are the worn ones of Ælfrida, the Alpha who dragged her unwilling Pack from the dying forests of Mercia to the New World all those centuries ago, and Seolfer, her Deemer.

The dozen or so pups run in and out among the

stones, understanding only that somehow this place is important and that every important place must be marked. So they do.

The stones are set. There are no bodies here. Those were quickly consumed by the coyotes, which is why we call them *wulfbyrgenna*. Wolf tombs. So death has been honored, and now we must get on with life.

As we walked back toward the Great Hall, I fell in step beside Evie, John's mate and the new Alpha. The fourth wolf I have addressed by that title.

"Alpha, it's time for me to come home. The 9th needs me. I have been Offland for thirty years"—it slipped out, but I quickly correct myself—"three hundred and sixty moons and—"

"And we need you protecting our interests Offland more than ever." She picks up a pup who is jumping at her ankles and rubs him against her jaw, marking him. He lies on his back, offering up his belly to be rubbed, but as soon as he hears another pup, he twists and turns, anxious to get back down. They are like that. They need love, but they need freedom too.

"The Pack is vulnerable now, and no one knows better than you how to protect us from the human world. I agree with you that the 9th needs its Alpha, but it doesn't have to be you. It is time for you to let your shielder take primacy; Celia's been holding the echelon together for years, and it's time, Elijah. It's time for you to let go."

Long after she left, I stayed staring down into the foundation of the Great Hall being laid on the still-blackened, smoke-scented foundation of the old one. It is cavernous and complicated because we need storage and because the frost line is so deep.

What Evie doesn't understand is that I am blind in a maze, with only this thread to hold on to. If I let go, I will never find my way out again.

At 3:00 a.m., when the city that never sleeps finally does, the twenty-four-hour fitness center of my luxury condominium building is finally empty.

That's when I drag out the cambered power bar that I store in my hall closet. Turns out that the cheap things they have at the gym develop a permanent kink once you load on eight hundred pounds.

Evie refused my request, and Evie is immensely powerful, but females take at least three moons to recover from lying-in. It has been only two. Meaning she will still be weak for one more moon.

I have spent over ten thousand days Offland. That's ten thousand days in skin. Ten thousand days without the earth of home under my paws, without the pine-scented breezes rolling down the mountainside and through my fur, without the bones of prey, real prey, giving up their marrow to my powerful jaws.

But I refuse to end up like Halvors: corned wolf hash, wrapped around a streetlight on the West Side Highway.

One.

I am going home.

Two.

I am going home.

Three.

I am going home.

Four.

I am going home.

"What are you looking at?" I bark at the balding man staring at my overloaded bar. He stumbles backward over the threshold to the gym. The lid to his water bottle trundles across the floor.

He leaves it.

Five.

I am going home.

Chapter 2

JEANS (D&G), T-SHIRT (ARMANI), JACKET (CUCINELLI). A quick squint in the mirror at the state of my shave. Left side, right side, lift chin. My hair is long and red brown, though the tips are banded a darker color. Agouti is common enough for a sable wolf. Less common for corporate lawyers.

The one time I cut it, I spent two moons fighting wolves who made fun of my crew-cut hackles and a near-constant chill across my withers.

I wonder if this was how Aldrich felt toward the end. If he felt a little sicker with every breath that came from the HVAC system. With every drink of water that tastes like chlorine. With every meal of denatured things from half a world away. With every cab that stinks of human.

"Keep the windows open, please," I say, leaning forward so the driver can hear.

I wonder if Aldrich was as desperate for the hunt as I am. Did he indulge in the same pathetic stopgaps I do?

Nothing marks Testa but a dark-green door and a brass number and a prime spot on narrow New Street in a location that is convenient to the courts, City Hall, and the Financial District. There are a handful of clubs like this scattered through lower Manhattan that offer privacy, exclusivity, and smoking. Testa charges five hundred dollars for a single night's membership. There aren't any other kinds of membership, because the owners want to be able to refuse the man who's already wasted and likely to be an embarrassment. The man who misbehaved last time. The man who is under investigation by the SEC.

Men. Women—if they're young enough, beautiful enough, trim enough, and well-dressed enough—get in for free. Members then stand them drinks.

The lights are always low. There are no large tables, only booths with high, tufted backs to mute the sound. It's all about giving the illusion of privacy, so we can hunt our prey without distraction.

I've learned that I don't need to bother with the booths. The bar is just fine. My back is to the room, but I can see as much as I need to in the mirror behind the brightly colored bottles of gin.

"Hey," says a voice. The voice's long blond hair falls in carefully blown-out waves down either side of her lightly tanned face with perfectly regular features. Dressed in a white backless dress with a low-draped collar showing supremely full breasts, she promises the warmth of summer in the dead of winter.

"Hey."

"My drink's a Moscow mule," she says, swinging onto the empty seat beside me.

I nod to the barman and then tap my glass for a refill.

"Wow," she says, putting her hand on my arm. "D'you play football?"

I shake my head, then, throwing my chin back, I bolt down a handful of wildly salty nuts.

"Basketball?"

"No. Not much for sports."

"Are you, like, in financial services?" she asks.

When you're hunting, all sorts of things happen. Without making a move, your heart starts to pound faster, your muscles tighten, your senses become razor-edged. Adrenaline primed, you are so ready to leap that the real strength, the real power, is in holding back until the moment is absolutely right.

It used to be like that, watching a beautiful woman, knowing that beneath the tape on her breasts, her nipples will be tightening, that she will be feeling an uncomfortable warmth.

Or will she? I can't really tell anymore.

"Lawyer."

"Oh," she says, a slight tinge of disappointment in her voice.

Noah, one of Testa's owners, comes over and hands me back my credit card. I lean up on one hip, retrieving my wallet.

As she watches me slide in the black-and-pewter card, she brightens. "Oh," she says. "That's interesting. I haven't seen you around here before."

"Hmm." Tomas, the mixologist, slides me my seltzer with bitters and lime. Wolves can't really drink. Does something awful to our livers. Tomas is discreet about my drinking habits because it's his job to be discreet, because the ownership certainly doesn't mind customers who don't use the bar as an all-you-can-eat buffet, and because I tip him well.

"Thanks, I guess," she says, lifting her Moscow mule toward me. She slides around on her seat, scanning the room, looking for someone who might be more responsive.

"Elijah Sorensson?"

In the mirror caught between the tall emerald-green bottle and the square blue bottle, the woman in white pauses as a sloppily drunk man I'm supposed to know slaps my shoulder. Pale-gray tweed jacket with black piping and a black shirt. Elaborately stitched jeans. He smells vaguely familiar. Like wild onion and rubber. I didn't say pleasant, just familiar.

"This man..." he slurs. "You remember, we bought Alacore? In 2015 we bought it. But the big abattoir around our neck"—I'm assuming he actually means *albatross*, not *slaughterhouse*—"was a busted-up cement plant up near... I don't know where." He waves his hand toward the Empire State Building so everyone will know he means north.

Now I remember. His name is Dante something. "Fort Miller," I say.

"I think you may be right. State says we're goin' to have to clean it up. For a lotta money." He rests one foot on the rung of my stool. "I don' remember how much, because this genius, he makes it out so that we don't have to do shit. Says the rotting concrete is good for climate change."

I'm not in the mood to explain the mechanics of concrete carbonation to Dante Something from the Mergers and Acquisitions Department at LMSC. It's part of my job. I'm very good at my job, and when I'm good at my job, I make money. Money that is used to protect another piece of land and a different wilderness up there. North.

"Well, anyway, the thing is still rottin' away." He guffaws again. "Rottin' from the inside out. Being good for the environment." He removes his foot from my stool but doesn't slap me again. Humans don't. They do it once to be comradely, but there's something about what they feel under my bespoke jacket that makes them nervous about doing it again.

I take another drink. The woman in white stands closer, her breast pressed against my arm.

"I haven't seen you here either," I say. Now I'm just going through the motions, mouthing the words to an old script. "I would certainly have remembered. No man could ever forget you." She looks exactly like half the beautiful women in this place. The other half have dark hair.

When she finishes her Moscow mule, I order her another. She's jabbering something about some start-up. An app that does something I don't have any use for, so I hear but don't actually listen. When her voice goes up in a lilting question, I nod or frown slightly, concerned. When conversation lags, I look intently at her irises for a beat or two past the norm and say something about sky or storms or chocolate, depending on their color. It's a body part humans set great stock in.

"Your skin is so soft." Lifting my arm is like lifting lead when I brush her hair back from her face and my fingers trace her cheek. "You should never wear anything but silk."

Her bleached-blond hair is dry and crisp, and feels like late-autumn sedge against the back of my hand.

~

Back when I first came Offland, there was something exciting about this game. Maybe it was just that it was unknown. *Cunnan*—the Old Tongue word for *sex* that

Pack use—that was something I knew. *Cunnan* serves two purposes: the pure feral joy of skin against skin and the infinitesimal chance that our chromosomes are at that rare moment in their slide along the spectrum of wildness when they are similar enough to create a new one of us.

In Intensive Human Behaviors for Offlanders, Leonora was quite clear. "Sex with humans has as much to do with *cunnan* as buying carrion wrapped in plastic has to do with hunting. Both will rot you from the inside out."

All juveniles are indiscriminate. No one has a bedfellow yet, just *schildere*, shielders, the wolves who serve as our companions and protectors. The wolves who watch over us during our more discretionary changes, so coyotes won't eat us when we're vulnerable. Who partner with us for our first real hunt so if we take a hoof to the head, someone can get help.

Shielders are fair game as long as they're not within the prohibited degrees of consanguinity, like Celia.

I was more indiscriminate and more priapic than most, which among Pack is saying something. I went to bed with an erection, woke up with an erection. Worked and studied and ate and fought with an erection.

My first week at college, I went through two whole boxes of Kleenex Mansize 3 Ply (soft *and* absorbent) before my roommate, Jeremy, asked if I could give it a rest for just a little while. Or take it into the shower. Or outside. Or anywhere that wasn't our room.

Leonora had been clear that humans frowned upon the public display of intercourse. She had not been at all clear that they frowned as well on the more solitary endeavors.

I didn't care what Leonora said. There was no way I was going to survive the coming years with nothing but my fist, so I started learning the human game.

There were many mistakes. When I slid my cheek along a girl's face to mark her. When I shuffled, stiff and engorged, at the foot of Marian's bed, staring at her, wondering when she was going to put her ass in the air and present already.

When I took the cords of her neck tight in my teeth and she screeched, deafening my sensitive ears.

It was Jeremy who took me under his wing and introduced me to pornography and the fertile imaginings of humans when it came to how bodies could be fit together.

Those movies were instructive, but also very hard to watch. Too often, men treated women like subordinates, doing things *to* them, rather than *with* them. They were gruesomely compelling, like a horror movie when all you can think is *Now, now she's going to do something very, very painful. Now*, I kept thinking, *now, she's going to get his balls in her carnassials and…*

Crunch, *snip*.

Wolves are always told that humans do things for one of two reasons: love or greed. In all my years Offland, I have seen all the many forms of greed—in which I count gluttony, betrayal, and envy—but I have yet to see something that counts as love.

I don't know when the thrill of the hunt died. My cock is so jaded now, but I can't help myself. It's like…it's like when you're a pup and the scent of prey hits you right in the back of the throat and everything tenses and you chase even though your tummy is little and full and all you really want is for that prey to escape so you don't have to eat it.

The woman in white doesn't. Escape, I mean. We end up, she and I, in the same old setting, one of the suites HST theoretically maintains for visitors from our offices in DC and Albany, but in reality, they serve all those politicians who need trysting spots in the City.

For a relatively small outlay and a useful tax write-off, it makes the power brokers quite pliable.

Every suite is exactly the same. Bold-patterned black-and-white wallpaper. King-size pillow-top bed in the middle of the wall facing the bathroom. Modern light fixtures and upholstered seating. Between bed and exit, there is a small table with two hard-backed chairs and a chilling bottle of midrange champagne. At one chair—always the one nearest the door—I take off my shoes and socks, then, with socks tucked neatly inside, slide them under, but not too far under. I fold my jacket across the back of the chair, followed by my T-shirt, then my jeans. My boxer briefs go on top.

From my breast pocket, I extract a condom, and not because I need one—we are too different to share diseases, and pregnancy is completely out of the question. I use them because of that thing Leonora said about sex with humans rotting you from the inside out. Humans take comfort from plastic-wrapping their carrion; I take comfort from latex-wrapping my cock. I am fooling myself into thinking that somehow it doesn't quite count.

She is stretched naked across the mattress, waiting for my appraisal. *Look at me*, her expression says. *I am young and beautiful, and you have money and power, so tonight*

I am giving myself to you. It is a transaction. She gives her body to me, I give mine to her, and we both bolster our positions within the elaborate human hierarchy.

Because I can't stand to see the calculating seduction in another woman's eyes, I hold her chest down with one hand, my finger and thumb working her nipple. The other hand holds down her hips while my mouth plies her furrow. I say appreciative things from time to time, but mostly I speed through my lines and my stale stage directions like an actor in his twenty-fifth year of a dinner theater production of *Death of a Salesman*.

As soon as she comes, I thread my semi-turgid member in, screw my eyes tightly closed, and find release.

It's certainly not *cunnan*. It's barely sex, because sex implies that at least two people are present.

In the end, I am left looking at the ceiling, waiting for her breathing to even and slow. I don't know how many Moscow mules this one has had, but it must have been a few. Her breath is sickly sweet, and she snores in the way that women do when they're chemically relaxed.

The senses of my human form are nowhere near as sharp as my wild self, but they are much better than humans, and the semidarkness of New York is as good as midday. Besides, my escape is so well rehearsed. I quickly pull my clothes on in the order that they lie folded across the chair, then pick up my shoes with the socks neatly tucked inside and head out.

I take the stairs to the back, where Juan, the night porter, is on duty. He doesn't say a word, just pulls out his key and opens the black door with the plastic panel that says *Luggage storage* and comes back with one of the broad, shallow, white boxes I keep there. It doesn't matter which, because the robes inside are all the same: small, like every woman I meet. Pearl gray, which suits every complexion. And silk. Just like I promised.

You should never wear anything but silk.

She told me her name. I know she did, but as I stare at the tiny white card with the circled *LP* on the front, I can't remember it. "Dear NAME HERE, I will never forget" is what I usually write, before promptly forgetting. Problem is, I've already forgotten.

Crumpling up the note, I ask Juan to deliver the box to whatever woman is in room 513.

I can't take this anymore.

Chapter 3

When I get back to my building, the night porter is busily polishing the brass.

"Nice evening, Mr. Sorensson?"

"It was fine, Saul. Thanks."

I lope past the acrid smell of polish, up the elevator that smells of takeout carrion lo mein, and into the apartment. Because I bought a model unit that no one had ever lived in, it didn't take long for the stench of carrion and steel and artificial sweeteners to dissipate.

Humans don't come here. The only thing I changed was the mattress. I left the queen in the hallway one Tuesday afternoon, so the men came and knocked and rang and eventually left the California king in its place. As soon as I was sure no one was around, I carried it into my apartment.

The only thing that is truly personal is the photograph, sandwiched between two pieces of UV-resistant glass, of my echelon the summer before we divided.

There are eighteen of us in the 9th Echelon. All born within five years of each other: Celia, my shielder, who runs things day to day, frames the left side; I frame the right. Between us are the other sixteen. Eight standing, eight crouching down, all side facing and squeezed together. Genetics as well as centuries of breeding to power mean we are very big on the human scale.

The reaction to one of us is dully familiar: "You play football?" We rarely go Offland in groups.

Some of us would go on to college and come back to run Pack businesses near the Homelands. Some of us would stay away longer. I remember staring at the shield on the acceptance letter to Yale Law School—with its crocodile, dog, and staples—and thinking with dread that from now on, I would be that dog, fastened far away, protecting my Pack from that crocodile.

The photograph shows a happy cluster of newly minted adults, but so much has changed. Nils was the Alpha at our *Daeling*, our Dealing. He was the one who watched as we fought for position within the hierarchy and cemented our transition from juveniles to adult. Not long after, he and his mate were shot by hunters. His brother, John, took over, and now, another bullet later, he is dead too, leaving his mate, Evie, as Alpha.

It has hit us all hard. I don't think humans could understand the ties that bind us. They have family, but the longer I live Offland, the more I realize that family has nothing to do with Pack. Parents do horrible things to children. Children ignore parents. Spouses divorce. The loss of an Alpha goes beyond the loss of a parent. An Alpha is like the woody trunk of a grapevine. Everything spreads out from it. Yes, you can graft the vine onto a new rootstock, but not without consequences.

Sarah and Adam, the 9th's Gamma couple, seem to have been particularly hard hit by John's death. This past moon, they huddled close to Home Pond and the burned-out remnants of the Great Hall.

Carefully setting the photograph back on my bedside table, I reach into my pocket for my phone. Then I open the app designated by a full moon sandwiched between a black, star-speckled square and the silhouette of our native mountains. Called Homeward, this app is not available in the Play Store or on iTunes. It was developed three years ago by one of our wolves so Offlanders who sometimes get caught up in the rhythms of the lives of humans do not forget our own.

Each morning, a wolf—the developer, I presume—intones "*Hāmweard, ðu londadl hǽðstapa*" in the Old Tongue before a computer-generated voice counts down the days until the next Iron Moon. "Homeward, you landsick heath-wanderer, in 27 days."

Whoever devised this must have known firsthand how desperate Offlanders became for the Homelands. How "landsick" we gray heath-wanderers—as men once called us—became.

If Homeward calculates that a wolf is too far away to make it back before the change, it chirps out one last phrase in the Old Tongue.

"*Ond swa gegæþ þin endedogor.*"

And so passes your final day.

Who says Pack have no sense of humor?

~

Usually, I set Homeward for a single reminder one day before the Iron Moon, but this time, I set it for a daily countdown just so I won't forget how important this particular change is.

Hāmweard, ðu londadl hǽðstapa, IN *26* DAYS.

Homeward, you landsick heath-wanderer, IN *26* DAYS.

From inside the elevator, I hear a door open, followed by tiny claws skittering on the carpet. My thumb is pressed so hard into the brass DOOR CLOSE button that it bends. We were told to be careful with human things. They are delicate and break easily, but it's hard to remember when you're in a rush.

"Hold the elevator?" says a lilting, questioning voice. My finger drops from the elevator button, and my heart falls with it. I smile at the woman with the black Dutch boy haircut, yoga pants, and raincoat. Alana is in her thirties. Her husband, Luca, is nearing sixty.

He travels way too much.

Usually, I would have been smart enough not to screw someone who knew where I lived, let alone lived where I lived, but the day I did it, she was wearing a raw wool poncho that smelled like sheep and made my mouth water.

"Elijah? How have you been?" She leans one hip against the wall of the elevator and smooths her hair over her ear. Left, then right.

"Well. And how is Luca?"

"Well?" she lilts again. She swoops down and picks up a fluffy, gray doglet whose hair has to be clipped from his eyes so he can see and away from his underbelly so he can walk and who is apparently full grown but is named, for some unaccountable reason, Tarzan.

Pulling Tarzan to her nose, she eyes me over the faux-fur collar of the dog's trench coat. "But Luca? He's out of town? In China?" she says as if to ask whether the distance is far enough to revisit our infidelity.

That damn poncho.

Before the implicit invitation becomes explicit, the elevator door opens, and Alana is pulled into a conversation about lobby improvements while I glare at Tarzan.

"You," I whisper to the little ball of coyote meat dressed in beige-and-black plaid, "should be *ashamed* of yourself."

Tarzan lowers his eyes, then whimpers piteously. The little bit of wild that has not been bred out of him recognizes that submission is his only option.

I know it's not his fault, but still, a little dignity. Please.

As soon as the elevator hits the ground floor, I mutter something unintelligible and race for the street, hailing the first car that will take me. The driver motions for me to wait while he pulls the seat forward, but I throw myself in along the length of the back and slam the door closed just as Alana extricates herself.

Halvors, Sorensson & Trianoff is housed in a tall yet squat postmodern building overlooking the last feet of the Hudson before it transforms into New York Harbor. The building is undistinguished except for its proximity to a huge, green-glass atrium holding sixteen palm trees. It's odd that humans will pay so much for exotics, as though that makes up for the native trees they are so profligate with.

There is a man at the top of the curved atrium entrance. Looking up, I see his feet and the thin pole he uses to pull at a wave of soap. A line tethers him to the wall of glass above. I wonder if he's ever thought of sliding down the slick of soap and leaping off, flying toward the not-so-distant smell of the ocean and the sound of the seagulls. But then the leash would tighten and pull him back, and he'd end up where he started, bumping against the glass.

"Elijah? Are you coming?"

The window washer starts toward the next tier of glass.

"Max." I nod to the little human before opening the door into the expansive lobby with its high wall of shaded glass, its marble floors and brass fixtures. The security guards behind their white desk wave us through the turnstile without demanding any ID.

Maxim Trianoff is in his late sixties. He'd spent his early legal career as a brilliant member of the SEC's enforcement division. He'd been, I've heard, a Democrat who believed deeply in social equity. Then, in the middle of his first very expensive divorce, he left the SEC for Zoerner, Marwick. By the time he was done with his second very expensive divorce, he was a Republican, committed to holding on to whatever money he still had and ready for something new. Ready to see his own name acid-etched in glass. That's when he was approached by Aldrich Halvors with a proposition from a silent partner who wanted to fund a law firm with lobbyists to represent its interests and turn a profit.

Great North LLC.

"And how are our silent partners?" Max asks as he always does when I come back from trips up to the Great North. He has no idea how silent our silent partners are. Gliding through the great tangled swathes of pine- and loam-scented hardwood that his firm, our firm, was created to protect.

"Fine, though John Torrance has stepped down." I hadn't been able to say it last time. It was still too raw then. I stare straight ahead at the bronze elevator.

"Well, he was there for a long time. Have they chosen someone new?"

Two elevators arrive at the ground floor.

"Hmm. Evie Kitwana." We get into the second

elevator, the one with fewer people making fewer stops. Looking down, all I can see is the thinning top of Max's scalp, but in the high shine of the elevator, his face is reflected clearly. Worn, with puffy eyes and cheeks that hang low like a bloodhound's. Taking out a large handkerchief, he blows his nose.

I look younger than I am, because left alone, we live a long time. We rarely do, because eventually, the most powerful wolves take a bullet, trying to defend the Pack.

Still, I'd rather be shot during the Iron Moon than deflate soufflé-like as Max is doing.

"And does Ms. Katana—"

"Kitwana."

"And is she looking for any changes to our arrangement?"

I can see my jaw tightening, and the door slides open onto Halvors, Sorensson & Trianoff.

"No. She wants things to stay exactly the same."

From her place within the white circle of the reception desk, Dahlia calls out to tell us that the associates are already in Conference Room A.

Six associates are seated at one end of the long, oval table in Conference Room A, leaving the two seats at the very end free for Max and me. I slide my tablet into the slot designated for it and plug into the USB so we can talk about bonuses without putting anything up on the big screen where potentially envious not-associates might see it.

Sinise from accounting has taken the spot at the head of the table and waits while Max pours himself a cup of coffee before beginning.

Of course, Max and I already knew that last year was

a banner year for HST. The three equity partners—Max, myself, and Great North LLC—have all done exceedingly well. Max will be able to not only pay his three ex-wives, but also make a down payment on a fourth.

I push my hair back while looking at Sinise's rundown of allocations on my tablet… What *is* that smell?

The door is shut tight, so it's coming from inside. It's not the coffee or croissants or carrion or cologne. Maybe the lox is off?

"Don't you agree, Elijah?" asks Max.

"Absolutely."

Smells like rancid tallow. I try to pinpoint it, but then Max turns to me, and I know it's my turn to discuss the clients we're courting. I know it like the back of my hand, since the *we* is really *me*. I scratch the corner of my eye, and the scent of rotting raccoon is almost overwhelming.

I stare down at my hands. I usually scrub them thoroughly after each Iron Moon, but I realize that I only washed them carelessly, and bits of raccoon—which was a delicious late-Moon snack two days ago—stink to high heaven under my human fingernails.

The humans are staring at me. Can they smell it?

"Elijah?" Max prompts. "You were saying?"

No, of course they can't. They're just waiting for me to tell them about all the rich people who will pay us retainers to represent their interests so we can pay out big bonuses this time next year.

Pressing my hands between my thighs, I hurry through the rest of my presentation, desperate to get to the bathroom.

"That's a lot of money," Max says once the associates

are gone. I shove my hands into my pockets. "What are you going to do with it?"

I don't know. The Pack pays for whatever expenses aren't covered by the firm. I don't know what they do with the rest. I have no money. I have only the facade of wealth.

"I don't have any real plans."

"I'm going to be honest with you. You've seemed off your game for a while now. You work hard, Elijah, and there is no one who knows how to reel in the clients like you do. But you've got to be on and be focused. You should do something. Travel. Buy a boat, for Chrissake. My brother-in-law over at Morgan got a boat a few years ago. Swears by it."

Lori, Max's assistant, knocks softly at the door, and Max waves her in.

"Mr. Sorensson, your eleven o'clock is here?"

"What eleven o'clock?" I always block out the entire morning for associates' meetings.

"Tony Marks apparently—"

"Oh right," Max says. "I've got this, Lori. Just send her to Mr. Sorensson's office."

"Sorry about that," he says, pouring himself one more cup of coffee before walking through the door propped against my foot. "I meant to tell you about this before you went Upstate, but it slipped my mind. Our great friend and client Tony Marks is very fond of his gardener, even though he lost him when he lost Southampton to Susannah. Now, apparently, the gardener's niece has found herself with some kind of legal problem. If what Tony says is true, it should take no time, so just take care of it, will you? Pro bono, of course. Neither gardener nor niece have any money. And, Elijah? Be as charming as you want, but keep your clothes on. Hard to credit from a man on his third alimony, but still, I'd appreciate it."

"You really need a divorce lawyer who can stand up to women," I say, starting for the southeast corner of HST.

Turning toward the southwest, Max shakes his head. "What I *really* need is a zipper that can stand up to women."

Chapter 4

Whoever this pro bono woman is, she will just have to wait. I dip into the men's room and lock the door. By the time I come out, the beds of my fingernails are red and my hands smell like Ajax.

"Mr. Sorensson." Sinise from accounting scurries into step beside me. I sniff my fingers again just to be sure. "That was a super presentation. But you always do such super presentations." It wasn't a super presentation. It was raccoon-tallow-distracted bullshittery. But then Sinise from accounting puts her hand on my arm and bends her leg behind her, leaning slightly to fix a strap of her shoe. When she stands back up, she shakes her head, tossing her long, oddly burgundy hair first left, then right.

So.

It has nothing to do with the quality of my presentation and everything to do with indicating that she is receptive.

My assistant, Janine, quickly insinuates herself between us, her back to Sinise. She tells me that a client is waiting and unnecessarily adjusts my tie, thereby marking me. Telling Sinise that I am already fucking *her*.

Having defended her *cunnan-riht*, Janine points with her chin toward my office and the client Tony Marks sent who is waiting there. I can only see her from behind. Her thick, black hair hangs down wildly, like flames pointing to the curve of an ass like a Japanese pear. Her strong, slim legs are encased in jeans, one leg of which is caught in the top of a pair of mud-spattered hiking boots.

Janine has returned to her office, which is really a windowless interior cubicle across the hall from my own. She has her hand on her mouse and her eyes concentrated on the screen. Unlike Sinise, this woman poses no threat. When she turns around, I see why. She is not beautiful in the way Janine recognizes. She does not have the tight symmetry that every cosmetic surgeon and every patient of one aspires to. She has a long nose in a face that is broad and soft below high cheekbones. Strong chin. Her mouth is wide and straight and unsmiling.

She is probably four inches taller and eight years older than Janine, and since she is not like Janine, Janine not only doesn't see her as competition, but doesn't see her at all.

This woman doesn't flick her hair or coyly lower her eyes with a half smile. She doesn't angle her hips or finger her collarbone or bite her lower lip. She is contained, quiet, still. And when I take a step closer, she smells nothing like carrion and everything like cold, damp earth.

"Elijah Sorensson," I say, holding out my hand. Her hand has cropped nails and no ornament. Calluses in the grip between thumb and forefinger.

She sizes me up quickly with eyes the color of ironwood and just as unyielding.

"Thea Villalobos," she says, and it takes me a moment to get my breath back.

"I'm sorry?"

"Thea," she says slowly, "Villalobos."

Wolves laugh about the madness and mutability of men. About how they are prey to the sudden whims of fate and their own emotional instability. From my jaded and indifferent perch, I have laughed about it too. Laughed about Max and his sudden passions.

But now, confronted by this woman with an ass like a Japanese pear, hair like night, eyes like ironwood, skin the color of golden rye, the ground shifts and topples me into a rotation around her.

Thea Villalobos. Goddess of the City of Wolves.

"Elijah Sorensson," I repeat, stalling while I try to remember what Maxim had said about her. Tony Marks's something. Daughter? No, that wasn't it. She'd have money if she were Tony Marks's daughter.

"Have a seat?"

I hit my toe on the corner of my desk and stumble into my chair, the Titan. That's what my chair is officially called. The Titan.

I discovered it after spending four years at college, three years at law school, two years clerking for Judge Baski, and two more years at Halvors & Trianoff crammed into tiny, human-size chairs. Then when I became partner, my assistant at the time—Barbara, pubic hair waxed into an arrow as though most men she'd had were too drunk to know where to aim—suggested the Titan.

Ever since then, each new piece of furniture has been upgraded, even the two chairs facing across from my big desk. Having clients sit with their feet dangling loose above the floor helps whether I need to intimidate or impress. And everyone who comes into my office has to be intimidated or impressed.

Thea Villalobos shrugs off her backpack and pulls out a file and a flash drive before settling into the corner of one arm of the chair, her knee propped against the other. I want to see her do it again. I want to see that economy of movement, deliberate and smooth.

“I think you’ll find everything you need here. I didn’t want to waste your time,” she says, “but my uncle felt that a letter from a firm like yours would send a stronger message than something downloaded from LawDepot.”

As I take the manila folder and flash drive, she settles back almost motionless. Almost but not quite. Her ring finger gently pulses against the upholstered back of the big chair. There is, I think, a restrained sensuality in Thea Villalobos, and I feel that long-lost prickling in my thighs, and my Pavlovian part stands up and remembers.

Leaning over my desk and her file allows me to adjust the suddenly awkward side tuck. My mind is only half there as I look over the papers she’s typed up.

Thea Villalobos is an environmental conservation officer living in Buttfuck, New York. Robert Liebling, lunatic, is suing her for springing the body grip traps he’d set on his land but right across the border from the wilderness she patrols. He set them again, and Thea tripped them again. The third time, he took video and decided to sue her for trespass. As she points out, by the time he’d taken the date-stamped video, trapping season was over.

“You’d done it before though? *During* trapping season.”

"Maybe." She watches me eject the flash drive. "But his case against me is based entirely on that video."

"It would still be useful to know the history."

She says nothing.

"You do know that everything you say here is privileged?"

"It's not germane, and I don't think you would understand."

I follow her unyielding eyes to the two shelves of my bookcase that are empty of books and filled with photographs of me with various high-profile clients. The head of the United American Energy Commission, the board of the Northeastern Developers Association, the CEO of Consolidated Information. A line of men, none of whom will ever make it into *Us* or *People* or *InStyle* and must make do, instead, with ruling the world.

"I am not my clients," I say.

She leans back, pulling an errant strand of hair away from her forehead. When she bends forward again, she sits closer to my desk.

"Have you ever seen an animal in a body grip trap?"

I shake my head. Hunters come during the Iron Moon, but we've only had one man set a trap on our land. Within minutes, it was marked so heavily with wolf urine that no animal would go near it until the Iron Moon was over, and John had the opposable thumb he needed to trip it. And once she had the words she needed, Josi, the 3rd Echelon's lawyer, took care of the silly little human.

"They say they're humane, but they're not," she says, fingering the flash drive. "I've released animals when I can, but mostly you just have to kill them.

"Liebling claimed he was a trapper. That he needed the money and had the right to trap furbearers on his land. *Furbearers*. Like they're nothing but the keratin on their backs. It'd be like reducing everything you were to 'hairbearer.'" She leans back into the corner of the chair. "See, I knew a man like you would think it was funny."

"No, not funny. Not funny at all. I agree with you completely. It's just the part about 'hairbearer.' I can think of a few men who would say that was an apt description of me."

"Bald men?" she asks, a cool half smile hovering around her lips.

"Mostly."

"Anyway, Liebling claims he's a trapper, but he doesn't have a license. I took pictures of the skins he's taken. They're shredded and unsalable. It's just so much pain and waste. So yes, I triggered those traps, and yes, I will do it again."

I like this woman.

"You don't like him much, do you?"

"No, he's a shit."

It's one of the things you learn about humans early on. They're always hedging their bets. Always putting things in the conditional, always making concessions. Leaving their options open.

Thea doesn't, which makes me like her even more.

I tap the edges of the papers she's given me, as though to even them up.

"Unfortunately," I lie, "there are complications you haven't accounted for here."

She doesn't say anything at first. Then she pulls out a pen.

"What kinds of complications?"

"He claims to be a farmer, so he doesn't need a license to trap on his land."

"He's no farmer. I put some stills on the flash drive. Every month for five months during spring and summer of last year when he first brought up this 'farmer' idea. He put some plants in old plaster buckets that never got big enough to identify before they died."

"I really am happy to do this for you, Ms. Villalobos—"

"Thea."

"Thea. I'm just saying it may take a little longer than we originally thought."

"And I'm saying I'd rather take care of it myself."

"It's all pro bono. Won't cost you a thing. We owe it to your… To Tony Marks."

Her ironwood eyes focus on mine. It is all I can do not to look away. "My uncle's employer's ex-husband?"

"He's a big client. Look, you live in Arietta? We have an office in Albany, and I have another important client up near Plattsburgh that I visit…frequently. I could meet you in town and—"

She laughs at that. The sound is deep and throaty and untamed, and I really want to hear it again.

Everything I knew about Arietta came from a road sign on one of my more meandering drives home for Iron Moon. Turns out that Arietta is 330 square miles with a population of 304. Her physical address is a set of coordinates. Her mailing address is a PO box near Piseco Lake over forty-five minutes away.

But she agrees to meet me at the HST offices in Albany. Next week. I'll have something drafted for her by then.

She pulls on her coat. Her eyes go to my photographs again before she tosses her backpack over one shoulder. Then she slides her left hand in her jeans pocket, her anorak caught behind her forearm, and takes my proffered hand with a smooth slide of her palm against mine.

After she goes, I look at those photographs. How is it that I never noticed before? Never noticed that my pose is the same in every one of them: left hand in pocket, my jacket on that side caught behind my forearm. My right hand taking that of my powerful client.

Holding my hand to my mouth, I breathe deeply the scent of Ajax and black earth, while from the office window I watch the stretch of sidewalk that gives onto Vesey.

After a few minutes, Thea Villalobos emerges from the building. She bends down to loosen the pant leg from her boots. A little beyond her, the leashed window washer continues to work on the glass.

In Liebling's jumpy movie, a woman in jeans, shitkickers, and a cable-knit sweater carries nothing but a long, thick branch. Standing far back, she pokes the thin, metal trigger until it snaps. Her makeshift staff snaps on the second one. She picks up another branch and heads for the most distant one, the third.

"Janine? Tell Albany I'm going to need an office next Wednesday."

Liebling waits for a little and then starts to move, whispering softly that he's going to the third trap now, so the GPS on his phone will record that she was still on his land.

"And, Janine? Where exactly is the Albany office?"

Then I message Samuel, the investigator I use most

often, to stop by as soon as he gets back. Two hours later, I slide him a copy of the video and a piece of paper with Robert Liebling's name on it. "Find out everything you can about him."

He pauses, flipping the paper to look at the other side. "Yes. About her too."

Chapter 5

Hāmweard, ðu londadl hǽðstapa, IN *23* DAYS
Homeward, you landsick heath-wanderer, IN *23* DAYS

THE DRY CLEANER AROUND THE CORNER WENT THROUGH an overhaul and came out green. *Organic*, a sign now says, next to a picture of the earth in a tidy jacket. One cheerful eye is plopped in the middle of the Atlantic, the other in the middle of Europe.

The man helping me is holding down the button on the rotating clothes hanger while looking at the ticket on my phone. Then he stops and pulls out a handful of shirts. The smell of perc is overwhelming and makes my skin prick.

"Those aren't mine."

"Yes, they are. Look." He shows me the ticket number on my phone and on the clothes.

"I don't care what it says, those aren't mine." I hold the shirts up to my front. The shoulders are inches short of where they need to be. The cuffs a half foot.

"You got a wife?" he asks hopefully.

"No."

With a sigh, he pushes his button again.

"I thought you were organic."

"We are. One hundred percent organic."

"Then why does it stink of perc in here?"

"Perc's carbon-based. That's what it means to be organic. Carbon-based."

He should've been a lawyer. He knows that's not what people think when they hear *organic*, but that's the thing about humans—they never say what they mean.

"There they are." I point to the long, white tails sticking out below the hem of a jacket. As soon as they come close, he reaches up with a metal stick and pulls them down, putting them next to the other shirts that look like they belong with a boy's First Communion suit.

Back at home, I toss my shirts in the closet, grab a fork and a glass of water, then angle the photograph of the echelon so that the 9th will see it and know that I am always thinking about them.

I usually set aside Saturday night to videoconference with the 9th. Talk over any problems they might be having, offer advice, make decisions. Since John's death, I've been trying to make it twice a week, though it doesn't always turn out that way because most of my weeknights are taken up with clients.

Lorin and Francesca sign in, naked and spotted with blood.

"Good hunting?" I ask.

"Just a snack," Lorin says, rubbing at the wrong place.

Francesca throws herself on the bed and licks the dark stains from his face. Then she sticks out her tongue, trying to pick something off with her fingers. "Fur," she says. "What are you eating?"

I look down at the Styrofoam container blankly. Pushing the contents around, I finally remember. "Falafel." I push some more. "Tabbouleh."

"I swear that's all you ever eat."

I'd rather they think that I'm unimaginative than

know that when I am Offland, I eat carrion and drink alcohol so that the humans will see me as a man's man. An Alpha male. But a real Alpha, like all wolves, doesn't eat anything he doesn't hunt himself. Unfortunately, being a vegetarian teetotaler doesn't fit humans' conception of what it means to be an Alpha male.

"There's a halal cart down the street. It's fast. Hey, Celia."

Celia, my shielder, has set her laptop outside her cabin—my cabin too, I suppose, though I've never stayed there. Because of the angle of the screen, I can't quite tell what she's doing, but her arms row steadily back and forth. If she were human, I'd have said she had a rowing machine, but Pack have no use for pretend work.

She stops for a minute, pushing her reddish-brown hair—the same color as mine—into a band at the nape of her neck. Her eyes are like mine too, bright blue. Littermates don't always resemble each other, but Celia and I do.

Celia nods and keeps rowing.

Our similarities stop at physical resemblances. Celia is whip smart but socially very awkward, and her few forays Offland have ended badly. She is happiest, I think, staying in the Homelands.

I hope.

The other members of the 9th sign on singly or in pairs.

I've done everything I can to keep track of my echelon, but this is a difficult time, and wolves do not do well when the hierarchy is disrupted. I didn't know that Trevor was working in the kitchen because he got injured defending his *cunnan-riht* to Ella and can't go

Offland until his leg heals. Dani has quit her job at the snowboard company, though she is sullen and it's hard to tell whether she quit or was fired. Lorin and Francesca will be mated as soon as the Alpha is healthy enough to do her part.

I didn't remember that they had become bedfellows.

Mostly, though, I worry about my Gamma wolves, Sarah and Adam. The first mated pair of our echelon, they are brilliant strategists, and Sarah is our best tracker.

But Sarah doesn't look well fed. Instead, she is gaunt and haunted. Any questions I direct toward either of them are met with surprise—as if they'd forgotten where they were—or with a noncommittal nod.

It is only when everyone else has gone that I ask Celia.

She stops her rowing and pushes her hair back from her forehead again, using only her bent wrist. Something metal slaps against wood. Then she starts again. "Sarah lost her pregnancy."

The falafel suddenly feels very dry and bulky in my mouth. I chew hurriedly before gulping down a long draft of water.

"*She was pregnant?* How far along was she?"

"Four months," Celia says.

"And no one thought to tell me?"

"You know how it is. We don't like to tell anyone," she says, "for precisely this reason. Things go wrong."

"But *you* knew."

"Because someone had to make sure that Sarah's work schedule was something she could safely do. That there was someone in authority in her echelon, in case of trouble."

She doesn't say, but I understand her criticism all too well. I should have known. It's already so hard for us to reproduce. In all the moons I've been Alpha, the 9th hasn't had a single successful pregnancy.

"When did she lose it?"

"A week after John died," Celia says and starts her rowing again. "Stress..."

Her voice peters out, and she stops rowing, wiping a dull blade covered with fur.

"Is that for Lorin and Francesca?" I ask.

"The deer we hunted during the Moon."

At least I was there for the hunt. Even if I am not there to scrape the deer's hide and won't be there when they cut the long, continuous thong and won't be there for the *Bredung*, the braiding, when Lorin and Francesca are committed to the land, to the Pack, and to each other.

That long, thin piece of leather, tanned with the oak from our trees, will represent our land. The blood of the Alpha represents the Pack. The release of the couple themselves represents the bond between the two wolves.

My buzzer sounds—loud and high and jarring. It's not the doorman. His buzz is softer and lower down the register. Someone is at my front door.

"Mark Sarah for me. Tell her...tell her that her Alpha thinks about her."

"Shouldn't you get that?" Celia cocks her head to the side, listening as the buzzer sounds again.

"No. I don't know who it is, and I don't care. And if Sarah and Adam need anything—"

"*They do need something. They need you home.*" I can tell the sound of the buzzer is getting on her nerves.

Celia has spent very little time Offland. The insistent, demanding pitch of the human world is almost intolerable until you learn how to ignore it. "The Great North's Alpha died. Our territory was invaded. There are still Shifters out there. Our echelon doesn't need a *boss*. What we need is a *leader*, someone who will lay down their hopes, their desires, for the echelon. Someone who will be the first to hunt, the first to fight, the first to sacrifice, the first to die.

"What we *need* is an Alpha."

Whoever was buzzing at my door is now banging at my door.

Celia must hear it. She starts scraping more furiously.

"Celia, I know it's hard, but I am trying. Last moon, I asked Evie if I could come home. She refused, said the Pack needed me Offland. But the 9th can't wait anymore, and I can't either. So I am going to challenge her for primacy of the Great North. I will win, and then you will be the 9th's Alpha."

Celia's head pops up.

"But the Alpha won't be recovered from her lying-in yet. She's not ready."

"The Pack cannot tolerate weakness, Celia. You know that. Evie knows it too."

Whoever is in the hallway has started kicking my fucking door now.

"You better go," Celia snaps. "Some human needs you."

Then the screen goes blank.

"Dammit." I slam my computer shut. "Coming!" I yell, tossing the remains of my falafel in the refrigerator. Alana's frantic face stares at me through the peephole. I open the door a crack.

"Thank god! I heard you talking in there, but you didn't answer." She plucks frantically at my arm. "Something's wrong with Tarzan. He's vomited up his liver."

Well, hallelujah. Closing the door carefully behind me, I follow her to her apartment. *It's about time*.

But as soon as she opens her door, I hear a high-pitched whimper. "I don't think so. If he vomited up his liver, he'd be dead already."

Alana looks at me with that expectant look human women get when they want you to open a jar or kill an insect or figure out a tip or deal with vomited dog liver.

Tarzan is indeed looking unwell next to a lumpy, purplish-brown puddle. Alana stands well back, her hand covering her lip and nose. "So, coyote meat," I whisper to the tiny head, "had your last hunt?" He whines softly with breath that stinks of bile and sweet and dark bitterness. "Jesus, didn't your dam ever tell you not to eat chocolate?"

I bundle Alana and Tarzan into a cab, because that many dark-chocolate-covered cherries will kill a dog this size. Alana won't let me go. She's afraid he will die. She's afraid he will vomit. She's afraid he will be incontinent. She wraps him in a towel and gives him to me.

"He likes you," she pleads.

The vet cleans out Tarzan's stomach and gives him charcoal to absorb whatever theobromine is left in his intestines, while I sit in the waiting room pretending to read an article in *Best Breeder* about cleft palate in shih tzus.

Simply being here makes me angry, because I am not where I should be. At home, helping Sarah. Reassuring her. Marking her. Hunting with her. *Being an Alpha*.

The Pack has so many stresses now. Snows come later. The bats are dying out, making mosquito season hell. Rains come in torrents or not at all. Humans hunt not for food but for sport. And unlike wolves, they take the strongest animals as trophies, leaving the herd weaker.

Then there are Shifters.

Someone pats me on the shoulder. A nurse with a sympathetic smile. "I can tell you're worried," she says. "But Tarzan is going to be just fine."

No, he's not. Because if I have to fuck Alana, I will rip his throat out.

I ended up fucking Alana, but I didn't rip Tarzan's throat out, because that tiny remnant of wild guided his little muzzle into the spot behind my jaw, where the scent is strong. He had just enough instinct to know that if I marked him, I was less likely to eat him.

He whimpers after me as I creep out of Alana's bed and head back to the gym.

One.

I am coming home.

Two.

I am coming home.

Three.

I am coming home.

Chapter 6

Hāmweard, ðu londadl hǽðstapa, IN *20* DAYS
Homeward, you landsick heath-wanderer, IN *20* DAYS

"MR. SORENSSON, YOU RECEIVED TWO CALLS FROM EVIE Kitwana. She says she's the new CEO of Great North?"

Janine looks at me expectantly, her fingernail tapping at the casing of the phone, because she knows that whenever Great North calls, I jump. But not this time. Celia must have told Evie that I would be challenging her for primacy of the Great North. Our laws require that I recite the ancient formula for a challenge at the next Iron Moon. They do not require me to chat about it over the phone.

"Should I put the call through?"

"No, I'll take care of it when I have time."

My assistant leans over toward my computer, pulling up today's schedule. A petite blond with slender hips, a cross-trained abdomen, and an overabundance of pertness: breasts, nose, lips. She is perfectly beautiful, in the cookie-cutter way of so many women now. Max warned me to stop screwing around with the office staff. I'd done my best, hunting primarily at Testa, but then Janine came…

I couldn't resist. It wasn't because of the way she looks; it was because of the way she smells. She uses some kind of vanilla scent that makes me so hungry. I'm sure she thinks it smells like cookies or ice cream, but, in fact, it smells like the excretions of beavers' castor sacs, located under their tails. They use it to mark their territory, and just a whiff will make any wolf go into salivating paroxysms of need for fresh, chewy beaver liver.

I shake my head, trying to clear away the scent.

Janine flailed and flubbed her way through college. After finishing—whether she graduated is unclear—she took a series of jobs under men and women she describes uniformly as "asshole sadists." That made for a terrible résumé, but because Max knew Janine's father from law school, she landed here. With a loft paid for by her parents, a cushy job she can't be fired from, and the guarantee of a brilliant recommendation from the man who was stupid enough to bed her.

Her fingers reach for a pale tendril at the nape of her updo, directing my eyes toward the tattooed tail that ends there. I know now that the tail belongs to a dragon that clings to her back and around her ribs and up, its jaws set on either side of the nipple tight like an apple seed on top of her left breast.

"Where do you want me to make reservations?" Janine asks, pointing to my dinner date with a potential client. Her softness presses against my shoulder. My cock responds not at all, and my wolf curls into a ball, his muzzle buried beneath paw and tail.

"Oak. No, make it Plank. At eight."

Max has largely relinquished new clients to me—and with good reason. No human understands the workings of hierarchy as well as I do.

Admittedly, establishing your place in the Great North hierarchy is much more straightforward. Either your jaws are strong enough, your claws sharp enough, your power fierce enough, your strategy cunning enough…

Or they're not.

Human hierarchy is complicated and subtle. The strength and strategy is in knowing how it works.

At dinner, for example, I will take this man, described to me as the King of Ball Bearings, to Plank, a restaurant just starting to trend, but where I've already established a reputation for generosity—fairly easily, because the maître d' was at a previously trending restaurant where I had already been established.

Shown to a table near the fireplace with its pattern of perfectly cut logs set into the slate cladding, I will sit with my back to the door. I will not crane my head searching the crowds.

The potential subordinate—I mean, client—comes on time, but I am already there, and with a quick look at my AP, which he won't recognize because he has a clunky gold Rolex, he immediately starts to feel awkward.

When I stand, I tower over him, and whether I have to or not, I bend slightly to shake his hand. Opening the button on my Hardy Amies jacket, I pull it back from my Charvet shirt. The hem of my pants breaks just so above my Berluti shoes.

We sit, and when the sommelier comes, standing at my elbow, looking first to me, I nod indicating my subordinate-to-be. It is by my grace that he goes first. When he orders a dully predictable cabernet, I suggest instead the Côte-Rôtie, a more interesting choice. The sommelier smiles.

Then the client orders a filet mignon because it's the most expensive cut. I order the sirloin because it is the best.

We start to talk. My subordinate is eager to impress me with his importance, to tell me all the amazing ways in which the world runs on ball bearings. On his ball bearings, in particular. I wait until he is finished and ask him an intricate question about counterfeiting and patent law, so that he knows that I have already gone far beyond his palaver and know why he needs me.

The switch takes place. Suddenly, I am no longer trying to get him as a client. He is trying to get me as a lawyer. He will have already started to scan the room, looking for any powerful person to bolster his standing. He finds one and nods to him. I don't turn my attention from the client. I do not court power; power courts me.

He takes out his cell phone. "I'm sorry. I've got to take this." He does it to prove that he is a busy man and much needed.

I nod, giving my permission. But I keep my phone off. It is a tool for my convenience. I am at no man's beck and call.

While he talks, a woman I've had walks past with another man. She gives me a small smile. I lower my head for one almost unnoticeable second, and her body softens in response. Another woman, one I haven't had, lifts her eyes to mine, her lids lowered. My eyes linger on her a little longer than necessary. She pushes her hair behind her ear, then pulls her hand back, letting it slide down her jaw toward her lower lip.

The subordinate notices everything, and if I've done it right, he will do anything to be in this world, my world.

With a twist of my jaws, he is down and I am Alpha.

At the end of dinner, I shake his hand and thank him. Noblesse oblige and all that. I watch until he is safely out of the restaurant and then head toward the back. There, I lock the door of the shiny-bright restaurant bathroom with its orchids and bowl of river rocks. I stick my finger down my throat and tickle my uvula until both wine and sirloin, alcohol and carrion, are purged.

I am so sick of this world. My world.

It takes me a long time to fall asleep. Stripping down to nothing, I curl on top of my big bed, staring out the window at the moon—unless the moon isn't there, in which case I stare at the East River, trying to find a bit of it that is not garishly lit by the Manhattan Bridge.

I don't sleep well in skin. Haven't been able to for years or maybe ever, but it's been getting worse. I've started having dreams now. Dreams in which I start the change, but it takes so long.

In this dream, I've stayed late at HST, so late that the Iron Moon comes, but this time, only my legs change. I stay there waiting, pretending to work with my human hands clicking stupidly and endlessly at my keyboard while my bent wolf legs dangle hidden beneath my big desk. I smile and wave as each person in the office leaves. Making excuses about the Makropulos case, which isn't a case at all.

Once everyone is gone, I drop to the plush carpet and scurry away on my human knuckles and my lupine feet.

Breathless and panicky, I wake up and grab my sweats and sneakers. I run downstairs.

"Can I get you a cab, Mr. Sorensson?" asks the doorman.

"It's all right, I'm having trouble sleeping. Thought I'd go for a run."

His eyes flicker to the empty darkness outside. "Be careful out there."

"I will, Mohammad. Thank you."

I follow the rumble of the cement under my feet toward the place where the air smells less of ocean and more of river.

At the 1 train, I swipe my card. A man in a frayed, black puffer coat with two wheelie bags is lying in one corner, his head cushioned on an overstuffed Babies "R" Us bag. He lifts one eyelid to see if I'm likely to tell him he has to move along.

I shake my head and turn away. I am the least of his worries.

Penn Station is quiet, though even now, it's not empty and there are more than enough police. Still, I've done this before and know my audience. Moving like a drunk bridge-and-tunnel partier, I head to the very end of platform 16, leaning heavily against the wall until I'm sure no one is watching. Then, with a quick turn, I sprint down the narrow metal stairs at the end, prancing carefully across the tracks. Another few feet, and I'm safely at the walled-off remains of the old tunnel that served as mail access to the trains. Beside one crumbling part of the wall, I drag out two concrete blocks and wriggle in.

Now comes the dangerous part.

There is no law more deeply held by Pack than the one against changing Offland. It is *felasynnig*, an Old Tongue word that doesn't really translate because it combines both criminality and immorality. Not everything that is immoral is illegal, and not everything that is illegal is immoral, but something that is *felasynnig* is the worst of both.

I've taken every precaution I can to not be seen, but if Evie ever found out I'd changed here in the heart of New York City surrounded by millions of humans, she would have no choice but to condemn me to a *Slitung*, a flesh tearing.

Still, I'd rather be torn apart as a wolf than to face life trapped in skin.

Shoving my clothes and wallet into my bag, I lie down on the dusty tile. My fading wolf lifts his head, hobbling slowly to his feet.

Wolves have different ways of starting the change. Some roll their shoulders, some arch their backs, some bend deep into their haunches. I stretch both arms in front of me with my palms flat, my wrists extending as far as they can go. Then my other self, my real self, takes over, and I relax into it. Muscles lengthen or contract, and bones do the same, bending in new ways. Organs move. I am blind and deaf as my features rearrange. I am immobilized as my bones and muscles shift. My skin goes numb as the sad coating of hair is replaced by thick fur. Or vice versa.

And unlike the werewolves of fiction, I am completely and utterly helpless.

When the change is over, it takes me a moment before I can bear to look at my front legs, to make sure that they are, in fact, paws and not the hands of my dream. The relief is almost a physical thing.

I tried once before to change in my locked bathroom, but a caged wolf is no kind of wolf at all. This may be a poor substitute for my forest, but in this world, the steel beams are my trees, the tracks are my rivers, the sirens are my birdsong, the distant rumble of trains is my bellowing moose.

And the rats are my prey.

A big rat, nearly as large as Tarzan, scurries in the dark. The big ones make for the best hunting, not just because they have the most flesh on them, but because they have been smart enough to avoid rat poison and are fast enough to avoid trains.

Leaping across the tracks, I chase after him, weaving in and out of the beams and splashing through the fetid puddles. Before he goes somewhere I can't follow, I jerk forward, clamping onto him and pulling him back out. As he tries to race away, my claws *scritch* along the ground, banging into an old plastic bucket. I grab his tail and throw him into the air and catch him on the way down. Then I let him escape and take after him again.

It is not a good kill, John, but this is what happens when you domesticate a wolf. You pervert him.

I savor every bit of the chase and every last gout of warm blood and every delicately crunchy bone.

Then I head back to my hole in the cinder block as despondent as always. A slow rat smelling of almond and carbolic crosses my path. I give it wide berth. Poisoned rats won't kill me, but they do tend to cause bloat.

"Good run, Mr. Sorensson?" asks the night porter.

"It was fine, Saul. Thanks."

As I wait for the elevator, Saul starts the floor polisher again and follows my dusty footprints as far as the elevator.

Chapter 7

Hāmweard, ðu londadl hǽðstapa, IN *16* DAYS
Homeward, you landsick heath-wanderer, IN *16* DAYS

LIKE THE HST OFFICE IN NEW YORK AND THE ONE IN Washington, the Albany office is based on hierarchies. The large corner offices have tinted plate-glass windows and huge desks of wood recovered from old barns or railroad ties. There is usually a large painting of either ragged spots in neutrals or bright scribbles. They are painted to order by a consortium of artists who all started off with big dreams but now make works that are the right size, the right color, and not representational, because representation will always offend *somebody*.

There are smaller offices and conference rooms arrayed alongside the windows. This is the part of the office that clients see. It is spare and antiseptically clean.

As in New York, the other side of reception is the messy heart of the place, a warren of cubicles for the paralegals, legal assistants, legal secretaries, and more support staff.

Patrick Holding, the head of the Albany office, runs out of his corner office, rolling down his sleeves. He looks like he hasn't slept for days and offers a thin, sweaty hand that feels like shellfish but smells like cruller mixed with salt and old leather, the scent of fear. Usually, I leave the lobbying side of our business to

Maxim, who has long experience in dealing with politicians and has a stronger constitution for it. My sudden appearance has Patrick worried.

I've got to wash my hand.

Whoever had to move out of the corner office that I will occupy for the day has removed every trace. It is clean and well lit, and the windows face in the general direction of the Empire State Plaza and the Corning Tower. The office is grimly empty. No one would believe that this was a place that I'd visited often or ever.

I need a coffee cup, some pointless files, a volume of session laws, anything to make it look like I haven't come up here because of Thea Villalobos. That I haven't made the three-and-a-half-hour drive because, for the first time in years, I remember what it's like to be hungry. What it is to want.

As with Halvors, Sorensson & Trianoff in New York, the only thing I'm going to find in this part of the office is a bell jar filled with seashells or a piece of driftwood impaled on a bronze base or distilled water from some Pacific Island. It all reeks of linen fresh room spray.

To make my office look like someone actually uses it requires going to the bullpen.

"A client of mine should be coming in half an hour," I tell the receptionist. "Make sure she is sent in."

The bullpen here is just like the one in New York, and the first thing that hits me is the stink of microwave ovens coated with fake butter and coffee makers where the last inch of coffee is constantly burning.

"Steroids," someone whispers. "S'gotta be. I mean, nobody gets to be that big without—"

I thump around a little and cough. Leonora always told us that we had to make more noise than we do at home so that the dull Offland ears can hear us coming. They still don't hear and continue right on with their conversation about steroids.

I always hear things I'm not meant to hear. I don't really care about the speculation about whether I take steroids. It is, after all, preferable to the speculation as to whether I'm a werewolf. It's just the way the conversation inevitably progresses.

"You know what happens with steroids," another voice continues. "They make your dick shrivel up like a peanut."

This time, I cough louder and lean over the top of the cubicle, looking down at a young man in the process of indicating the size of my sex by wiggling the top joint of his little finger against his thumb.

The man's face immediately turns a shimmering gray, and he begins to scratch at the offending joint as though he's erasing it. Men who had been standing around him now inch away, their smiles fading. But I don't see them or hear what they're saying, because behind them is a picture of a wolf standing in the snow, against a scrim of pine trunks.

It looks *exactly* like Sarah. It isn't, of course. It's a forever wolf, but it's a female with the same reddish-brown coloring and the same dark-gray saddle, the same pale point on the tip of her tail.

And someone...someone has covered her body with crosshairs.

Fifty points for a head shot.

Thirty for her chest.

Ten for her empty belly.

The cubicle wall crashes on either side of me, and as I step over it, the little humans run and trip, skipping away from the destruction.

NEW YORK:
LET THE HUNT BEGIN!

I cover Sarah's belly with my hand and then tear down the picture of my sad wolf.

"*What the fuck is this?*" I shove the picture at the shimmering gray man who is hardly half my size and doesn't know that I couldn't give less of a crap about his peanut crack.

He opens his mouth, but nothing comes out. He blubs twice more, a stranded guppy.

"*Answer me!*" My face is against his, spit hitting his face. The insides of his pants turn dark, and the air stinks of ammonia.

In the suddenly silent bullpen, tiny heads peek around padded half walls and then dodge back down.

Patrick appears, plucking nervously at my sleeve, showing me a foam dart gun. The stink of salt and old leather becomes almost unbearable while he jabbers something incomprehensible about clients.

The dart gun in my hand hits the window, and I stand up straight, looking over the cubicle walls. There are at least four of these huge posters of Sarah, of my broken-hearted wolf, on the walls.

"I want every one of those"—I point to where two guys are busily tearing their own copies down—"and every one of these"—I pick up the crushed remains of the dart gun—"and every one of *you* in the conference room in three minutes."

"But..." say several voices, including the thin one at my elbow.

"Anyone who is late is fired."

Patrick raises his hands and opens his mouth, but I stop him before he can find his voice.

"I represent two-thirds of the partners of this firm, so don't think for a second that Max can do anything for you."

Holding the poster to my chest, my teeth tighten around a feral howl building in my throat.

"Mr. Sorensson? Your—"

I ignore the receptionist and slam open the glass door, heading toward the biggest conference room.

Two associates and a handful of paralegals have already claimed the room with their piles of papers and boxes. With a quick jerk, I lift one end of the table, sending the papers and boxes and pencils and tablets scattering to the floor.

"What do you know about this?" I clip the *ǣcewulf* to the board.

"It's from the New York State Predator Hunters Association." An associate who has just filed in with everyone else starts to rattle on quickly. Apologetically. "They're a small client. We're helping them find a sponsor in the legislature for a bill delisting wolves," he yammers on. "Get them off the endangered species—"

"There are no wolves in New York. New York slaughtered its wolves over a century ago."

"This guy says he was out hunting a couple of months ago and saw some big, white wolf. Wants to make some money as a hunting guide. Maybe aerial..."

One wolf. That's all it takes for the humans to go apeshit. He keeps talking, but I don't hear anything else he says. Nothing terrifies us like the planes that sometimes sweep low over the Homelands. The Pack Nunavut was destroyed by hunters in the sky they were powerless to escape.

Why is it that humans are so eager to hunt forever wolves, the only species that ever befriended them?

God, what a mistake that was.

"No one," I say, taking off my jacket. "No one will sponsor that bill."

"Actually, I have a senator in Brooklyn who—"

"No one will sponsor that bill, because no one in this office will eat, drink, sleep, or piss until the legislature is locked up."

So it starts. I have the office manager find out exactly how much we have been paid by the NYSPHA and send a legal secretary on the four-hour drive with a personal check.

Then we get a color-coded image with the names of 213 state legislators projected on the white board. I want a check mark next to every single name. Assistants and other junior staff take those with a strong record of conservation voting. Patrick starts to protest, his voice shaky until the plaster wall behind him crumbles under my hand and onto his shoulder.

I handle the trickiest ones myself, including the Brooklyn senator who irritably shoots down my politely phrased query about his potential support. I don't say anything more. Just tell him to give my best to Becca, his wife. And to Amirai, the young man he's been screwing in the back of his Impala every Thursday for the past eight years.

The handset is suddenly muffled. "Daddy's on the phone!"

"Damn you to hell," he says, and then after a long pause during which I don't say anything, he mumbles a muted "Fine" and hangs up.

I might not much like lobbying. Doesn't mean I don't know how to do it.

It takes time, but by the end of the afternoon, every name is crossed off. Most were easy. Some saw it as a way of calling in favors; others had to be convinced. In the end, this issue that nobody in the office or the legislature gave a damn about is dead and cremated and its ashes mixed into cement and sunk to the bottom of the Hudson.

When Patrick leaves the conference room, he shakes his head in disbelief over the wasted man-hours and the squandered leverage, but I really don't give a fuck what the humans think. By the time I am alone again, the light is a low amber rim against the skyline. I lean back against the edge of the table, my legs splayed in front of me.

The place is a mess of coffee cups and ramen and popcorn and pizza. Donuts. A vegetable platter that no one touched. I stare at the floor. I want to tell her, tell Sarah, that it's going to be okay. That she and Adam will have another chance. That things will get easier, and some day, her Alpha will carry her into the Meeting House for her lying-in and the 9th will celebrate its first live births.

I want to tell my Pack that I love them. That just because I'm not there doesn't mean I'm not thinking about them and working for them.

Someone knocks on the glass wall of the conference room and points toward the door. Toward Thea who is standing there, wearing a dark-olive button-down shirt that drapes, soft and yielding, over her tight curves. Black jeans. Backpack slung across one shoulder. Her anorak over her other arm.

I stare at her for a minute. I had forgotten. The first woman in a long time that I didn't want to forget, but I did.

"Ms. Villalobos, I—"

"Thea."

"Thea. I don't know what to say. Except I lost track of time." I look at my watch for the first time since I went into the bullpen. "You...you weren't here the whole day, were you?"

"More or less. Got drinkable coffee for some of the associates a couple of hours ago."

Patting my jacket pocket, I extract my tie. "Jesus, I'm so sorry—"

"For what? I'd taken the day off."

"But to waste it hanging around here—"

"It wasn't a waste." She leans against the table just a few inches away. "How often do you get to see someone with real power move heaven and hell for something they care about?"

Sliding the tie back and forth a couple of times until I like where it sits on my neck, I tie the knot with a practiced hand.

"Don't get carried away. This is just what HST does. Partly anyway. We're lobbyists." I look at my reflection in the window. "It's how we make money."

"Really? You make money by firing clients and

threatening lawmakers until you've undone everything the client wanted? If wolves had any clout or money, I'd say you were working for them."

In the reflection of the window, I tweak the dimple under my half Windsor. The tiny hairs on the back of my neck are standing on end. This conversation is creeping uncomfortably close to the truth. I need to get it back on script. I roll down my sleeves, check the fold of the cuffs, and pull the chain cuff links from my shirt pocket.

"Look, let me make this up to you." I thread one platinum cuff link through the left cuff. "There's a restaurant nearby." I thread the other platinum chain through my right cuff. "A chef from the City. Downstaters swear by it."

"Well." Her voice is suddenly cooler. "That's certainly high praise."

I pull on my jacket, making sure the seams are seated snugly on my shoulders. "Good. Then let me get my coat."

"I was being facetious. There's pizza in the staff room. Not to mention a completely untouched vegetable platter here." She picks up a green pepper slice. "Okay, so not *completely* untouched."

"Please, Thea, I'm not going to let you eat cold pizza. I forgot our appointment. And no man should ever forget you." I hold her gaze for two fractions of a second over the norm, and then I lean in to sweep her hair back from her face. "Your skin is so soft." I sigh, making sure that my breath caresses her ear. "You should never wear anything but silk."

She bites into the green pepper. "*And* there he is again."

I turn quickly to the glass wall looking onto the hallway to see which subordinate is getting in the way of my seduction. "Who?"

"Just a pompous ass. Don't worry about it."

"Did someone insult you? Did—"

"Like I said, don't worry about it."

I pull my shirtsleeves one last time so they emerge just a centimeter from my jacket sleeves. "I'll get my coat and meet you in reception."

Ten minutes later, standing alone in the lobby, I look at my watch. The receptionist is packing up her bag, getting ready to go. I ask if she saw my client.

"Tall woman?"

I nod.

"Long, black hair?"

I nod again, faster.

"Carrying a pizza?"

Chapter 8

A RUNNER IN IRIDESCENT, BEADED, DOVE SATIN DIGS INTO my skin while I peel off my socks in the "Royal Suite" that the office manager at HST arranged for me. Why would a hotel in Albany have a Royal Suite? Everything is tasteful gray: ash walls, graphite headboard, pearl bedspread, gunmetal rug with a vaguely oriental pattern.

I'd asked specifically for a California king, because I was sure I'd need it.

Pack courtship is a very straightforward affair. It starts with a deep breath to see if a wolf is receptive. If not, the courtship is over. If yes, the next step depends on whether said wolf has a bedfellow or merely a shielder. If there is no bedfellow, then the female presents, the male covers, and everyone hopes for the best.

If there is a bedfellow, then you must fight. Lose, and the courtship is over. Win, and the female presents, the male covers, and everyone hopes for the best.

No one messes around with mated wolves.

I think about the pretty young woman with the short gauze shift over a tight, black underdress. She smiled at me as I walked past, making it clear she was receptive, but just the thought of her naked body beneath mine makes the traitor in my pants sag glumly.

I've never really worried about whether a human has someone already. Technically, Alana has Luca, not that it makes any difference to me. Why should it bother me if Thea has someone else? Why should I care if she's eating my cold pizza with him? If she's tossing the box aside and kicking off her mud-covered boots and sliding out of her jeans, and he's grasping her ass like a Japanese pear, lifting her above his…

And of course, now, *now*, my balls tighten and my cock hardens into a lead pipe. I drag myself wearily into the shower. Elijah Sorensson with the lead pipe in the bathroom. I turn on the water and bend my left arm against the wall, my right hand fisted, trying to remember when there was pleasure, not just release.

When it's over, I collapse onto the bed covered by nothing but a damp towel and that itchy, jeweled runner over my feet.

I don't know how long I'd been asleep when I wake bolt upright from another dream, the panic thudding in my ears, my arms aching. My breath comes in broken gasps, and I am drenched in sweat.

My wrists feel like they're about to break.

It was so real, this dream. I was trying to change. But no matter how hard I pushed and stretched, all I could see were my manicured and clean hands with their masculine but not bestial smattering of hair emerging from the perfectly starched cuffs: French, with cuff links made of platinum chains. I must have been trying to change even in my sleep, or my wrists wouldn't hurt so much.

But nothing happened. What if my wild is dead, and I'm trapped in skin?

Pulling the still-damp towel around my waist, I look through the plate-glass windows over the buildings of Albany to the black strand of the Hudson. If I follow it south, it will take me back to New York.

North, the Hudson will take me through many twists and turns to Lake Tear of the Clouds on the southwest slope of Mount Marcy. On a clear day, you can see Mount Marcy from the mountains of home. It would take me only a few hours to get there, and then I could change and run and hunt. My heart aches for it—my body too—but this is not the time to talk to Evie. I have nothing to say until I officially announce my challenge.

There's an Alpha way of saying things. It's not rude, just firm, as though the outcome is already decided. Usually backed with that slight tone of menace that makes compliance seem mandatory.

And then there's the money, of course.

The pimply valet slides another twenty into his pocket and lets me into the garage so I can retrieve my Land Rover. I can live with having some teenager shrug off my eccentricity, but I cannot abide the thought of driving for hours with the stench of human in my car.

I know all the routes through the underpopulated Upstate. Most of them, at least. After all, I've made the drive up and back once a month for the better part of three decades. And when the usual route through Gurn Spring, Gansevoort, and Glens Falls got too dull, I took the route that skirts Lake Desolation before turning north to Hope.

Or west to Arietta.

The car slews on the damp asphalt. At the off-ramp, I find a small, boarded-up white building on a patch of flat snow. Maybe it was a gas station years ago. Or maybe with a little paint, it becomes a farm stand, servicing summer tourists.

It takes me a second to find the video Liebling took. After I key in the GPS coordinates, my phone calculates directions to Liebling's property. I'm guessing that Thea lives somewhere nearby, because how far would she walk with only a cable-knit sweater in an Adirondack winter?

In the empty darkness, I race down two-lane roads, then travel slower down country lanes, and bump as far as I can along rough, stone-strewn paths, until I dead-end near a farmhouse. No humans have lived there for a long time—that much I can tell, even in skin. Still, someone must have mowed here last fall, and that's enough humanity to make me nervous.

Tucked behind the farmhouse, my car gets colder and colder, my hands tight on the wheel, my eyes on the thin, waning crescent above the forested hills.

Then I take off my seat belt.

Chapter 9

On the floor of the passenger seat, I set my shoes with the socks carefully tucked into each. I drape my jacket across the back of the passenger seat with cuff links and tie inside the pockets. Shirt glowing brightly over the top. Then I fold my pants on top of my shoes. My boxer briefs come last, lying on top of my pants.

The cold is a relief on my naked body. The shivering has nothing to do with the cold and everything to do with my fear that I will stretch out my wrists and nothing will happen. What happens if my wolf has been so poisoned that he can no longer struggle up?

What is the point of living, if all you are is human?

Sitting on the cold damp ground, I awkwardly hold my wrists out in front of me. Nothing happens. I press harder, pushing toward the dark hills, waiting for the faint, buzzing electricity of my wild to take over. I look back to the road, in case someone comes.

I try again. In the dim light, all I can see are my manicured and clean hands with their masculine but not bestial smattering of hair.

My wild has to be all right, doesn't he? The universe can't be that pathetic. It couldn't allow the holiest thing about me to die with no more warning than a dream about French cuffs.

Could it?

I try again and again. I try different things—twisting

my shoulders and tightening my haunches—but nothing lights the spark. In the back of my mind, I keep worrying that the human who mowed this land in the autumn will come back and find me sitting naked on the damp ground and ask what I'm doing.

Yoga, I suppose.

The moon's path hovers over the prickly heights of the pine trees on the ridge above me. It shines down expectantly.

Well? she asks.

Well, what? I'm trying as hard as I can. But suppose a human comes and sees me mid-change. What then?

Strangely enough, the moon speaks to me with Gran Sigeburg's impatient voice. *Why do you worry so much about humans?* she says in that same snappish tone. *They are like blackfly, an irritation whose season the earth will survive. Must survive. You are something else. You are wild. The wild and the earth are intertwined, one and eternal.*

This time, I lay myself belly down, stretching out my arms and legs so that more of my skin touches the damp ground, so that my face is buried in it, so that the cool breeze caresses my back and shoulders, so that my fingers can dig into the muck, so that I feel the heartbeat throbbing deep in the soil. My consciousness grows beyond the me of this poor form, and I am bombarded by the smell of moldering autumn cuttings, the scrabbling of small claws on rough bark, and my fingers reach deep into the cold where life waits patiently to begin again.

This time, when I press the heels of my palms out, power rushes in. My body coils and my skin tingles and my head tilts back as the muscles contract and lengthen.

My mouth waters, and my tongue stretches out across teeth that grow and thin from my jaw. As my eyes and ears and throat contort, I am blind and deaf and speechless and immobile.

Eventually, consciousness, real consciousness enters into me. The cold is no longer cold. The dark is no longer dark, and the emptiness is full. I remember that I am a link in the chain of the world.

Pack used to like open spaces, back when we earned the name heath-wanderers, before we realized that open spaces meant a clear shot. Now we really prefer the shadowy and protective embrace of the woods. But that ancestral longing to race at full speed is still there, and I can't help but charge across the shaved bowl of grass, jumping into the air and twisting mid-leap only to twist again, and coming back on legs that are already churning at the grass.

I run back and forth across this bit of land until a distant car horn pulls me to my senses and I sprint for the forest.

The woods here are not like the Homelands. We have been expanding out from the plot of land we bought in 1668, and the whole of our territory is marked in the way of wolves. It may look trackless to humans, but to us, it is a rich web of greetings and warnings and signposts.

The paths through this forest smell like polyurethane and steel-toed boots and Cheetos. No wolf has been here for over a hundred years, and the things that have thrived in their absence have lost all sense of perspective.

In an attempt to restore some perspective, I eat two of them.

Loping back and forth through the woods, I search for

Thea's scent until I find an unmarked track with fresh tire prints. At the end is a tiny cabin, maybe an old fire watch cabin, though there's no lookout tower nearby.

Thea's scent calls to me, unlike the two other scents here. One belongs to a man who uses her front door and smells like sex. The other belongs to one who circles her cabin but never goes in.

Thea is not here. Her car is, but the engine is cold. She left recently on foot, and her tracks lead around the back—past the cistern and the propane tank and the tarp-covered compost and several cords of firewood—into the trees. I do not smell the circling man, the man who doesn't use the front door, here.

I follow her for a mile or so until the path hits a trail and the trail hits a trailhead. There are people there with trucks and lights too bright for my eyes. Guns. It's a staging ground. A lot of people wearing acid-yellow jerseys saying *CASART: Central Adirondacks Search and Rescue Team*. I sniff the air for Thea. She was here, but she isn't anymore, so I trace a wide circle until I find her tracks again, but this time, she's not alone. Now she is with the man who enters through the front door.

"Do we really have to talk about this *now*?" she says.

"Well, when is going to be a good time?"

Thea says nothing. He's a bulky man, this front-door man in the sheriff's T-shirt. From the smell of things, he is a moderate drinker and an immoderate consumer of saturated fats.

"Thea," he says, a plea in his voice. *THEEE-ah*. "We have a *good* thing here."

"I know we do. I just don't understand why you want to change it."

"Not change it. Grow it. I'm not like Lee. I'm not going to try to get you to move to town with me. But there are things we could do to make your cabin more… just *more*. Put in a TV and a sofa? That'd be nice, right? A real refrigerator. You've got to have a refrigerator. I mean, you can't live like this forever."

She doesn't respond at first. Just pulls tight on the straps of her backpack.

There's a hoarse voice echoing up ahead. It belongs to a man, human and fiercely frightened. But neither Thea nor Front-Door Man can hear.

"I've been through this before. You want *more*, but what you want more of, I don't have. You already want me to go out more. You want me to see people, to entertain and be an audience, and I'm not good at that. Any of it."

Why can't they hurry up? This man is screaming. He's so close and so…unwell.

And who is this Timmy he keeps yelling for?

"You know…" He pretends to laugh. *Ha-ha. You won't believe this*. "Lee said you were a sociopath. Hold up, babe. I've got a stone—*ow*—right at my heel."

Thea waits patiently while Front-Door Man holds on to her arm and digs around with his finger. "Got it," he says, pulling his low boot back up.

"A sociopath lacks a conscience. I didn't go to his nephew's christening, and he thinks I don't have a conscience? He didn't want to go either, but the difference between us is he did it and fumed for weeks after. Look, I've never made a secret of it. I like to be alone. I *need* to be alone. I like you, but—" She stops suddenly. "Shh."

"'I like you.' *I like you?* We've been together for a year, and all I get is—"

"*Doug*," she snaps. "Just *listen*."

Doug listens and finally—finally—hears. I chuff out a long breath, because the man was driving me nuts, all that screaming for Timmy. They move faster but still cautious over the rough terrain, calling out. The owner of the desperate voice holds his forearm up to his eyes, shielding himself from the bright lights.

"Are you the police? Have you seen Timmy?" he asks. His voice is hoarse from screaming. "Have you seen my son?"

"Mr. Fanning?" Doug holds out his hand. "Doug Glenn, sheriff's department. Your son's fine. He's waiting for you at the trailhead."

"Oh, thank you, God," the man says, his voice shivering. "Thank you, God." He is too lightly dressed for a human in this time when the woods are trying to decide between winter and spring. Between the two of them, winter always wins.

"I don't know what happened, but he wandered off. He's never wandered off before."

Doug radios the staging ground to tell them they've found Mr. Fanning, while Thea quietly unhitches her backpack. She gives him a bottle of water, shakes out a down jacket wrapped tight in a little bag, hands him gloves, a hat. Then helps him put on a headlamp.

She offers him a bar of something, but he pushes it away.

"Did they feed him? He needs water. My wife must be... My wife..."

"He's fine, Mr. Fanning. We're going to get you there as soon as we can."

"Look." Doug pulls out his radio. "Why don't you talk to your—" Before he can hand it to Mr. Fanning, Thea plucks the radio from Doug's hand.

"What are you doing?" Doug asks.

She twists the dial, finding nothing but static. "That's unfortunate. The reception up here is so spotty."

The three of them start very slowly back toward the staging ground, Mr. Fanning talking disjointedly, worriedly, though Thea's quiet responses seem to calm him just a little. Doug stomps and grouses behind them. When they stop to let Mr. Fanning rest, Doug pulls Thea aside.

"What are you doing?" he whispers angrily. "Just let him talk to his son already."

"I think it's better to wait till the trailhead," she whispers back.

Mr. Fanning comes closer, trying to listen. "Is there something about Timmy? Something you're not telling me? Did he get hurt?"

"Mr. Fanning. Give me a second, and I'll get him on the radio."

"Doug, plea—"

Doug ignores her.

"Mr. Fanning?" He holds up a finger and then calls someone on the radio. "Here's your son."

"Dad?" I recognize the voice on the radio as one of the men from the trailhead.

"Dad?"

The old man blinks and then holds the radio away, staring at its dark face. "What the hell are you trying to pull?" He drops the radio. "Where is my son? *Where's Timmy?*"

The radio falls, still faintly echoing with the man's voice. "Dad? It *is* me. It's Tim. Dad? Dad!"

The father lurches back toward the mountain, screaming for the boy who is so vivid in his memory.

Thea leaves Doug sweeping the ground for his radio while she follows Mr. Fanning. She lopes across the rough terrain and catches up to the old man. She doesn't try to stop him, just parallels him, talking to him in that quiet voice. After a while, she moves slower and he slows down too.

Doug shouts, giving directions as the trail fills up with EMTs, rangers, CASART, and Tim, the burly forty-five-year-old with a fringe of gray hair and a fringe of rosy fat, who probably hasn't been called Timmy for thirty-five years. There's a lot of frightened shouting between father and son.

I stay well back, lying in a dirt hole left by an uprooted oak. There are too many eyes and too many lights that, if they shine my way, will catch the green lucidum of my eyes, and someone will shoot. I lie below the level of the fingery roots and wait. These people all know each other, so there is the endless human ritual of promises that no one intends to keep.

Get together.

At the pond, at the bowling alley, at church.

With the kids, with the wives, with the team.

Soon, soon, soon, soon.

Never.

Thea says nothing. Just recovers her jacket, hat, gloves, and headlamp from the EMTs and heads back into the trees, returning the way she came.

"Thea!"

She stops but doesn't turn around. Doug's booted feet come running after her.

"You knew he wouldn't recognize his son?"

"Of course I didn't *know*. But listening to him…I just thought maybe it was best to wait."

"Oh Jesus, The. Let me give you a ride."

"It's all right. It's not far," she says and starts walking into the woods. "It'd take longer in a car."

"But it's the middle of the night."

"I'm good," she says, but before she can take another step, he grabs her arm, pulling her close.

"Thea, please. Promise me you'll think about what I said." And for some unaccountable reason, I hate this man who is touching Thea and still smells like her.

"I'm sure I will." Then…she rubs the back of his hand. It's a gesture that looks a lot like *There, dear, don't fret* and nothing like *You make my spine tighten and my legs clench, and later when I touch myself, it is your name—oh, Doug—that I will scream into the night.*

And I can tell that Doug knows it.

"You're going to regret it some day," Doug yells to the bright light bobbling into the black forest. "When you wake up in that cabin in the middle of nowhere with no one to talk to but cats."

"You're right about that," she says, her voice fading in the distance. "Always been more of a dog person."

With a little gleeful kick of leaf litter in Doug's general direction, I trot along parallel but hidden by the dark woods and my own silence, because neither Doug nor I want her walking alone.

For a human, she moves quietly. To a wolf's ears, it sounds about like an arthritic bull moose, but still, unlike most humans who blunder around in a shell of disruption, treating the rest of the world as an inconsequential backdrop, she is aware. She pays attention to everything, gives everything its due.

She stops to listen to a woodcock call out his heart (*meeep meeep meeep*), and because he is doing something really important, she slowly moves away so he can have a little privacy.

It doesn't take her long to get to her cabin, and when her door closes, I lower my head to the ground. The man who doesn't use her front door has been back. Even worse, he has used her front door. He went in and came out again, but to be sure, I run to the side window and jump up, the pads of my front paws landing silently on the windowsill.

Thea's cabin is so small that I can see immediately that she is alone. She's already hung up her coat. Her boots are side by side next to the door as she crouches in front of a cast-iron stove, scraping away ash. She puts on new kindling and prods it into place. Then a new log. The stovepipe creaks as the fire starts, and smoke mixes in my nose with the slow ferment of pine needles dampened with snow.

She sits on the side of her bed, her hair falling forward over her shoulders and touching her knees. She stares at her knuckles for a long time.

Eventually, she stands, her hands at her buttons and then at her zipper, then her thumbs hook over her waistband and pull low enough for me to see the top of her hips.

Oh god. Just one more minute, I tell myself. She shifts her hip; her jeans lower on one side. *Just one more minute*, I tell myself. She shifts the other hip, her jeans below the level of her black underwear. *One more minute…*

The wind changes, bringing the stench of the man who has now used the front door. The man who stood here, doing exactly what I'm doing.

I am better than this. At least that's what I tell myself. A shiver runs across my withers, and lowering my head, I follow that man who has gone uninvited through her front door. His stench leads east through the spotty woods. I move carefully, keeping close to uneven ground near trees, because I know this must be Liebling, and however strong I am, if those traps are still out there, I will be broken.

A possum scurries across my path, heading straight for a tree. I'm full, but I eat him anyway. Because of that perspective thing.

Liebling lives in a trailer. Not an RV; there is no vehicle here, just a white trailer with a beige-and-brown curlicue painted on the corrugated-metal side. It isn't old, but it's also not well maintained. A wire from the trailer loops around trees, heading, I presume, to the roadside and an illegal hookup.

The lights are blazing inside, so I circle the trailer cautiously, giving the rusting jumble of traps in the back an especially wide berth. With more of a bump than a jump, I put my paws carefully on the metal lip of the window, looking through the thin, lopsided blinds. He must have about as much room as Thea, but it is full, crammed with the thinginess of humans. A big boom box. A small TV on top of a VHS machine surrounded by piles of black plastic tapes with scraped-off labels. A microwave sitting on a propane stove. All sorts of objects I can't identify but that were probably once "As Seen on TV": a high casserole, a giant dumpling press, a plastic dish with fine combs for holding bacon upright. I know because there is still bacon in it, sitting in a puddle of cold grease.

Liebling is asleep on a bed that takes up all of one end of the trailer. He is still in his clothes, his feet hanging over the side of his bed, his boots kicked higgledy-piggledy to the floor next to a clear bottle of gin or vodka.

A gun rests on the beige-and-brown plaid arm of the built-in sofa next to his head.

I really don't like this man. The most satisfying thing to do would be to break through the flimsy front door and grab his neck in my jaws, then disembowel him. Satisfying but also messy, a potential PR disaster for the forever wolves, and a *Slitung*, if the Pack found out I had changed Offland and killed a human.

Besides, Pack law dictates that life not be taken frivolously and that anything we kill must be eaten. I really don't want to eat Liebling. I ate part of a state trooper once. He tasted like fat and Styrofoam. It was a week before I could eat anything other than oatmeal.

As soon as I'm in skin again, I nudge the door, because it's always worth trying the easy option first.

There is no latch, just a loose circle of string on the inside that keeps the door closed. All it takes is tracing one finger up through the gap to unhook the string and open the door. Unfortunately, the door is poorly hung and swings against the metal side of the trailer with a violent bang.

Liebling wakes with a start, his bleary, bloodshot eyes fixed on my naked body crowding in through the door of his cabin. He shrieks, and everything moves very fast. Grabbing for the gun on the sofa arm, he knocks it to the floor, then throws himself after it, dislodging the bacon cooker, so that when he tries to right himself, he slips on the bacon grease and hits his head on the edge of the white table holding the TV, which shudders for just a second before falling onto his neck. The gun in his hand goes off, and his hips jerk up, then settle back down with a sigh.

Blood seeps from under his body, mixing with bacon fat.

Well.

I lean over to feel his pulse, careful to avoid actually stepping inside. No matter where I place my inexpert fingers, there is nothing. I don't feel anything about his death. Humans think that their deaths are somehow more significant. Wolves don't see it that way. A human's death is no more significant than a deer's, except for that thing about humans tasting so much worse.

I only meant to tell him that I knew he'd entered Thea's cabin unlawfully and would be serving him with a cease-and-desist letter. What killed him was his humanity: carrion and guns and too much stuff.

When I leave, I don't close the door.

Folding myself back into the front seat of my car, I check my reflection in the rearview mirror. My hair bristles with forest detritus. My naked skin is caked with the scabrous bits of mud and the drying gore of that possum and the last gluey remains of my fur.

Okay, maybe I did have something to do with his death.

Still not going to eat him.

Chapter 10

Hāmweard, ðu londadl hǽðstapa, IN *15* DAYS
Homeward, you landsick heath-wanderer, IN *15* DAYS

I RUBBED AWAY ENOUGH OF THE MUD AND GORE TO SLIP past the somnolent parking attendant and the distracted night desk. In the shower of the gray suite, rivulets of mud and blood flow down the drain until finally they don't and it's just soap. I'm almost asleep when a waiter knocks on the door with breakfast. But instead of the continental breakfast I'd ordered yesterday, he lifts the bell on a full American with extra bacon. I wave him away, the taste of last night's superfluous possum rising suddenly in my mouth.

At nine, I call Samuel to ask him if he's found out anything about Liebling. There's a long pause.

"I left it on your desk yesterday."

"I'm not at my desk. I'm in Albany."

"You know I don't like transmitting anything electronically." He whispers elec*tron*ically with this odd emphasis like it's an obscenity.

"Samuel, just send it to me."

It turns out that Robert Liebling's real name is Robert Darling. There is an outstanding warrant for criminal trespass in Orlando where an old girlfriend had gotten a restraining order. Another outstanding warrant from some small town outside Oklahoma City. Samuel says he has dispatch records as if I needed further evidence that this is a man prone to violence against women.

It's about what I expected. There are two reasons humans live so far off the grid: either they see themselves as woodsmen, the heirs to Thoreau, or they're thugs on the lam.

I've known heirs to Thoreau, and they do not crap up their living spaces with a lot of stuff that is "As Seen on TV."

Before heading back to Thea's cabin, I call the Hamilton County Sheriff's Department, and by the time I arrive, there's already a black SUV with a big, gold star parked in front. Doug himself is parked in front of her door, talking to Thea.

"And you are?" Doug props his hand on the top of his holster.

"Elijah Sorensson." I bend my head in Thea's direction. "Thea's lawyer. I was the one who called about Liebling."

"Darling, you mean."

"Exactly. Did you get him?"

"Manner of speaking," Doug says, looking at me suspiciously, but at least he drops his hand from his holster. I try not to look at Thea. "We went to his cabin. Seems he shot himself."

"Suicide?"

"Doesn't look like it. As far as we can tell, he was drunk, reached for his gun, slipped around, the gun went off, he fell. The place was a mess. Animals got in."

"Uh-huh," I say, grimacing. "Animals."

"You called from New York?" When I hesitate, he explains that he knows most of the lawyers in Hamilton County and that my phone has a 917 area code.

"I had work in Albany when I heard from our firm's investigator and was worried. Due diligence, you know."

"Are you normally *this* diligent?" He's five inches shorter than I am, but I have to give him credit for not backing down, the way most humans do when they're forced to crick their necks to look at me. "Calling us," he says, "that I understand, but coming up here? Even from Albany, it's a schlep."

"Halvors, Sorensson & Trianoff is very thorough."

He sucks at his lips and then lets them go with a pop. "Okay, well. See you around, Thea. You know you can always call me."

She stands behind him on the threshold. "Thanks again. And I am sorry."

"It's all right. I should've known. I guess I always did."

He closes her door and then gives it an extra pull until the latch catches properly, as though showing me that he is someone who has learned how to close this door.

"You've got me blocked in," he says, nodding toward my car.

Doug pauses, his foot propped on the running board of his SUV.

"Eli?" he says.

"Elijah."

He looks from his high perch directly into my eyes. "You know, last year, I was standing right where you are. And it was Lee, the guy before me, getting into his car. Getting ready to drive away. I'll tell you what he told me. 'You think you're going to make her right, domesticate her, but you're not.' So now I'll tell you the same: you're not."

"I don't know what you're talking about. I'm just her lawyer."

"And I was just her drinking buddy," he says with a shrug. Then he clambers into his SUV and slams the door. In my Land Rover, I watch him pull the seat belt across his chest and catch his eyes in the rearview mirror.

I don't belt up.

Thea's cabin is spare and self-contained, the exact opposite of Liebling's trailer. Everything has its place: the backpack she took to find Mr. Fanning hangs from a cast-iron hook screwed into the wood. Ropes in differing lengths and thicknesses—each neatly tied and whipped in yellow—hang nearby, along with an ax.

Hanging from a hook up above everything is a long, dusty, mud-colored canvas case with H. VILLALOBOS stenciled in red letters.

The only furniture is a chaise with worn black-and-white floral upholstery that is clearly not original. A single wooden chair, a small pine table hinged like a school desk, and a bed.

"Coffee?" she asks. "I was just about to start another pot. Late night last night."

"Yeah. Sure. Thank you."

She pours some water into the teakettle and sets it on the cast-iron stove.

"It's the least I can do for your help," she says, retrieving a mason jar filled with ground coffee and another of sugar.

I try to imagine how to spin what little I did into something impressive. Magnificent. Something that will make her crave my power and my position. Make her feel how utterly imperative it is to see me again. To be with me.

Unlatching what looks like a small safe built into the side of the cabin, she pulls out a carton of milk. From a low shelf above her sink, she retrieves a single cup and a bowl with steep sides.

"Here's the truth. I didn't do anything. The letter you wrote for Liebling? The one that you showed me in New York? It would have been just fine as it was. A change or two maybe to make it stronger. Our letterhead, sure. But it was fine as it was."

"So why did you say it was more complicated?" The smell of coffee hits the back of my throat as she spoons the grounds into the filter.

"Because I wanted to see you again."

She stops for a moment before screwing the lid back on and returning it to the cold box.

"That's kind of pathetic."

"I know. I'm not used to being pathetic, but there it is."

A thin wisp of steam starts to curl up from the kettle.

"And why are you here now?"

"Same reason. I wanted to see you again, and after yesterday…I wasn't sure you would."

"You're right. I wouldn't have." She raises her arm, stroking her cheek with the back of her hand. "Your skin is so soft," she whispers, low and deep and urgent. "You should never wear anything but silk."

If I weren't so humiliated by the words, the sound of her voice would have made me come right there.

She grins and hands me the mug and a spoon.

"When you're done with that, give it back."

"What?"

"The spoon. I've only got one."

She pours milk into the bowl in front of her and then coffee, and then taking the spoon from my hand, she swirls the clouds of milk through her bowl of coffee.

It is so terribly, achingly intimate.

There is, I realize, looking over the rim of my mug, only one of anything here. A single cup. A single bowl. A single small skillet. A single pot. A single chair. A single plate. A single towel hanging from the bathroom door.

The only thing that might accommodate more than one is the bed with its thick duvet and four pillows.

Doug wanted to expand Thea's cabin. Install a refrigerator, a sofa, a TV. What did he say? "That'd be nice, right?" He wanted more. More noise, more stuff, more *him*.

But he missed the point of this place. Thea's cabin isn't just a shelter that could use modernizing and expanding; it's a bulwark protecting her solitude. And no matter what he thought could be done, should be done, it would not be done, because there was no room here for more Doug or more of any man.

But...I am not any man. I am not a man at all. And as wolves, we understand what it is to be wordless. We understand the primal importance of silence.

She stirs distractedly, staring at the silence beyond the window.

"How long have you been here?"

"Four years," she says, "give or take."

"That's a long time to be in the middle of nowhere. Do you ever get bored?"

"Bored? Never. I like the quiet. Helps me focus. For

me, things get muddled when there are too many voices telling you what to do or how to be. Can I warm you up?"

You have got to be kidding me.

I glare down at the mountain ridge in my pants, pointing out that the only thing this woman with a steaming pot in her hand is offering to warm up is my coffee.

My cock does not listen, and my brain suddenly goes all curious about whether Doug is out of the picture. Because I don't want him or anyone else offering to refill *her*.

"You don't get lonely?"

"Sometimes. Not a big deal. Then I just make more effort to see friends. But most of the people I see need me. I like it. It feels more real than when someone's squeezing you into their schedule, praying that you'll cancel at the last minute." She taps at the window with her finger, then wags the same finger. Even I, who am a creature of the forest, can't see who she's reprimanding. "Do you?" she asks. "Get lonely, I mean."

"Me? *Pffft*. I see people all the time."

"That's not what I asked."

I think of all the clients I have spent time with, laughing and impressing and cajoling. And all the women I have spent time with, laughing and impressing and seducing. And in the end, have come home, vomited, and crawled into bed with a wolf-shaped hole in my chest.

"Yes. Sometimes."

There's a narrow shelf above the window at my eye level. Arrayed across it are a handful of things, none of them "As Seen on TV." An elaborate corkscrew of woody bracket. An almost baroquely gnarled branch. The perfectly intact skin of what looks to be a rat snake.

Several small cardboard boxes that read 20 CRTG. 7.62 MM LONG RANGE 118 in sun-bleached lettering.

And a gleaming white skull that I recognize instantly.

I freeze.

"You can hold it if you want," she says, standing on her toes, her fingers feeling carefully along the shelf. "It's not going to bite. Not now, anyway."

Stepping closer to help, I get too close, so that when Thea turns around, her hand accidentally brushes a mother-of-pearl button, which grazes the top placket of my shirt, which touches the bottom placket, which touches my skin. She hands the skull to me.

Dust motes shimmering in sunlight float down around her.

"I found it," she says, stepping away. She rubs the back of her hand. "A marten skull, I think? Anyway, it's beautiful."

I gently follow the arabesque of its jaw with my finger. The fine crested ridge.

"Have you ever seen them hunt?" I finally choke out.

"A marten?"

"Fisher. It's a fisher. They... It's like gravity doesn't apply. If they're hunting, they'll just jump off a rock and"—my arm traces a spiral in front of me—"swim. Like an otter, except there's no water, only air."

Carefully, I put the skull back on its shelf. I was forty-two moons old when Nils put my fisher on a shelf of First Kills next to all those bunnies and squirrels. I didn't pay much attention to it after, because there were all those skulls, and some of them were ancient, and like the *Gemyndstow*, they were a reminder of the persistence of the Pack. I didn't realize how fragile that world was until I was older. Until Nils was gone and John was gone and the Great Hall was gone and the shelf was gone and that fisher was gone.

Now. Now I know how fragile it is.

"I miss it so much." I stand back, looking at this other skull arrayed on this other shelf. "I miss it all."

Thea holds me with her ironwood eyes, her head cocked to the side. I think I may actually have spoken.

Chapter 11

Hāmweard, ðu londadl hǣðstapa, IN *11* DAYS
Homeward, you landsick heath-wanderer, IN *11* DAYS

I SHOULD PROBABLY GET A MATE.

A bedfellow at the very least.

Bedfellow. Leonora once tried to explain that a fiancée is like a bedfellow except neither of you have to fight challengers claiming *cunnan-riht*. Fucking rights.

Celia has been a stalwart shielder, but she is too closely related to be a bedfellow.

Besides, being Alpha of the Pack is different from being Alpha of the echelon. Especially in the beginning, one cannot afford even the appearance of weakness or indecision in front of a pack of wolves just spoiling for a fight. For that reason, it is helpful to have someone who can talk you through any doubts and concerns in the privacy of bed. Wolves tend to be receptive to Alphas, so the list of possible candidates is long. Limiting it to strong hunters narrows the list down somewhat. Limiting it to fund managers who can offset my weakness with numbers narrows it to Tilda.

She's been at Bank of Boston for seven years and is probably anxious to come home.

I try to imagine Tilda by my side and in my bed. I even try to picture her wearing the braid of a mated wolf around her neck, with her coal-black hair and her skin the gold of rye and her ironwood eyes and her ass like a Japanese pear.

Except that Tilda has hazel eyes, ruddy skin, fine blond hair, and the body of an East German shot-putter.

"Good morning, Mr. Sorensson. I believe Mr. Trianoff is looking..."

I nod distractedly and keep walking.

At my office, I flip on the light and turn to the large envelope in the emptiness of oak next to my telephone.

Personal and Confidential, it says. The opening on the back is sealed, and across the seal is a signature. *Samuel Borston*.

There are two folders inside. The thicker one has a tab with LIEBLING/DARLING printed on it in ballpoint. As he's uninteresting and dead, I put it aside.

Instead, I open the other, thinner one, the one that says VILLALOBOS.

There isn't much. She is thirty-five. Born in Fort Benning, Georgia. Her mother was a housewife. Her father was a sniper, first for the army, then for the Tucson police force. Both dead in a car accident nearly five years ago. DUI. She went to college in Texas for one year before transferring to Syracuse, which must have come as a shock to a girl who'd apparently never made it north of the 34th parallel before.

She kicked around a little. Worked at a cider brewery. At a veterinary clinic. As a tour guide in the Finger Lakes. Did some work—mostly clerical—for the police department in Ithaca. Then went to Pulaski to train as an ECO. Spent some time in the City and Long Island before transferring to Hamilton County.

And that's it. She has managed to glide through a

third of a century leaving barely a trace. Barely. Samuel did include an article from the *Austin Beacon* about a girl who died in a fall from the roof of a campus building. It wasn't much of a story, but Samuel has highlighted both the caption to the photograph and a few lines from the story. "One distraught young woman started ripping off her clothes before school officials escorted her away. 'Our students were all deeply affected by the tragedy,' said school counselor, Solange Marisco. 'Some more than others.'"

The other side is blank.

The photograph shows a building: a wood-sided house with Greek letters under the gabled roof. A group of girls and boys stand to one side, the girls almost all burying their heads in the boys' shoulders. But standing alone is another girl. I turn on my desk light and look closely. It looks like Thea, and it doesn't.

She has been "dolled up" as humans sometimes say. I'm used to seeing women "dolled up" and never really cared enough to notice the difference between a simulacrum of a woman and the real thing.

But none of this looks right on Thea. Not the hard black around her eyes, not the soft black above them. Not the dark lips or the pale skin or the waved hair or the jewelry or the cropped T-shirt laddered down the back. Nor the tiny, tight skirt that she is in the process of removing.

She looks both utterly calm and completely furious, her thumbs hooked around the waistband that is already at her thighs. The *Austin Beacon* reporter is probably himself barely more than a child. He's got a story that combines death and nudity and coeds. To him, a hysterical college girl makes good sense and makes good copy.

A girl who has decided she is done with make-believe... That requires experience.

Another light snaps on in the office, and Maxim stalks past windows lit by the pale-purple morning light, looking as dark and threatening as a man with a face like a basset hound can look.

"Good morning, Max. What are you doing here so early?"

Even though Dahlia is the only other person here and the architectural glass is quite soundproof, Max closes the door. There is no disguising his fury as he turns on me, his hands splayed on my desk.

I ease back in the Titan, my fingers woven behind my head, and watch him yell. With his mouth yapping furiously, he reminds me of Tarzan.

"I don't know what is going on with you, Sorensson." He's used my last name to indicate the high degree of his pissedness. "But you need to get a grip. Do something. Get a wife, have some kids, settle down. Or go fuck a string of women. I really don't care. But don't ever waste this firm's time and money and political capital on a stunt like that again.

"The political capital," he snaps again.

Slowly and deliberately, I unweave my fingers. Then I just as deliberately push my computer's On button.

"*Did you hear me?*"

I deliberately stand and deliberately lean forward, bending my back until my nose is an inch from Maxim's. A low rumble burbles in the depths of my chest. My wild remembers the image of Sarah in the crosshairs and strains with the need to claw flanks and rip muzzles.

I am the Alpha of the 9th. This time next week, I will challenge the Alpha of the Great North. Then I will fight, and I will win. And I will *be* the Alpha of the Great North.

The growl escapes, and any wolf would recognize it as the prelude to an attack. With a sprightly *drrriiing*, my computer comes to life.

"Close the door on your way out, Maxim."

I pull out a tissue to wipe away the lingering damp handprints.

Chapter 12

Hāmweard, ðu londadl hǽðstapa, IN *5* DAYS
Homeward, you landsick heath-wanderer, IN *5* DAYS

THERE IS SOMETHING TERRIBLY WRONG WITH THE intercom link to reception, and Dahlia's voice burbles and screeches from the speaker like a panicked fox. "Mr. Sor*#%sson? Umm, the*#% someone *#%? Says he's %&# Gr*#t North LLC?"

"Did you say the Great North?"

"*#&"

Was that a yes? And what the hell is the Great North doing here? There's no law about it, but there is definitely an understanding that our size makes any gathering of wolves Offland a cause for comment. We don't want humans commenting about us. We don't want them noticing us at all.

"Who is it?" I crane my head to see where Janine has gone.

"He won't say. But"—her screeching-enhanced yell drops to a screeching-enhanced whisper—"I think you *#% get out here."

"He." I don't know who it could be, but at least it's not Evie or Tara, her Beta, the two wolves I least want to see right now. I pass Janine's desk; her coat and purse are both gone.

Nestled between the offices that hug the plate-glass

windows and the architectural glass of reception is a spacious and elaborate waiting area. Empty leather Knoll chairs are scattered here and there, each attended by concrete-topped side tables, fresh flowers, and glass bottles of water imported from places too cold for humans to have mucked up. They all attend upon the pleasure of clients who never come. Our clients pay too much to wait, so the whole thing is just a symbol of success. HST is so rich, it says, that we can afford to be profligate with space on the tiny, crowded island of Manhattan.

Several members of the staff, who all have better things to do, start tidying and adjusting: moving water bottles, plucking stray leaves, fluffing pillows and then chopping them so they are slightly dented in the top. Lauren, from Client Services, rearranges the hollow balls made of lacquered vines. As soon as she sees me, she holds my arm and nods toward the wall next to the elevator, as though I could miss the huge man who is leaning there reading because his body is too big to fit into the large, commodious furniture we provide for our large, commodious clients.

There is one other wolf that I really don't want to see.

"Tiberius."

"Elijah," he says, pulling himself upright.

"Should we go into my office?"

"Probably for the best." He looks impassively at the swarming humans busily doing nothing.

"Do you mind if I take this?" He holds the *Atlantic* up to Dahlia who bobbles her head like it's not fastened on quite right.

The water movers and tchotchke arrangers and leaf pluckers and pillow fluffers stop what they're doing and head toward their desks, all via the hall leading to mine.

"Did you have a nice trip?"

"It was fine. A little tie-up at the GWB, but other than that, no complaints. Nice setup you have here."

"One makes do," I say jovially as we enter my office.

As soon as the door closes, I turn to face him.

"So what the fuck are you doing here, Shifter?"

"I'm here on Great North business."

"You should have used the phone. Now I'm going to have to make up some bullshit about football. I hate talking about football."

"I would have used the phone," he says, leaning forward, his eyes mute, "but seeing as you wouldn't take *your Alpha's* calls, I had no reason to think you would take mine."

Neither of us backs down. I turn over the picture of Thea that I left on my desk. "Which brings me back to my first question. What are you doing here?"

"The Pack needs a new copy of the trust, because the one at the Homelands went up in flames."

"That's it?"

"That's it. We need to rebuild. The Alpha also wants to familiarize herself with the changes you've made."

The changes I made because it turns out that Tiberius's father had found a loophole that would have allowed him to control all our assets by the simple expedient of turning the Pack of four hundred into a Pack of one. Well, two. His son and the crippled runt Tiberius would do anything to protect.

It's hard to hide my resentments. My resentment over the destruction he has brought to our Pack. My resentment over the rebuilding that is taking place without me. When I am Alpha, it will be my turn to decide what to do about the Shifter.

Unlocking the safe, I pull out the thick, green letter box holding the voluminous pages of the Pack trust. I toss Thea's file into its place.

I call for reception. "Dahlia? Did Janine go out for lunch?"

"I haven't seen her."

"I need someone to do some—"

Tiberius pushes a button and hangs up on Dahlia. "*We* copy the trust." I start to object. "Soon after you brought the trust to the Homelands for us to sign, my father knew every detail. I believe, and the Alpha agrees, that someone here—"

I cut him off before he can say any more. "Or maybe his son gave him access to the copy in John's office?"

He looks down at the desk for a moment, then lifts his hand in front of him. Tiberius's right hand is branded with the Ur rune. It was meant as both a punishment and a reminder to him of the importance of the wild. His left hand, though, the one he holds up to me, was not branded but impaled. The third and fourth finger overlap slightly, and there is a giant, ragged starburst in the middle of his palm.

"If I had done what my father wanted, he wouldn't have found it necessary to nail me to a post with a dog spike." He tightens his fingers into a fist and then stretches them again. I can tell by the way he moves that the hand will never be whole. "I'm not saying it was you, Alpha. But until I know otherwise, I don't trust anyone."

He picks up the letter box from the floor beside me,

as if I can't even be trusted to carry this thing that I've tended for more than two decades, my only fucking progeny. Then, with an elaborately courteous sweep of his arm, he indicates the door.

Wolves. I cluck with disgust and lead the way through the pale halls, past the associates' offices and conference rooms, through the waiting area with its pointless water bottles. Opening the transparent glass door to reception.

"Dahlia? Could you have someone look into my intercom?"

Then I open the opaque green-glass door into the bullpen. Here, the whispered voices are crowded around, close at hand.

Sinise from accounting laughs with one of the clerks. "That's not what Janine says. She says he's hung like a fucking bear."

"You mean 'bull,'" the clerk corrects her.

"Whatever. I mean, a bear's gotta be hung, right?"

"I don't know anything about bear prick, but I do know that the expression is 'hung like a bull.'"

Sinise snorts. "I'll tell you what. When I've seen it for myself, I will give you a *full* report."

"Pretty sure of yourself, aren't you?"

"Look, it's not even a thing. He'll do anybody who's clean and has a decent set of tits."

Oh my god, that's sad. I would say how pathetic to be that man, but, of course, I am that man. I know just how pathetic it is.

Tiberius's senses are freakish in skin, so he hears—how could he not?—but he doesn't react. Before he came to the Homelands, before he met Quicksilver, he was just like me. A man of the world. Of this world.

He asks loudly where the copy room is.

Sinise pops her head out of one of the cubicles, her face ashen. She pulls it back in and starts babbling noisily about billable hours.

"Almost there."

There are two clerks in the room. I kick them out and close the door. There is no lock, so Tiberius unplugs one of the copiers and pushes it against the door. Dust snakes that had been hidden beneath are suddenly exposed and trundle across the floor. "Now," he says, "which one do we use?"

"This is why we have staff," I say irritably as I search around. There are several machines. Some are big; some are smaller. One is very big, as if maybe the bullpen uses it for all those stupid *Calm Down and Lawyer Up* posters.

I head toward one that is centrally located. Tiberius and I both stare at it blankly.

"Where do the originals go?" he asks.

"No idea," I snap again. "*That's why we have staff.* Maybe here, where the rectangles are?"

Tiberius pounds the edges of the sheaf of papers.

"And who among that staff had access to the trust?" Tiberius asks, piling the pages in a tray.

"No one. My assistant copies only the signature addendum when we are adding to the Pack. But she doesn't handle the trust itself. And only John—well, now Evie—and I have the combination to my safe."

Tiberius pushes the green button with a circle and a line in the middle. A light goes on, but nothing happens. "You're sure she didn't touch anything else?"

"Absolute..." But even as I say it, I can't help but

think of the times she flitted around my office either being professional or very, very unprofessional. I was always careful to put the trust away. I was always careful that the safe was closed and locked. Even when I was in the middle of that raging castor-induced hunger, I was always responsible.

Wasn't I?

I look at the machine. When did things get so complicated, and what *are* all these buttons for?

Suddenly, Tiberius pushes something, and the machine starts its rapid-fire suck and cough. "Don't touch anything," he says.

"I wasn't going to touch anything. Jesus."

Tiberius stands silently, stooped over the shelf holding the Pack trust, drawing in deep breaths as the pages fly in and out of the machine. When it's done, he picks up the original and riffles the pages.

"But someone else has had this," he says, fanning the pages once more toward me. My senses in skin are strong compared to the humans, but they are nothing like my wild senses. And even my wild senses are nothing like the freakish array of Tiberius's mixed Pack-Shifter heritage. Still, I would definitely be able to catch the unmistakable carrion-and-steel stench of humans.

"I don't smell anyone."

"You're not scenting for someone; you're scenting for some*thing*. It's faint, but it is there. Try again."

This time when he fans the pages against my nose, I catch the slightest whiff of something I can only describe as a mix of lavender breeze and the off-gassing of polypropylene carpets.

"What *is* that?"

"Industrial smoke remover, but Shifters sometimes use it to wash their hands when they're trying to hide what they're doing from other Shifters."

"Oh please." I slip the still-warm trust into its brand-new letter box. "Offland is full of fake smells. Don't be so paranoid."

I shove the box into one of the bags floating around the office from a charity run that HST sponsors.

"You should change the combination."

Tiberius is starting to get on my nerves.

I thrust the bag toward him. STRIDE TO SURVIVE, it says in bold, white letters. The handles of the bright-pink bag are not long enough to fit over his huge shoulder.

"Oh, and Silver thought I should tell you that I will be challenging the Alpha for supremacy of the Great North this coming moon."

"*What?*"

"I will," he repeats slowly, "be challenging the Alpha for supremacy of the Great North this coming moon."

"I heard you the first time. There is no way—*no way*—the Great North would...accept...a Shifter...as..."

I know what he's doing. He has no interest in challenging for the Alpha spot. This is not about fighting Evie; this is about fighting *me*. According to our law, two wolves who challenge for the same position must fight each other first. Then only the winner is allowed to proceed.

With Evie weak, Tiberius is the one wolf, the *only* wolf, who might have a chance at stopping me from coming home.

"I hope there are no hard feelings?"

We are Pack. Fighting is how we settle status. It

would be like a human holding a grudge because his cousin wore pricier shoes to Thanksgiving dinner.

"No, of course not."

As he walks away, the pink satchel swings daintily from his forearm. Tiberius knows his wild now. He holds it burned into his skin and safe in his heart. And these women who smile at him with half-closed eyes and these men who scuttle out of his way are as meaningless to him as dried leaves to the wind.

Chapter 13

Hāmweard, ðu londadl hǽðstapa, IN 2 DAYS
Homeward, you landsick heath-wanderer, IN 2 DAYS

PACK LAW EVOLVES VERY SLOWLY. OUR CULTURE IS OLD, and our nature is wary. John liked to say that "an Alpha cannot lead via Skype. It has no teeth." Maybe Skype doesn't, but I do. Because there is no law that says an Alpha must be on the Homelands, anyone who has had an issue with my primacy of the 9th has had to take it up the way wolves do: with tooth and claw.

Plenty have tried, but I am too strong, and now after thirty years of challenges, I am the most formidable fighter in the Great North. I know better than any of the Great North how a wolf fights and how a wolf wins.

Tiberius may be a killer of men, but the one time he fought wild was when he and Silver paired off against the 14th's Alpha pair.

What a fucking mess that was. Tiberius stumbled around, letting Solveig get the better of him over and over, until lulled by a kind of lupine rope-a-dope, she raised herself to strike the final blow and he lashed out, almost killing her.

Quicksilver simply grabbed Eudemos's balls with her teeth and held on for dear life while the big lug scratched at her like a deer tick.

Still, I am leaving nothing to chance. At 9:00, the gym

is still populated by a posse of humans hoping to retain sexual viability into late middle age, so I pretend to grunt and strain over two hundred pounds until they go.

Then I start the real work.

I smell Janine before she knocks on the doorframe, so I nod without looking up when she does. My desk is more cluttered than usual with loose ends I am trying to wrap up before I leave for good. Janine moves things around, clearing a space for the mail that needs my personal attention. She usually leaves, but this time, she doesn't.

"You going back up to visit *the silent partners*?" she asks.

"Hmm." I scribble something I need to double-check in LexisNexis. *Why the odd emphasis?*

"What do you do up there?"

"Business."

"That doesn't sound like a lot of fun. But maybe it would be more fun if, you know, you had company."

The trace of her fingernails along the back of my neck is like nettles.

I sit back to see what she really wants. The hand that had been scraping so irritatingly across my skin falls. The other is holding an ivory envelope with a black embossed snowflake and an inscription that reads *"Because of the cold, they kindled a fire and received us all." –Acts 28:2.*

Then I know. This is the invitation to an event that everyone calls L-Cubed. Maybe not everyone, because officially, it's some combination of Homeless or Hospitals or Help or Hearts, but most everyone knows it as L-Cubed because while there are always a few celebrities, the guest list is overwhelmingly lawyers, lobbyists, and lawmakers.

It is the most important networking event of the year, and HST always buys a table.

"Should I take care of this for you?" Janine asks, picking it up and tapping the edge of it on her lips. Not terribly subtle. She has clearly heard that I buy clothes and shoes and bags and cuts and colorings and waxings and whatever other treatments are necessary to assure that my plus-one reflects well on me and maintains my place in the hierarchy.

Naturally, she presumes that as I have plumbed the mysteries of her dragon, she is the most plausible recipient for clothes, shoes, bags, cuts, colorings, and waxings.

"I'll take care of it," I say, turning again to my computer screen. "Later."

Now she taps the envelope against the desk, unwilling to let it go. She doesn't understand, and I can't tell her that I am not saying no to *her*. I'm saying no to parties, no to the Plaza, no to lawyers, no to humans.

No to Offland.

I'm saying I don't give a damn what happens with this, because in five days, my challenge will be fought and won. The Iron Moon will be over. And Tara will call Maxim to tell him that the board of managers has voted for me to replace the interim CEO of Great North LLC.

Then there will be no lever long enough to shift me away from the Homelands again.

"What do you think this is?" Janine says, shaking a small box against her ear. The scent of pine wafts to my twitching nose, and I hold out my hand.

T. Villalobos is scrawled on the top left-hand corner. *Fragile*, it says. *Personal*.

Janine watches expectantly like a child who believes every box, no matter how small, must include something for her.

My hand covers the box completely, because whatever it is, it is Personal and Fragile and is from Thea to me. *To me*.

"I don't know."

She doesn't leave at first, not until she sees my face stripped of the practiced look of consideration and compromise, revealing instead the millennia of Alphas whose rock-hard will is my legacy.

Janine backs away from my desk.

"Close it, Janine."

In the bottom drawer of my desk, hidden under everything else, is my seax, the dagger that every adult Pack wears. It slides easily through the tape holding the brown paper recycled from the local Publix. An envelope on the outside reads DON'T SHAKE.

So you don't miss "it" quite so much.
Thank you.
Thea

Poking one finger through the dried fir needles she used as packing, I feel the high ridge and the graceful arabesque of the jaw. I dig out the fisher skull, blowing off the dried duff until the skull lies pale and slender in my palm.

Maybe this was meant as a goodbye gift, but it's

nothing like those pearl-gray silk robes that served as a sop to my underwhelmed conscience. Those shallow white boxes I left for whatever woman was in room 513.

When I take over the Alpha's office, I will put the fisher skull front and center on the shelves holding the Pack's First Kills, even though it's not Pack and not First and not a Kill. My mind is already spinning out a future that has nothing to do with taking Tilda as bedfellow. It has entirely to do with spending nights in Arietta and comforting this huge, overfull erection between Thea's thighs.

I'm afraid to adjust it, afraid the touch of my hand will set it off.

Why couldn't I have felt this with one of those hundreds of women who laid themselves down and made every orgasm a chore? Why for this woman? Why for this one who hasn't tried to seduce me? Whose only touch was a handshake. Oh, and the accidental flick of her hand against my button, which touched my top placket, which touched my bottom placket, which touched the skin above my heart. She touched my skin.

Slamming the door shut to my executive washroom, I barely manage to push my cock down before the great bone-white streaks explode in pulses that match the rhythm of my heart.

"Mr. Sorensson?"

Gripping the side of the sink, I look at myself in the mirror. My still-hard sex mocks me between the open zipper of my vicuña trousers and the tails of my high-count white twill shirt.

"Elijah?" Janine says more softly this time. "Are you all right? Do you need something?"

"I'm fine. Just...just spilled something. On my shirt." After zipping up, I run water over one of the fine towels by the side of my sink and use it to wipe the mirror. Then I dab at my shirt, so when I head back out to Janine, I have a plausible wet spot.

I shouldn't have worried. Janine's eyes are locked on the bathroom mirror with its filmy smear of drying wolf semen.

Chapter 14

Wilcume, ðu londadl hǽðstapa.
Welcome, you landsick heath-wanderer.

At the rusted sign saying *Private Drive*, I yank hard on the steering wheel, heading onto the rough, narrow road with deep trenches on either side. It is a nearly impossible entrance, but we like it that way. All but the most practiced hands will find themselves spinning their wheels in the gutter.

A few yards in, the road takes a curve at the deserted fire watchtower, and here, hidden from the asphalt, I hit the brakes. Looking up through the windshield, I let the stillness of the place I love take me over. The pale-gold-and-gray sky is a cutwork pattern through the bare branches of the hardwoods and the spiky tops of the evergreens. Through the windows come the smells of damp bark and needles, the sounds of mallards overhead, which must mean that the ice is breaking on Home Pond. The land stretches and expands as the deep layers of frost recede and it starts to remember that spring is a possibility.

I will never leave again.

Everything that is of any importance to me is in a paper bag from Whole Foods I found in the trash room. Toothbrush, the trust, degrees, seax, the picture of my echelon, and the fisher skull nestled in its box of pine needles. I didn't bother to bring any of the bespoke suits or shirts.

"Hello, Mei."

The wolf on gate duty waves me through but does not look happy about it.

"Want a ride?" I call through the open window.

Her back toward me, she threads the thick chain tight through the fence and clicks the padlock. Then, without a backward glance, she lopes through the trees toward Home Pond.

I take it that means no.

Parking beside the assortment of Wranglers and Land Rovers, I slam the door. There's something particularly satisfying in that *thunk*, as though the Land Rover's door is the door on another life.

At Home Pond, only the pups are wild. The adults are all in skin as they are in the hours before the Iron Moon, because the Moon is like a current, pulling us further along our feral spectrum. If she finds us in skin, she makes us wild. But if she finds us already wild, she makes us *ǣcewulfas*, forever wolves. Real wolves. Because the pups are already at the wildest end of the spectrum, they cannot be pushed any further.

She allows them this kindness until they are juveniles. Then they too must greet her in skin.

I don't know where the 9th is. I can't find anyone. None of them are in their cabins, and as I search for them, every member of the Pack looks at me angrily. Wolves I've known my whole life turn their backs to me.

There's someone at the Boathouse. I was right; the ice must have broken, because there is a slow splashing in the water. At the edge of the dock, watching the mallards at the dark center of Home Pond, her feet breaking through the thin brittle ice at the edge of Home Pond, is a small female with a long mane of silver hair that glows in the fading daylight.

She sprints up as I approach, her bare feet and jeans wet with icy water. Silver has always been more wolfish than the rest of us. In skin too. It's not just her silver hair or the long eyeteeth; it's something that's harder to pinpoint. It's almost as though the earth talks to her in her human form, the way it talks to the rest of us when we're wolves. Even the way she moves—the sudden reactions, the loping steps—all are more wolf than woman.

"Did you set him up to it?"

"Tiberius?"

"Yes, Tiberius. I don't believe he would have challenged me if you hadn't told him to."

"Tiberius was going to challenge you. I only advised him because he doesn't know our law. He hadn't understood that if he challenged you instead of the Alpha, it changed nothing. That even if he had won, you could still fight Evie. Now, if he wins, you can't."

"I've been fighting wolves longer than he's been alive. He will not win."

"Don't underestimate him, Alpha."

She stamps her naked feet on the grass. She is more resistant to cold than most, but even she feels the iced water of Home Pond.

"And why are you so set against me, Quicksilver?"

"I'm not set against you. I barely know you. But *you* barely know the Homelands. Everyone's in a bad mood. The Alpha's control is weak at least until she is fully recovered. There is a lot of anger against Tiberius. They blame him for John's death. And then you decide to challenge Evie for what? For more power?"

"I'm not doing it for power. I need to come home. I need—"

"*You need?* We just lost four wolves. We lost our Alpha. We lost the Great Hall. We almost lost our pups. *We* do not need or *want* an Alpha who is so human that he puts his own needs first."

Her head cocks slightly, her eyes shooting toward the horizon. "It's almost time," she says, already struggling out of her sweater.

I run toward the Meeting House, pulling at my tie. By the time I get there, the Great North is assembled around the steps, huge and fierce and naked, too proud and too hot-blooded to huddle under blankets even in the sharp cold of the last breath of an Adirondack winter. Evie closes the door and stands at the top next to Victor, our Deemer. Her face is expressionless, but Victor nods once.

The Deemer is exempt from hard work so that he can devote his time to thinking about and teaching our law. He is also exempt from challenges, so that fear does not have a role in the dispensing of it. Unlike the rest of the Pack, his body is thick, almost heavy, in stark contrast to Evie. Without her clothes, it's easy to see how much she lost. She is a tall woman with broad shoulders and strong legs, but pregnancy, lying-in, and nursing have drained her, and her bones seem about to break through her espresso skin.

Her expression doesn't change as I push my way through the Pack. Everyone clearly already knows, but a challenge has its formalities. As soon as I open my mouth, an angry rumble of suppressed growls flows through the Pack. It stops again when the Deemer holds up an imperious hand.

I strip as I speak. Shoes, socks, and pants are easy enough to slip out of when we change, but if the change hits before you get out of your button-down shirt and tie, you're stuck with it for the next seventy-two hours. A wolf in a silk tie and Egyptian cotton is a fool, and the Pack does not suffer cowards, weaklings, or fools gladly.

"Evie Kitwanasdottir. By the ancient rites and laws of our ancestors"—my tie falls to snow and earth churned under the Pack's feet—"and under the watchful eye of our Pack, I, Elijah Sorensson"—I struggle out of my shirt, straining to pull it over the expanse of my shoulders—"challenge you for Primacy of the Great North." My cap-toe Oxfords land in the muck, followed by my socks. "With fang and claw, I will attend upon you the last day of this Iron Moon."

Hopping on one leg, I kick off my pants and briefs. Damp mud soaks through the camouflage I've worn so long. When my foot comes down, it lands on the silk tie, and my Offland leash sinks into the icy sludge.

The Pack rustles and then parts, letting Tiberius through. Silver walks by his side, snapping at a wolf who doesn't get out of their way fast enough.

"Evie Kitwanasdottir," he repeats. "By the ancient rites and laws of our ancestors and under the watchful eye of our Pack, I, Tiberius Malasson, challenge you for Primacy of the Great North. With fang and claw, I will attend upon you the last day of this Iron Moon."

The rumble starts up again.

"Our laws are clear," Victor says. "If two wolves challenge for the same position, only the dominant may continue forward. On the last day of this moon, Elijah Sorensson and Tiberius Malasson will meet to determine which is allowed to fight for primacy of the Great North."

Then Evie and Victor walk down the stairs to stand among the assembled wolves. I still can't find anyone from the 9th.

"You will win, Alpha," says a voice behind me. Victor stands at my shoulder but takes care not to look at me.

"Of course."

"Good," he grunts. "The Pack has strayed. We need an Alpha who will bring us back to the Old Ways. Bring us back to greatness."

He glares at Tiberius with his mate. Silver runs her hand along the scars at his neck before her pale hand pulls his dark mouth to hers for one last kiss before the change.

"*Min coren*," she says in the Old Tongue. *My chosen, my beloved*.

Victor has a sour, evil look in his eyes.

"*Ēadig wáþ*." Evie calls out the traditional blessing, wishing her wolves three days of happy wandering and hunting. She was not raised in the Great North, and her accent has always rung strange.

When I repeat the blessing, it is perfect, unaccented as befits a wolf descended directly from the wolves of Mercia. The Deemer and a few others exchange smiles in recognition of my flawless diction.

The 9th has finally joined the assembly. Clearly, they waited until the last minute. I run toward them, leaning in to mark each wolf as I do at the beginning and end of every Iron Moon. They all receive my mark, but they are stiff and resentful. Even Celia doesn't look at me.

There is something going on in the Pack that sits uncomfortably with me. I need to talk to them, find out what it is, and at least explain that I'm not doing this for something as trivial as power. But it's too late: the little bones in my feet start to shuffle and change. My jaw begins to thrust forward, my tongue lengthens, my mouth rips open into my cheeks, and I collapse onto the slushy soil. *This* change I can't control. It doesn't start with my wrists; it hits me all at once. My feet, my shoulders, my hips. My face. Then my eyes and ears begin to rearrange themselves in my skull, leaving me deaf and blind. The only thing I hear is the thumping of my heart against a background of dull static.

The prickling of my skin subsides and is replaced by the prickling of little pup claws clambering over my back as they search through the carpet of writhing adults, waiting for someone to hunt with. The bigger the wolf, the longer the change, and by the time my wolfish ears can hear the snuffling and shaking of fur and clacking of claws, most everyone else is turned. Tiberius is still in that awkward between moment. His little silver-furred mate doesn't like me looking at his still-twitching body and lunges at me.

I leap into the air and fall back to earth. I have no fight with her. I have no fight with any of them, because I love them all.

I love them all.

They think I am too human. They think that I have forgotten that our only real power is the power of sacrifice.

The sacrifices John made were evident to everyone. In his hard work, in the scars on his body that he gladly took at every *Bredung*, when his blood was required to symbolize the bond of Pack and land and mates.

They can't see the sacrifices I've made Offland. No amount of blood or sweat could ever equal the pain of the alienation and the slow rot at my core.

Evie is having trouble steering the Pack. They recognize weakness in a new leader and in a female still recovering from her lying-in. When she pushes a couple of the echelons to hunting grounds farther up the mountain, some wolves challenge her. Even weak though, she is a decisive fighter. She wastes no time in posturing and goes straight for the throat. Her flank glistens with blood.

Victor is everywhere. Some wolves accept his marking; some do not. He does not approach Eudemos, Alpha of the 14th, Silver and Tiberius's echelon.

Celia, my shielder, snaps at him when he approaches the 9th. But then she snaps at me too when I try to approach Sarah.

There will be plenty of time to prove that I have what it takes to be a great Alpha. My paws break through the brittle crust of snow as I follow the scent of a tick-weakened buck mingled with foraged wintergreen. When he is down, I gnaw only on the gristly lower hind leg, leaving the best parts for my echelon and the rest of the Pack. Though pups and the lower subordinates are the only ones who deign to eat from my offering.

At night, the haunting calls of wolves echo around the mountains and make my heart ache. When I respond, my own howl breaks in the middle.

Challenges all take place on the last day of the Iron Moon, and like everything else, there is a hierarchy. Wolves fighting for *cunnan-riht* to the 13th's Gamma male start. Then, slowly, we move up to the most important challenge of each echelon. Tiberius and I will come last, as we are fighting for the highest position of all.

Next to last. The last will be my fight with Evie.

The paddock of low logs where we will fight is sprayed with the dark blood of old fights and the brighter blood of recent ones. Claws have already churned the icy earth into cold mud. Pacing back and forth, I watch one fight after another, waiting impatiently for my exile to end.

The losing challenger to the 3rd Echelon's Beta spot drags herself over the paddock wall, a large hunk of her hind leg hanging by a thread. Tara throws back her head in a long, sustained howl that lowers and then rises again before dying away.

A high response that falls and then quickly rises and ends abruptly comes not from Tiberius but from his mate. I add my own low, menacing howl to the mix, just to remind the Pack that I, at least, know *how to fucking howl*.

Tiberius breaks through the trees beyond the Boathouse and lopes toward the paddock. He is huge in skin, but wild, he is as big as night. The little silver wolf joins him, her muzzle dark with blood from the hunt. She leaps up, her front legs splayed across her mate's shoulders, then gives him a big, open-jawed kiss across his ear.

As he jumps over the low wall, I see he has become more graceful than the last time when he fought Solveig under the watchful eye of John. Both dead because of him. It is no small irony that he is defending Evie against me.

Everything is crystal clear at the start. The silent

wolves standing watch around the paddock, thin, gray clouds streaming from their mouths; the prickling of my shoulders as my hackles rise; my snarled greeting; the circling of his immense body.

Tara's howl to start.

But then the clarity is lost, swept up in a blur of details that are sometimes relevant, sometimes not. The awkwardness of Tiberius's body as he tries to back away from my first rush. A red-winged blackbird announcing its homesteading somewhere nearby. The feel of thick wolf hide giving way under the tearing pressure of my claws. The smell of blood. The anger in Celia's eyes. The curled lips over the flash of sharp, white teeth. The whipping of winter-bare branches in the wind blowing down from the mountains. The taste of blood. Sarah's distant, empty face. The high-pitched barks of tussling pups. The splashed landing of ducks on the water. The scent of skunk cabbage on some wolf's paws.

It is all there, swirling around my consciousness, but nothing distracts my focus as I wait for Tiberius to slip. As my jaws move almost on their own, directed by the memory of a hundred fights before, to Tiberius's suddenly vulnerable throat.

I feel his fur on my tongue.

The sadness in Evie's face. The triumph in Victor's. There is something wrong here. I know it.

I stop in midair and turn, my jaws closing on nothing. Tiberius lunges, his teeth around the top of my muzzle, close to my eye, with jaws capable of breaking bone. John had specifically commanded that we not maul each other's faces as it raised comment Offland, but John is dead and the Shifter doesn't clench tightly, but it's enough, and the narrow passage of the sinus near my eye socket collapses with a crunch.

My body hits the ground. I do not lower my ears, I do not pull in my tail, I do not submit, but if I try to get up, Tiberius's canine will put out my eye.

Tara finally gives the sharp bark signaling the end. Tiberius opens his jaws as gently as he can, but his fang still grinds along the bony orbit.

Everyone leaves except Victor. As soon as we are alone, he jumps into the paddock and scrapes dirt at me with his hind leg.

I don't leave. Ours was the last fight, because, of course, Tiberius didn't challenge Evie. He couldn't have become Alpha if he'd wanted to, and he didn't want to. Everything is as it was.

The night falls, and my eye circles around in its socket exploring the pain. The other helplessly twinned with it watches the repeated procession of starry sky, looming mountains, old wood, and bloodstained earth.

My sky, *my* mountains, *my* wood, *my* earth.

Đu londadl hǽðstapa.

You landsick heath-wanderer.

Chapter 15

THERE'S NOTHING LIKE ICED WATER AGAINST NAKED SKIN to signal the end of yet another Iron Moon. One eye opens and swivels around the spattered wood before resting on the tall figure of my shielder.

"Get up," Celia says. "You can't go to Iron Moon Table looking like that."

"Naah goin' do dable." I spit out something that feels hard. A piece of bone, maybe. Or a piece of Tiberius's tooth.

"Are your bones broken?"

"Na."

"Are your internal organs damaged?"

"Na."

"Then it is just a flesh wound, and you are expected at table."

"Fu' you, Thelia." I pull myself up and, with the newly reconstituted fingers, touch my right eye. It feels like a cantaloupe, but when I pull open the swollen lid, light leaks in, so at least the eyeball is still there.

"Close both eyes." She throws more icy water into my face, numbing the bruised, punctured skin and sending a stream up my nose. When I sniff in, the water screams its way into my sinus and mixes with blood. A huge clotted gob goes down my throat.

Except for my face, the only other damage is the tears

in the fascia of my abdomen where Tiberius anchored his hind claw.

"Here." She throws me something.

Because I have only one eye, I misjudge the distance and fumble to catch it. Of course, my Offland clothes are in the mud where I left them, and I didn't bring any other clothes because *I was going to be Alpha and I wouldn't need them*.

The Pack's dry storage went up in the fire, so the pickings are slim. Sitting on the wood logs, I thread my blood- and mud-spattered legs into gray sweats. The worn, loose ribbing at the ankles flutters well above my ankles. The purple hoodie with the green-and-black fleece lining is simply tragic.

Celia drops a pair of navy-blue flip-flops in front of me.

I don't put them on. Instead, I stare at the rough outlines of the Great Hall. The foundation is set, and a floor and studs mark where the walls will be.

"Alpha, we are expected at the Meeting House."

As far as Celia is concerned, I challenged and I lost. Happens all the time. I'm still Alpha of the 9th. La-di-da. She doesn't understand that I've given up my one chance to come home before I become as human as the Pack already thinks I am.

She doesn't understand that I did it at least in part for her.

Stumbling on the low steps heading up to the construction site, I pull back a tarpaulin over what will be the big double doors. Memories flood through, filling the space between the studs with beloved detail. The floor pitted by generations of claws. The sofas covered with fur. The staircase buffed by pup's bellies because we all sledded down with our legs outstretched until we grew big enough to manage it with more grace. The smell of cheese chews hidden in every corner to be tussled over whenever we got bored. The tables populated by a forest of strong legs and powerful arms that were always reaching for us—to feed us, to clean the blood from our muzzles, or simply to mark us. The surprised skittering at the end of one of our countless games of hide-and-stalk.

Running, forever running.

Because fragrance is as important as any visual detail for us, the Great North spent what it needed to on cedar wood, so it would smell like home. In the back, the little room that used to hold supplies for the cold frames is gone. But the kitchen will be expanded, the medic station too. I suppose that's all good.

Except for the addition of another window, John's office—*Evie's* office—will be the same though. I stand in the place where John's creaky, oversize banker's chair used to be. Stuck between two of the studs is a small cardboard box holding three blackened First Kill skulls and two white ones. Rabbits, all. I don't know who made the two more recent ones. I barely know the names of any of the wolves younger than the 11th.

"We will have the walls by next moon," Celia says. "Roof too. You'll see it when you come back."

When you come back. I feel almost sick at the thought of another moon spent Offland. And another and another, until when? Until I can no longer change except with the Iron Moon? Until I can no longer change at all?

I rub the heel of my hand against my chest. "Something is happening to me," I whisper. "*Inside me*, something is falling apart. I'm not sure how much longer I can—"

“Table is beginning,” says a cool voice.

Always the good little wolf, Celia bolts down the stairs, racing for the Meeting House, for this one time when we are all together and we all have words and opposable thumbs.

Tiberius doesn’t run though. He looks at me, with his big arms crossed in front of his thick chest.

“What are you staring at?” I spit out, glaring at him through my one functioning eye.

“Why did you lose?”

“Why did I lose? I lost because you’re a giant freak.”

“You and I both know that’s not true. You had me, but you stopped. You stopped yourself,” he says.

“You don’t know the first thing about me, Shifter. So don’t pretend you do.”

He holds open the tarp and looks toward the Meeting House.

“I do know one thing about you. Something that no one else here understands.” His voice is so soft, and despite myself, I strain to hear.

“I know how it feels when your soul starts to die.”

Chapter 16

Hāmweard, ðu londadl hǽðstapa, IN *27* DAYS
Homeward, you landsick heath-wanderer, IN *27* DAYS

HOMEWARD HAS RESTARTED.

It wasn't supposed to happen this way. From the bubble of my car, I look at the forest. I try to care when my phone beeps with road closures and alerts about the impending superstorm that might hamper my return to the city.

I can't say—I won't say—my return *home*.

My hand is still holding the car door. I need to let go. I need to start the engine. I need to put the damn thing in Reverse. My mind rehearses the procession of towns and landmarks that will mark my return Offland—Dannemora. Plattsburgh. Ausable Chasm. Schroon Lake. I can't do this again. Saratoga, Albany, Hudson.

My single eye falls to the bag on the floor and the little box sitting on top. Suddenly, the tires *graunch* against the loose stones as I throw the car into Reverse and bump down the road away from Homelands, aiming for another wilderness, the one north of Desolation Lake and west of Hope.

Feeling quickly in the underside of my visor, I find the card from the president of the New York State Sheriffs' Association that has his personal cell scrawled on the back. Then I race toward the same coordinates that I loaded into my phone on that earlier visit.

When I pull up beside Thea's Jeep, she's already at her door, alerted by the crunch of rocks and *thunk* of my wheels. Standing with her hands flat in the back pockets of her jeans, she looks through the windshield. I clutch the steering wheel, suddenly wondering what I'm doing here.

I keep looking straight ahead when she comes around to the side and opens the door, taking me in: mauled face, purple travesty of a sweatshirt leaking blood, the short sweatpants and flip-flops.

Thea stands back, pulling the door open wide. "You'd better come inside."

I clamber out. The snow has already started, and its incongruous flakes cover my flip-flops.

Thea pulls at my arm. "Come on," she says, pushing and pulling me toward her cabin.

As soon as the door closes, I collapse against it. "I had an accident," I start. "A deer crossed the road—"

"If you don't want to tell me, don't, but please don't lie."

I watch her move quickly and quietly around the cabin. She puts a pot of water on the stove.

"Let's get you fixed up," she says, heading into the little bathroom. "Watch your head."

On the edge of the bathtub, I unzip the hoodie and start to shrug it off, opening up the claw marks that start at my rib cage and keep going below my waistband.

Thea purses her lips and releases them with a *pop*.

She hands me a small towel. "Take off your pants and"—she looks at the navy-blue flip-flops—"shoes. I'll be back in a minute."

The gray sweats fall to my naked feet. My body is covered with mud, and when I touch my hair, there are burrs in it. I stretch the hand towel across my front and start to pick them out.

"I got into a fight," I say when she returns with a bucket and a big first aid box.

"Hmm-hmm." She drops my filthy clothes in the corner, then reaches past me to turn on the water. When it's warm enough, she fills the bucket, then motions me in. It's tight in here, much smaller than the bathroom in the apartment. There's barely enough space for me to turn, and the water from the showerhead only hits my shoulder blades.

"Put your head back."

I tense immediately, my muscles coiled. I have to remind myself that she isn't Pack and has no idea what it means for a wolf to expose his throat. She has no idea that it's what we do when we don't have words and need to say *I am vulnerable, but I trust you*.

How did I end up here? Battered and exhausted and looking for help in this little cabin from this little human with her little bucket and her ironwood eyes?

I ended up here because there's something about her that I do trust. Her edges aren't smoothed down and polite. She isn't all about compromise and accommodation. Maybe I trust because I know that to be honest with someone else, you have to be honest with yourself, and I believe Thea is. Honest. With herself.

I close my eyes and lean my head back, my neck stretched out long. The ladle clunks in the bucket. An audible sigh escapes under the cascade of warm water and gentle progress of Thea's hands combing through the length of my filthy hair. The small towel is wet and molds to my hips, and there is no way it can adequately disguise what the flow of warm water and the scrape of Thea's fingers are doing to my body.

She mixes something from her first aid kit, and when she turns back to me, she is armed with a nozzled container. "Close your eyes," she says and irrigates the punctures left in my face by Tiberius's fangs with something that smells acrid and medicinal.

"Move that over," she says, pointing with her chin at the towel that feels like a postage stamp and tents so far from my body that I can feel cool air on my balls. She doesn't meet my eyes as she irrigates the claw marks on my torso.

She grabs the clothes in the corner, bending over. My single eye swivels around her ass until she stands up and warns me that she has a small cistern.

Of course she does. It's made for *one*.

I nod, because whatever she thinks, I am not from the city where water appears as if by some inexhaustible magic.

Once the small towel is soapy, I turn off the water and wash everything. I scrub my arms and shoulders and chest. I scrub my feet and legs, trying to ignore the engorged thing that refuses to be ignored. But as I touch my ass and my lower back, I realize that the tightness in my balls and cock has spread to my spine, and if I don't find release here, I will almost certainly find it in a less private and water-tight place.

I have never fantasized before. Pack do not waste energy on females who are not receptive. And as for all those humans, once I was done with them, I wanted to forget them entirely, not summon up Technicolor recreations during my most intimate moments.

But now, I can't help it. As I pump forward into my terry-covered hand, against the dark screen of my eyes, I see Thea. All gold and black. Noble colors. Her nipples will be bronzed and her breasts will be perfect size for my hands and they will feel soft, not at all like those big ones that feel like ziplock bags overfilled with pudding.

Her voice echoes in my mind. *You better come inside*, she says, but this time, it is more urgent. This time as she says it, she parts her thighs. My fingers carve runnels into the skin, and I pull her open wider and fit my...

With a barely contained snarl, I come.

Still panting against the wall, unsure what to do with the contents of the soaked terry cloth. I rinse it as thoroughly as I can in the shower before stumbling out and drying off. The old crate that serves as her medicine chest is just a little deeper than a printer's box and has no front to it, so nothing is hidden. Not that much is here, no first aid. Some aspirin, lipstick, skin lotion, coconut oil.

Then I catch sight of myself in the mirror glued above her sink. Of course, I couldn't be injured the way movie heroes are—an elegant scrape below the cheekbone or a clean cut above the brow. They never have something disfiguring, like a right eye that has turned purple and swollen shut. Or a nose that has become mottled and distended.

I look like a perverted eggplant.

There's a rapid knock on the door. "Hey."

"Yes?"

"This is all I have." Thea snakes her arm through the crack in the door and hands off a tiny stack consisting of a long-sleeved T-shirt that says *Pittsburgh Steelers* and is seriously too tight and basketball shorts that are too short. They are clearly from some earlier man, maybe Doug, but because he was on the stout side, the shorts fit me where it counts.

Thea is sitting on her bed, her back to me. There's a tiny sliver of skin the color of rye between her sweater and jeans. As soon as the door opens, she pulls at her sweater and picks up a tube from the bedside table.

Antibiotic. I don't need it, but I can hardly explain to her that I heal quickly and am not susceptible to infection from whatever is on a wolf's claws or teeth. Besides, she might stop touching me, and more than anything, I need the trace of her fingers.

I need her touch.

Thea smooths antibiotic ointment around my nose and my cheek and my eye socket. "Look up?" she says, moving in close. I part my knees a little to give her access to my eye.

Okay, no. This…this was a mistake.

The ointment glistens on her fingers as she moves toward the tear at my hip. "I've got it," I mutter and smear the antibiotic on the claw marks. Two inches over, and Tiberius would have castrated me. Which, I think as I try to figure out how to readjust the gourd in my shorts, might have made life easier.

"Your clothes are on the dryer," she says, leaving me to wonder, *Dryer? What dryer?* There's no way she has a dryer, but then I understand why she said *on*. My clothes—washed and wrung out—are laid across what looks to be the side of a crib suspended from a line-and-pulley system near the fire. The loose end is wound around a metal cleat screwed into the amber wood of the wall.

"You should be okay, but the snow is getting worse. I need to get food before the roads are closed." She pulls on her jacket. "Do you know how to stoke the fire?"

I nod. "Wait, you're just leaving me here?"

"You go if you want, but be careful. These roads aren't the first ones plowed."

"That's not what I mean. I mean, you're just leaving me in your house?"

"What? Were you going to take something? A bowl? My teapot? A library book? Okay, that'd be a nuisance. But there's no lock on the door, so anyone could. If you do decide to go before I get back, just make sure to close it tight. You may have to pull it a little." She takes her car keys down from a nail by the door.

"Wait, Thea?"

She stops, her head turned slightly.

"Why are you doing this? Why are you helping me?"

She swings her worn rucksack across one shoulder and shrugs.

"Because you need it."

When she closes the door, she pulls it that little extra bit until it clicks.

Chapter 17

THERE REALLY ISN'T ANYTHING HERE TO STEAL. A random collection of books—a biography of Walt Whitman. A history of dueling. *The Tale of Genji*. Thrillers and mysteries and books with buff-chested men who look like miniature versions of me. Except none of them have the rotting-gourd face. All with bar codes and bookplates saying *Property of the Crandall Public Library*.

I pick up a selection by Aldo Leopold and curl under the quilt that lies loose at the foot of her bed and begin to read.

By the time I wake up, the snow has started in earnest and the sky is charcoal. And though the cabin is still warm, the fire is dying down.

I push the glowing logs around with a poker and lay on two more logs, close but not touching. I don't need the lamps. My sight is good enough with just the firelight and the dull remnants of day that seem to spread out from everywhere and nowhere. I lean my face along the window toward the road, feeling the cool glass against my damaged eye, and wait. A limb overburdened by snow cracks and falls.

I wait. I need Thea to come home. I mean, come back. To her home.

Finally, lights come bouncing along the rough road, picking out the thick clumps of snow and making them glow brightly. Stone and snow crunch under her tires, and a door bangs. Then another door. I run out in my bare feet, and Thea hands me two bags before taking the other two and slamming the back door closed.

"You're not going to make it out now," she says. Her black hair is netted with melting droplets that shimmer as soon as she gets into the cabin. "But I brought extra food. You can take the bed."

I start to argue, but she stops me, saying that she frequently falls asleep on the chaise.

Settling her bags on the floor, she shakes out her coat and hangs it from the corner of the "clothes dryer," next to my clothes. She puts her boots to the side of the stove and her gloves on a mitten dryer on the chimney. Melting snow drips onto the hot iron with a staccato hiss.

"You hungry?"

"Very," I say, because I really am.

Opening the bags, she pulls out bread and cheese and butter and spinach and eggs. She puts butter into the cast-iron skillet and layers bread along the bottom. While the cabin fills with the smell of toasted bread, she stirs cheese and eggs and tarragon and spinach and pours the mixture over the top.

She cuts one piece for me and puts it on a large plate. Another smaller piece for herself on a small plate. I try to push away the knife and fork, because that leaves her eating with a spoon, but she pulls a wicked hunting knife from her backpack.

Too pumped to eat since that gristly buck-leg snack, I'm suddenly starving, and I swear that of all the fine foods I've eaten, nothing has ever tasted so good. The bread is buttery and crispy at the bottom and soaked in cheese and eggs and tarragon on the top. And I don't have to purge after.

She puts away the rest of her groceries while I wash and dry and put each thing on her single shelf. At the Homelands, everyone works. Everyone. We do laundry and scrape hides and wash toilets, and good Alphas lead by example, not by delegation.

Thea heads into the shower, and when she comes out a few minutes later, her hair is a damp black tangle over a white Henley and gray leggings. She puts two more logs on the fire and adds water to the kettle. A dinged metal cylinder with cherry blossoms on it makes a little squeak as she unscrews its lid. "Tea?"

"No. I'm okay."

So that when the water boils, she can use the single mug.

"I'm sorry. I'm not really set up for entertaining," she says, setting her teacup on the pine table next to her chair.

I can't tell whether she's apologizing for her lack of a television or some more intrinsic absence in her personality.

"We could just talk," I say.

"Talk or chat?"

"There's a difference?"

"Chatting means asking questions with answers that don't matter." She slides into her chaise and pulls the throw over her legs. "I don't much like chatting."

"Talk then."

"So. How come you have claw marks on your gut and tooth marks on your face?"

Tapping my fingers against my chin, I give her a tight smile. "You know, maybe I don't actually need to be entertained."

She digs a book out from the slot between her chair's

seat cushion and arm and opens it, wrapping the dark-olive grosgrain ribbon she used as a bookmark around her finger and rubbing it gently over the top of her lip.

Well.

Gingerly, I pull myself onto her bed and move an extra pillow around to keep my head up. On the other side of the bed, the side closest to the bathroom, is a row of books without plastic covers or bookplates. The top one is beyond dog-eared. The fore edge was originally reddish but has faded to pink with bleached-out drops and a dark-gray middle where the oils of her fingers have rubbed it repeatedly. The cover is gone, though there are traces of tape that she must have used to try to keep it together.

"That's the one thing I'd hate to lose," she says, still looking at her book. "I've had it for a while."

"I can tell." Although the cover and first pages are missing, I know what it is. John and Nils both taught English literature, so we are better read than most Packs. Better read than humans goes without saying.

"'The great man'"—I try to remember the quotes and strip away the emendations that John made, altering them to our circumstances; "the great wolf" was what he actually said—"'is the one who in the midst of the crowd'"—John said "of humans"—"'keeps with perfect sweetness the stillness of the forest.'"

She stares at her book for a moment and then puts her finger on a passage.

"The quote is 'keeps with perfect sweetness the independence of solitude.' I like yours though."

"My old English teacher loved Emerson. But I learned it a long time ago. Must have mixed it up."

Of course I didn't. The summer before we were to go

Offland, Leonora did her best to make sure that those of us who were leaving understood how to appear human in the world they had re-created in their image.

John tried to do something altogether more subtle and difficult. Whatever disguises we were wearing, he wanted to make sure that we preserved the Homelands within us. He wanted us to make sure that there was a place for the wild inside, even if there wasn't a place for it anywhere else.

"You liked your English teacher?"

"What? My… Yes. Very much. He was more than an English teacher. He was kind of the…head of our little rural community. We're very tight-knit, but tempers can run short. He worked hard to keep everyone together."

"But not anymore?"

"He died. Suddenly. A couple of months ago. His wife is trying to take over, but it's hard, and I think I've made everything more difficult for her."

She dunks the tea bag a few times before fishing it out with a spoon and, wrapping the string around it, squeezes it dry. "Was it worth fighting for?"

"I didn't win, if that's what you mean."

"Not really. A good fight isn't about the outcome. It's about knowing that you've made things better by trying."

Then I hear Victor's voice. "You will win, Alpha," he says. My one advocate with his sour, judgmental voice and his sour, judgmental face.

"Honestly, I don't know if it was worth fighting for. I don't know anything anymore. And no one seems to know who I am."

When she blows across her tea, she sends the damp-orchid-and-honey scent to my waiting nose.

"Do you? Know who you are?"

"Of course I do," I snap, all the Pack's skepticism and my own self-doubt suddenly brought to a head by this woman who doesn't know me from Adam. Then I remember what she is. A woman. A human. "I am a partner in one of the most powerful law firms in the country."

"You're not just a lawyer, any more than I am just an ECO."

"So what else would you say you are?"

"All sorts of things. I'm a woman who doesn't listen to music in the background, because that's not actually listening. Who is a vegetarian gun owner. Who makes her living helping people but likes to be alone. Whose ancestors were on this landmass when the people who yell at her to 'go home' were sleeping with pigs in Europe. Who likes caffeine and Cheetos. Who was in a sorority for four months. Who is the daughter of dead parents and the sister of a dead brother."

She lifts her tea to her lips and blows across the surface.

"What happened to your family?"

"You're changing the subject. I'm saying that I've never met anyone who was just one thing. Who was just 'a lawyer.' So, Elijah Sorensson, *Esquire*, what *else* are you?"

What else am I? I'm an exile. A disappointment. An Alpha without a Pack. A leader no one wants to follow. A flashy vessel hiding something unspeakably sacred and undeniably fragile. I am a monster: neither one thing nor the other, belonging nowhere.

"Lost," I say, staring at the fire until my single working eye begins to dry out. "Just. Fucking. Lost."

My throat feels achy and full, and I turn back to the page, pretending to read, because I feel her ironwood eyes on me, and I know what she sees: an angry, defensive, broken, defeated man in a human's castoffs and with a wolf-ravaged, bruised-gourd face.

And then I feel something else. I feel Thea's hand hanging loose between us. She has returned to her book, but the wordless invitation is there. The cabin being what it is, when I let my hand drape to the side of the bed, I'm close enough to touch her.

In the snow-muffled peace of no expectations, I stare sightless at the pages, every nerve focused on the shared heartbeat between our fingers.

When I finally look up from the blurred pages, the mottled fire is reflected in the warmth and welcome of her eyes. I can't stop myself. I collapse to my knees, my head at her lap, my arm wrapped around her knees, silently asking if this woman who makes a living finding people can find me too.

She slides the ribbon back into her book and tucks it into its place between the cushions and smooths my hair back from my face, careful of my swollen eye. With each pass of her hand, she erases one jot of despair. Then another and another, and it adds up until I feel...still.

I catch her hand and settle it against my mouth. She smells like soap and steel. There are callouses on her hand.

For the first time in years, in decades, my jaded body longs to touch and be touched. I want the most intimate touch. I want to be inside Thea. I try to tell myself that she is different. But what if she's not different enough? What if, in the event, her face is filled with the familiar calculus of seduction? Just one more Offland transaction?

If I don't look, I won't see. So when she curls around me, laying a soft kiss on my blind grapefruit swelling, I close my one functioning eye and raise my head to the soft brush of her lips, painfully gentle and undeniable. I weave my hands through her hair and turn my head so my lips are firmer against hers, testing how deep this restraint of hers goes.

Her mouth softens under my tongue flicking at her top lip and then her bottom, and she opens to me, unbearably receptive. Her hair falls around us like a damp curtain, and she takes me in, tasting my mouth with her lemon-and-tea tongue. She is slow and deliberate, one hand reaching around the top of my shoulders, the other to the small of my back. Her finger takes up that almost unnoticeable pulse, the one she played against the upholstered back of my big chair the first day I met her. It's so slight, but it builds with each light touch until I am holding my breath, waiting for the downbeat. Her hip bone finds the heavy ridge of my erection and settles against it with a sigh halfway between contentment and ache.

That's it.

Wrapping one arm around her, I push up from the chaise and lay her out, pulling off her leggings while she struggles with the Henley. I still can't look at her eyes, looking instead at her body. It's not like the dozens of young women I've had before. Her breasts spill a little to the side. There is a soft bulge under her navel and a scar on the left side of her abdomen. A burn on her forearm. A small constellation of freckles at her cleavage. A sprinkling of tiny lightning bolts at her hips.

Holding her hips down with one hand, I push her chest down with the other while I kiss and suckle every baroque decoration time has stitched onto the canvas of her body, moving down until I reach her furrow.

I don't want her to touch me, because if she does, it will be all over, and this needs to be slow. I want her to burn. I want to burn. I want this to leave a scar in my memory that can't be forgotten. I need to slow down.

I need to slow down. *Ineedtoslowdown*.

Then she says my name, substituting a clipped sigh for the last syllable—Eliii*zhah*—and I lose control. There's no slow or fast, just all that pent-up need breaking past my lower spine, through my pelvis, and out. Like a teenage boy, I hold her tight and come undone in vast desperate bursts.

I groan twice: once for the coming and once for the humiliation.

"Elijah, turn over," she says, pulling the pillow away from my face when she comes back from the bathroom. When I don't, she pulls me harder. "On your back."

I cover my eyes with my forearm because I know what she's going to do. She's going to lick her lips, suggestively, naughtily, making sure I understand the awesome gift of her mouth. As if there wasn't something so hopelessly banal about lips on a cock. As if I hadn't had a whole sodality of sucking. I wait for the mattress to bend under her knees, but it doesn't, and when I lower my arm, she is standing over me holding that wicked hunting knife and a handful of disposable restraints.

I take it back. I have no idea what she's doing.

"What are you doing?"

She holds up a single restraint. "Probably exactly what you think."

"Is this… Do you do this often?"

"Never." She looks at the restraints, trying to remember something. "I only used these once. Two years ago, on a crazy drunk hunter."

"But...why me?" I mean, really, *why me?* You didn't do this to Doug, but you're going to do it to Elijah Sorensson, who is an Alpha of the human hierarchy and, if it hadn't been for that sudden attack of doubt, would have been the Alpha of the last truly great wolf pack as well?

"I've never met someone who needs control as much as you do. Over other people, but mostly over yourself. Like there's some part of you that you're afraid to let out. It makes me wonder: What happens if you don't have it? Control, I mean. What happens if you give control to someone else? And just let go? Would it unleash you?

"Free you?"

My wild cocks an ear. I finger one of the restraints, feeling its strength.

"Is there a safe word?"

"No, there's no *safe word*. I told you, this is not what I do. All you have to do is say 'stop' or 'no' or 'I've changed my mind' and"—she twists her knife in the air—"you're free."

Slowly, she moves my left foot to the outside of her bed and threads the double cuff around my ankle and her bedpost. "Trust me?" she asks.

I don't say yes, but I don't say no either.

She slides along my body to my left wrist. She doesn't make the cuffs too tight; when I pull on them, they don't loosen, but they don't tighten like a noose.

I don't say yes, but I don't say no either.

With a warm breath, she plants a kiss on my palm,

and a bolt travels up my body. My cock jumps slightly. She kisses my nipple and drags the rough side of the two remaining restraints across my chest.

Then my right ankle is secured, and because my ankles must be on the outside of her bed frame, my legs are stretched wide. There is no place for me to hide.

I don't say yes, but I don't say no either.

At my right wrist, before she puts on the last restraint, she turns my chin toward her, making sure I'm watching her. She smiles at me.

I don't say yes, but I don't say no either.

She circles plastic gently around my free wrist. The loose ends feather against my skin, then I am immobile.

The heat from the cast-iron stove slavers up my legs.

She lays her body next to mine, lets her hands run gently down the slope of my shoulder and to the hard curve of my chest. My skin has gotten way too tight. She leans over me, her hair falling onto my chest before sliding down to the sheets. I feel every strand. "Breathe, Elijah," she whispers against my mouth. "Let me love your body."

My breath escapes in a low hiss like the air from a punctured tire. I pull slightly on the restraints but then let go. There is nothing for me to do here. No games to play, no scripts to follow, just the feeling of Thea's tongue and her fingers and her hair and her skin.

She reads my body like it has a narrative. Every touch responds to the one before and builds to the next. She starts in places that I've never given a second thought to—the spot just inside my knee—and builds from there. I almost climax *again* when she nips the skin of my pelvis, my cock sliding over her soft cheek and under the tangle of her hair.

But then she goes places where humans aren't allowed. My neck. She plants a line of kisses along the most vulnerable part of me. I'm just about to tell her to stop, but she makes it even gentler, until she reaches the top and opens her mouth on either side and exhales. Doesn't even touch me, just exhales. Nothing but whispered warmth and trust.

When I grow too ecstatic, she pulls back, leaving me in the dark, straining toward the heat of her skin and the weight of her body beside me on the mattress. Then she leaves the bed altogether.

Please, Thea.

Don't leave me.

She comes back a moment later, pulling at a little packet with her teeth. It's funny. I'm usually so careful about condoms, but I'd forgotten completely.

She tears it open and straddles my hips. She holds the crown of my cock tight in her fist and pulls it on. Then she uses me in long strokes along her seam before taking me in. With her free hand, she traces tight, hard circles until her expression softens, her eyes become unfocused. She arches her back into a perfect curve and comes with a broken cry. She collapses against me, the last remains of her climax sobbed against my lips. Flexing my hips, I follow the rhythm of her orgasm until, finally, I come with a howl, and every animal in the woods knows what I am and shuts the fuck up.

I am, my wild screams, *here*.

Chapter 18

Hāmweard, ðu londadl hǽðstapa, IN *26* DAYS
Homeward, you landsick heath-wanderer, IN *26* DAYS

CURLED UP IN A COCOON OF SWEAT AND SEED AND SALIVA and the thin curl of blood from my reopened wounds, I sleep like I haven't slept since I was a pup, one indistinguishable part in a writhing warm pile of fur.

I sleep so deeply that when I wake up, the sheets are cold and the cabin is empty.

"Thea?" I feel for her, finding only the cut remains of the restraints.

She stoked the fire and left the coffee on the table, but for the first time, I am the one left behind, and I can't help the sour panic creeping up in my chest.

It doesn't take me long to find the note she left under the coffee mug on the plain pine table. *Srry*, she scribbled. *Hd to run*.

That's it? "Srry. Hd to run?"

Srry. Hd to run?

I don't even warrant vowels?

I should have known.

Jeremy, my college roommate and mentor in the realm of human sexuality, warned me. He warned me about seeming too eager, too open.

"You can't jump around her like an incontinent

puppy," he'd said after I'd sat next to some girl in the dining hall. "You will lose all hand."

"Hand? What do you mean *hand*?"

"The *upper* hand?" He must have seen by my expression that his explanation hadn't really explained anything. "What planet did you say you come from?"

"Upstate."

"Look, Jethro." Never clear on the difference between the Adirondacks and Appalachia, Jeremy insisted on calling me Jethro when he felt I was being especially green. "The reason you can't go jumping around a girl like an incontinent puppy is because they will either (a) take advantage of you or (b) dump you, because, you know, what every girl wants is a real alpha male."

Now, I already was a "real Alpha male." I'd left every challenger scarred and scared, and it amused me no end to hear him say "alpha male," his skinny, little arms crooked and his tiny fists all balled up.

It was really very cute.

He never did say "alpha female."

If I wanted to have the upper hand, he said, I must never call a girl I'd slept with or go with her to have coffee or sit next to her in the dining hall.

With Pack, the equation is simple: receptivity = mounting. This "hand" business seemed like unnecessarily awkward confusion and led to long delays between mountings. Generally, it was easier and faster just to start over.

But I don't want to start over.

I want Thea.

Removing my clothes from Thea's "dryer," I slip them on, stiff and bone dry and warm on my skin. I untie the rope, pull the dryer back up to the ceiling, and secure it again around the cleat. I fold the borrowed clothes.

Chewing on a crunchy end of bread, I bend over a new piece of scrap paper, trying to think of just the thing that straddles that line between cool disinterest and pathetic availability. That will say Alpha male, not incontinent puppy.

I feel like I did that day in the Year of First Shoes, when some adult Pack member helped me wrap the unfamiliar fleshy fingers of my human form around a pencil.

I put the pencil back down.

Back in New York, I'm no better. I sit on my bed with my laptop balanced on my crossed legs, Thea's email address typed in and my cursor at the subject line.

Cool disinterest and pathetic availability.

I end up typing *FJFJFJFJFJFJFJFJ* until I run out of space.

My doorbell rings. Unaccountably, my heart leaps, and bouncing off the bed, I run to the door like an incontinent puppy. Through the brass frame of the peephole is Alana, the only person it could ever be.

I've got to sell this place.

"What happened to you?" she shrieks. "Was it an accident?"

"Something like that." I start to pull back into my apartment. "Alana, I really have a lot of work—"

"Luca is out of town again?" She scrapes her nails across my chest, her eyes studiously avoiding my battered face. "San Francisco?"

Well, of course, nothing says *cool disinterest* like

fucking your neighbor. But I discover that all the upper hand in the world is worth nothing if the lower parts refuse to cooperate.

Alana is already down to nothing but a shelf bra of burgundy lace and matching panties, and the only thing I've got in my pants is a parboiled squid.

Trying to wake up the squid, I pretend to scratch at my thigh. *Leave me alone*, says the squid.

"Is he going to stay here?" I nod toward Tarzan, who is watching me, his head cocked to the side.

"He was here before?" she says after a quick look. "You didn't mind then?"

"He wasn't watching before."

"Ooo, waz de madduh?" Her voice floats up the register. "Is de big man afwaid of the liddow doggy?"

Oh sweet fuck. Get me out of here.

She drapes herself around me, her chin on my shoulder, her breast against my shoulder blade, her fingers toying with my waistband. I pull her hand away.

"You seem kind of off your game, Elijah? Did you…like…hurt it in the accident?"

"It? What acc…?" Then I remember the "accident." The one in which an enormous wolf tried to eat my eye. "No, but the accident… Maybe it's just that coming so close to death so unexpectedly has made me more aware of the transience of life."

That should do it. Nothing unnerves humans like talk of death. They simply can't wrap their minds around the idea that their own spark—divine, they call it, to distinguish it from every other creature's unsanctified ember—might sputter like a waterlogged Roman candle.

"Well, that's kind of a bummer?" Alana says and swings her leg around the other side of the bed. She toddles toward the en suite and pulls her robe around her. "Maybe we should wait until you stop thinking, you know? About 'transience'?"

My squid and I share an overwhelming sense of relief. There will be no tomorrow. No amount of upper hand is worth this. When I start to pull my shirt back on, Tarzan stares straight at me.

I know what you're thinking, you minuscule mutant.

"*You should be ashamed of yourself.*"

One of these days, Tarzan.

One of these days, I am going to eat you.

Unable to concentrate on anything, I push stuff around. Socks into the hamper, batteries into the smoke detector, new ice cubes into the ice bucket, clean towels on the towel bar.

I'm just pushing the toothpaste tube up when my pocket buzzes with a pleasant, pulsating buzz, the one I'd set for Thea. In my rush to get it, the corner of my phone catches on the inside of my pocket. I fumble and scuffle, and it flies toward the toilet. Diving, I grab the phone, but not before it stops ringing.

In the full-length mirror on the back of the bathroom door, I catch sight of myself on my knees in front of the toilet, cupping the phone to my chest. *Like a frigging incontinent puppy.*

No incontinent puppy, I wait for nearly two hours before I dial her number, lying on my bed, the phone cradled in two hands.

"Hey," she says. "I have to put logs on the fire. Do you want me to call you back?"

I think for only a second. I know what she's doing. She'll call me back in two hours, and then she, *she*, will have the upper hand.

"I'll hold," I say and press the phone tighter to my ear, listening for the creak of the stove's door. If I concentrate, I can hear the cindered wood crumble under the heavy poker, the dull thud of one new log, then another. I can almost smell the damp earth and woodsmoke that surrounds her and the cushion of silence everywhere and Thea's hair sheltering me.

The metal door of the stove squeaks closed again, and the latch clicks into place.

"You still there?"

"Yeah."

My wolfish ears strain for the sound of her chair as she leans into it.

"I'm so sorry I had to run out like that, but you seemed like you could use your sleep. There was a woman trapped in her car overnight. The snowplow had covered her. It took a while to find her, but she'll be fine." Thea shakes out the throw with a light swish before pulling it over her legs.

"Anyway, I'd really like to see you again," she says and blows on something. I can almost smell the warm tannic steam from her tea.

And just like that, she upends everything I know about the way humans play the game. She had an emergency. Not just a silly pretend emergency. A real emergency. And she wants to see me again. My wild pricks up his ears and gets to his feet, his tongue lolling excitedly.

Like an incontinent puppy. I turn over on my front, my hand underneath me, the weight of my body pushing my raging-hard Pavlovian member against it.

"Yes. Yeah, I'd like that. When?"

"I was going to come into the city to see my uncle this Friday. If you have time."

"Friday? You mean this Friday?" My wild gets up and prances around and stands with his paws on the sills of my eyes looking out, his tail wagging. "Yeah… No… I mean…" I think for a moment about Jeremy and the all-important hand.

"That's great," I say, because I know that whatever I have on Friday is going to be canceled.

Fuck the hand.

And I do.

Chapter 19

Hāmweard, ðu londadl hǽðstapa, IN 25 DAYS
Homeward, you landsick heath-wanderer, IN 25 DAYS

CHECKING MY REFLECTION IN THE BRIGHT, BRASSY shine of the elevator, I tighten the textured silk tie and shift the lapels of my Fioravanti jacket, just to be sure it sits properly on my shoulders. Then I pull the cuffs of my white Ascot Chang shirt, checking reflexively the platinum-chain cuff links.

The ravaged face looks back at me with a wolfish smile, and the elevator doors slide open with a ping.

"*Oh. My. God!*" Dahlia shrieks. "Mr. Sorensson, what happened to you?"

"Accident." I pick up the Whole Foods bag with all my worldly possessions and beam brightly at the HST staffers. "Hit a deer."

From the far end of the hall comes the hurried whisper of satin lining against nylon. Hobbled by her long, green pencil skirt piped in snakeskin and high alligator heels, Janine manages only a mincing race walk as she hustles toward me.

"Janine, I—"

"Oh. My. God! What happened to you?" In my absence, the law seems to have discovered the deity.

"I had an acci—"

"Didn't you have your seat belt on?"

"The windshield—"

"They didn't give you any stitches? What kind of doctor did you go to? That is definitely going to scar. I suppose that means you're going to skip the blood drive *again*?"

She says "again" with full significance, because every six weeks, a nurse and her volunteer sidekick come around looking for blood. And every six weeks, she eyes me with disdain while the little men who have never fought a bobcat in their lives sit in comfortable chairs in the main conference room while the women fret over them before offering them a plate full of chocolate-chip cookies and a red plastic glass of orange juice. They emerge ostentatiously rolling down their sleeves and for the rest of the day sport red-and-white stickers that warn everyone *Be Nice to Me, I Gave Blood Today!*, the opposite of which is *Be a Shit to Me, I Kept My Blood to Myself!*

But they all have blood types that are easily recognizable. I don't. The oxygen content means that the color isn't even quite right, shining a noticeably brighter, more vibrant red than is the human norm. So, every couple of months, I—who ripped out the heart of a heavily armed Shifter, who has the sunken hollow where a wolf crunched through my sinus, whose First Kill was a fisher—have to put up with the *tsk-tsk*ing of humans as they show off their cookies and their tiny, carefully bandaged punctures.

"Yeah, no. Probably not a good idea."

Janine follows me into my office. I know she wants me to ask her what's on her mind so she won't have to bug me. I'm not really up for it though. The two picture hangers are right where I left them. Janine leans against the wall next to the bleached rectangles, tapping something against the heel of her hand.

"Oh," she finally says, like she's just noticed. "I almost forgot why I needed to talk to you." She shows me the white card with the black embossed snowflake. "Lori needs to finalize the list for L-Cubed. For the seating arrangements. She says she needs to know who you're taking."

I pull one framed degree from the bag, following the wire with my finger, making sure it's angled onto the hook.

"I doubt that seriously."

"Doubt what?"

"That she needs to know who I'm taking." I step back to check that it's level. "Lori's never needed to know my plus-one before."

Janine stops leaning casually on the wall.

"A what? *I* am not a fucking *plus-one*. Your other women might have been, but don't ever make the mistake of treating *me* like that."

She pulls herself up tall on her spindly Gianvito Rossis, smoothing her Cinq à Sept skirt over her tight hips. Maxim insists his old law-school friend hasn't given Janine an unlimited Barneys charge card, but there is no other way Janine could maintain her steady diet of Proenza Schouler, Dries van Noten, and Prada.

For Pack, all our offspring are the same. Beloved by all, protected by all, marked by all. They are our future. But humans are not like Pack. They see their children not only as their legacy, but as accessories signaling their personal success.

Mother, father, son, daughter. The words seem odd on a wolf's tongue. Like we owe them some responsibility that we don't owe to the Pack as a whole. The only right that is peculiar to those closest to us is First Blood, the right to kill your child or your mate. The responsibility to take a life you have failed.

"*Hello?*" Her voice breaks through. "Do you even remember who my father is?"

How could I forget? A day doesn't go by when you don't—

"My father is Judge Wilson Unger. And he—*Judge Wilson Unger*—has always said that I could be a great lawyer."

"But?" I pull the other frame out from the bag and settle it above the first.

"But what?"

I lean back again. Adjusting them both until they are straight on the wall and even with each other. "You said 'could,' and 'could' is conditional. What is the condition? You could be a great lawyer if what? You actually worked for once?"

"If I *decided* to! The reason I'm not is because I don't *want* to be. I don't want to be tied down like you, like everyone in this office. I want to live. Really live. This is the only life I've got, and I am going to carp dime."

"It's carpe diem, Janine." I feel sick that I ever touched this callow girl whose version of independence is a Barneys charge card and a one-bedroom in a doorman building supplied by her parents. *Carpe diem*. The battle cry of the perpetually indulged. We have nurslings who have more sense of responsibility than this supposed adult. "I can't listen to you anymore."

"You can't listen to me?" she sputters. "*You* can't listen to *me*?" She crumples the invitation and throws it at me. "You better listen to me now, *asshole*. You think you're God's great gift to women, but this is one girl you're going to be sorry you ever screwed around with."

"Believe me, Janine, I already am."

She tears across to her office, grabs her Alexander Wang coat and her Victoria Beckham Tulip bag, and storms out.

Chapter 20

Hāmweard, ðu londadl hǽðstapa, IN *21* DAYS
Homeward, you landsick heath-wanderer, IN *21* DAYS

SHE DIDN'T COME BACK FRIDAY EITHER. THE THOUGHT that Janine might have extracted herself from my life with so little effort on my part is a small but very real adornment to my day.

Most of the day is spent running and rerunning my backward calculations: Thea will be at Penn Station at 4:43 p.m., which means she boards the train in Amsterdam at 1:20 p.m., which means she left home maybe at noon. I keep my phone in my pocket, compulsively checking her train's progress on the Amtrak app.

At 4:15 p.m., I can't wait anymore. "Penn Station," I tell the cabbie, then throw myself back against the cold vinyl. The cab's smell is a stifling combination of chicken, hot dust, and the adhesive backing of duct tape.

"Keep the windows open, please."

The streets are crowded with pre-weekend traffic. I pay the driver and run the last mile.

Passengers are already pouring from the doors of Thea's train by the time I get there. I search through the masses of little humans, sniffing my way through jasmine and the leathery scent of fear and caramel mocha and tobacco and Jamba Juice and salty misery until I hit the musty smell of damp earth and my spine tightens, pulling me like a leash toward the tall woman with the long, black hair who is just out of reach, swerving in and out of the crowd. When she reaches the escalator, I'm blocked in at the bottom, and all I can see is her hair licking against her back.

"*Thea, stop.*"

She turns and looks for me, and when she finds me, she smiles, her body relaxing. There is no "hand" at all. Just the courage to be open and joyous in a world that always seems so calculating.

At the top of the escalator, she stands to the side, shrugging her worn canvas backpack a little higher on her shoulder, and waits until I finally get to her. I can't help but pull her up while she slides one arm around my neck and the other around my back. Her body pressed against mine, she raises her face to me. If Penn Station didn't serve as Hell's Vestibule, I would mount her right here.

Grabbing her hand, I race for the street, throwing my body in front of a cab and helping the elderly couple out. "My treat!" I shout as I bundle Thea in. I give the cabbie my address, tell him to take the West Side Highway ("Yes, I know it's out of the way"), and cram a handful of twenties through the partition. Then I slide the window closed. Someone has scratched HOME into the plexiglass.

Thea straddles my lap, and when I look down, her eyes follow mine to the enormous bulge bent to the side. She chortles against my mouth, and I find myself laughing, something I haven't done for so long that the memory of it feels like a dream.

"If you don't move me," I whisper, "I am going to break."

She slides her hand down and under, rearranging, but she doesn't let go, and with every curve and halt of the cab, her hand jerks a little, and this part of me that simply could not get heavier and thicker does.

I run through the lobby with Thea's backpack held to my front so as not to offend civilized humans for whom sex is something that is best kept offstage.

At the door, I fumble with the key, then open it wide, suddenly anxious. I've never had anyone in here, and last night, when I tried to imagine it through her eyes, it was so sterile: the asbestos-white carpeting that I never walk on, the hard, narrow sofa I've never sat on, the white resin cast of coral that I've never known the purpose of, the glass-front refrigerator that holds nothing but batteries and ice and an untouched bottle of pricey vodka left by the broker.

The two dozen roses I bought from the twenty-four-hour deli—hoping they would add a little life and color—have remained perfectly tight and symmetrical. They smell like paper.

This isn't home, I want to say. My home, my real home, is rich and complicated and alive. Stretching up the great folds of mountains are forests that are old and baroque with the huge roots of ancient blowdown surrounded by the opportunistic suckers stretching to take their elder's spot in the sun. Lichen and moss fight over massive rocks, and water carves tortured paths and it's all bent and crowded and even the boggish smell of rot stinks of new life.

She leans against the wall, untying her boot. "It's very...clean," she says, seemingly at a loss for anything else. Just then, she loses her balance, dropping her boot.

Little flecks of dried mud and leaf fly across the pale wooden floor. She grits her teeth.

"I'm sorry," she starts to say. "Do you have a broom..."

No.

I don't want to clean it up. I don't want her to be sorry for bringing something real into my life. I envelop her, my back shielding her from all this crappy nothingness, and her body relaxes into mine, lengthening against me. Her hands slip around my neck and my waist, her lips brush my cheek, the sunken wound near my nose, my eye. My mouth.

My tongue breaks in, at first just tasting the sweet bitterness of mint and coffee. My hand struggles with the button at her jeans.

"Let me," she says. She doesn't pull her body away from mine but slides her hand down between us. I press closer so that when her fingers twist against her button, that twisting rubs against my crown. When she pulls at her zipper, her hand glides down to the root and rests momentarily against the heavy weights beneath.

Then she lets go, and I hook my thumbs through the belt loops on either side of her jeans and hold them still while Thea shifts her hips, holding me around the waist, so I'm tight against her. By the time she's finished with her shifting and pulling, I'm hurt and achy. Then she crosses her hands in front of her sweater, and when she pulls it over her head, she looks at me with an expression of pure lust.

Humans apparently categorize lust as a sin, like wrath or sloth or envy or anger or those others that I'm forgetting right now. We understand those; they have consequences for others.

But lust? That overwhelming need to please and be pleased? How is that a sin? How is it anything but pure?

Thea clearly has little experience with ties and snorts in frustration when the knot grows too tight to get the tie off. All the civilized buttons and cuff links and knots that lock up my body.

I grab the tie and pull it over my head, then slide my hands under each placket and tear, sending little shirt buttons scurrying under the radiator in the process. I squeeze two fingers between skin and French cuffs and yank at those, freeing my wrists. My pants follow. Pinked, hand-sewn, bespoke, ripped, destroyed, and beyond repair—and I could *not* care less, because I am naked with the Goddess of the City of Wolves in my arms, against my skin. I pull her up until her thighs are wrapped around my hips.

"Wait, I've got to get a condom."

"I've got dozens."

"Dozens? I find that both really reassuring and really not," she says.

"I didn't say how many dozens. I've just always been very careful." I don't want to be careful with her. I want to feel her slick grip on my cock and come in vast waves until she is inundated with me. I just don't know how to explain that STDs and pregnancy are not a worry, will never be a worry, because I'm a werewolf and she's not.

In a few steps, I lay the Goddess of the City of Wolves on my bed. She refuses to let go. "No, you don't," she says, and her legs tighten against me, pulling me lower until my erection is trapped between my belly and her rolling hips.

She sighs happily, with no sign of calculation or

coyness or guile. This isn't a transaction. It's just... sweet, feral joy.

Her body shivers under me like aspens do in the late fall. With my mouth and teeth, I nip and suckle at her skin, sinking lower and lower until I feel her pulse under me like the warm blood of a fresh kill.

Something is rising in my blood, something old and terrible and wonderful and very, very untamed. I reach for the drawer of my nightstand while I still have the wits to do it.

"You're panting," she says, watching me fumble with the damn condom.

"What?"

"Breathing fast. Wheezing, even. Do you need help?"

"Just maybe don't watch so closely?"

"If that's what you need," she says, and she turns away, raising her hips and her perfect ass in the air and *ohmygodican'tfeelmybrain*.

I lunge. The only thing that stops me from taking the cord of her neck in my teeth is the thick waterfall of black hair. I lay across her back, gasping.

Thea watches me over her shoulder. Watches me pull back from the spot where shoulder and neck join.

She forces her hips tighter against me until I am positioned at her entrance, my body shivering. "Do what you need to, Elijah," she whispers, her head to the side. "Trust me to take care of myself."

Silly human doesn't know what she's talking about. But then, with a gentle sweep of her hand, she sends her hair tumbling down to one side, leaving exactly the spot I'd been looking at completely exposed.

My wild takes hold, and I strike. She startles, like

even our females do sometimes, then stills, the muscle of her shoulder tightening under my teeth. I growl softly against her skin, to reassure her.

Her head cocked slightly to the side, she seems to be considering what she feels. There is no safe word between us. If she tells me to stop, I will stop. However much I don't want to, I will stop.

Then she relaxes against my teeth, and all I can do is hold on, keeping her in that tight balance between pleasure and pain. She shudders as my fingers explore, making sure she's ready for me. And then big and heavy and hard and near breaking, I take her.

Shattered, I watch Thea fall asleep, watch her kick off the blankets in this overheated apartment, leaving just a corner of the sheet covering her waist. On her side, her legs drawn up, revealing the seam of her body, which seems so inexcusably strong and terrifyingly vulnerable.

Is that what love is for humans? Is that where it lives? At the juncture of strength and vulnerability? Wolves don't think that way. We join strength to strength. We have no room for weakness.

But here—I lie down next to Thea, my chest tight against her back, my thighs around hers, my arm over her waist and bent up across her torso—I understand that there is enormous strength in vulnerability.

When Thea wakes up, I am still watching her, my head propped on my crooked elbow. She smiles at me, and I know I have lost all hand.

Chapter 21

I USE UNSCENTED SHAVING FOAM MADE "FOR SENSITIVE skin," not because my skin is sensitive, but because I have enough trouble with skeptical wolves without coming home stinking of amber and oud.

"I hope you're hungry?"

"Starving," she calls back from the bedroom. "What do you have?"

I lift my chin and stare down my nose, carefully pulling the razor along my neck. The rough glide of the blade against my stubble echoes the sound of her legs sliding into her jeans.

"Three-day-old falafel, a bottle of vodka, and a reservation at a place a few blocks from here."

The door is angled so that I can shave and still watch her in the full-length mirror. Watch the soft fold at her belly as she bends over for her bra. Watch the way she gently cups her hand under her breast before nicking the bra closed.

Watch the way she threads her arms through her black sweater, pulling it over her head. She slips her hand under the hair trapped in her turtleneck and picks up the frame from my bedside table.

I stick my head out from my bathroom, my mouth full of mint. She pushes her hair behind her ear, looking at the picture of the 9th.

"You look very happy here."

I rinse and spit. I join her, wiping my face with the towel. I don't say anything until I'm sure that my voice won't catch. "That was taken at home. I mean, my old home. I was very happy. And I am. Here. Very happy."

She looks at me oddly. "If you say so."

"Of course I am." Grateful for the change of subject, my eyes light on the wrinkled, heavy-stock invitation with the embossed black snowflake that Janine threw at me before she stomped off. "Hey, do you want to go to a party on the twenty-fifth?"

"No."

"Maybe you want to find out what it is before you say no?"

"Can I wear what I'm wearing?"

"Hmm, it's black tie. But I'd—"

"Will it have lots of people?"

"It is a party."

"Will there be lots of chatting?"

"Ditto."

"Networking?"

"Ditto."

"Posturing?"

"God, yes."

She swipes her lips with something that makes them look soft and slightly ruddy.

"Now I know what it is," she says, "and oddly, the answer is still no." Then she kisses me with a mouth that smells like cherries.

I have second thoughts about my reservations the moment I come through the revolving doors at CU. It's supposed to be cute, like *See You?* but also CU like the copper that lines everything from the beaten sconces and pendant lights to the mottled copper bar top to the dining-room chairs, sharp and folded like mean-spirited origami.

This was all explained to me by Alia, the maître d', who I'd cultivated from an earlier trending, now-failed restaurant, Faux, which itself was a play on pho, the chef's signature dish.

One has to know these things to stay ahead of the game.

Thea refuses to relinquish her coat or her backpack, which the coat-check girl takes as either a personal slight or at very least a sign of cheapness. When I hand her my own coat, I include twenty dollars as an initial goodwill gesture.

Thea drapes her pack over the back of her chair and spreads her coat over the front, sitting on it. It gives her some slight reprieve, I suppose, from the mean origami, but also detracts from the clean line.

The waiter stands at attention, the smile hardening on his face as she orders salad and soup and a beer from Brooklyn.

I lean over, my hand on hers. "My treat. Order whatever you want."

"I did," she says.

The unhappy waiter suggests the venison noisette.

"No, thanks."

The yarn at the left shoulder of her turtleneck is pilling.

I order the oysters with bottarga and coffee oil. Venison noisette with quince au jus and a side of purple potato chips with burgundy truffle. I don't want any of it. What I do want is for the waiter to stop the disapproving *tick-tick-ticking* of his pencil on the order pad.

I order a bottle of Achaval Ferrerra Finca Altamira.

Thea says a few words to the busboy in Spanish. He brightens and smiles sweetly. Despite the venison and wine, the waiter continues to make his disdain clear, but I have never been so generously supplied with water and clean cutlery.

She won't try my venison because *she doesn't eat meat*. She does not, of course, understand the riotous irony that she—a human—isn't eating carrion while I am. She swipes her bread through the remains of her soup.

This really was a mistake, I think as the coffee appears. CU is a place in the neighborhood, but not really a neighborhood place.

"Sorensson, is that you?" calls a hopped-up voice behind me.

"Dean." I smile tightly, readjusting my cuffs, my fingers checking the platinum links on both. I don't feel like dealing with Dean Latham (international commerce, Sarnath & Keene) right now.

But I have no choice. He's right here, sniffing around, taking Thea in. Her face, her hair, her pilling sweater, her mud-spattered boots, her anorak and worn backpack absolutely ruining the spare grace of the chair.

"Thea Villalobos," she says, extending her hand when it becomes clear that I'm not making any introductions.

When she smiles, the copper-tinted lights overhead pick out the fine lines at the corners of her eyes.

"Dean Latham. The pleasure," he says, smiling a smile that tells me he's seen everything, "is all mine."

I can almost hear what he's going to say to the boys at Sarnath & Keene. *Guess who I saw at CU? Elijah*

Sorensson. Not a client, a woman. Let's just say his standards are slipping.

It's like Pack. Always looking at the higher ranks to see if they're getting sloppy or slack or stupid, and it might be the right time to take them down.

"We should make a squash time," he says, finally dragging his eyes back to me.

Thea puts her hand on my hand, whispering that she'll be right back.

I swish the thin, tan foam of the coffee around in my copper-glazed cup. I'm going to have to purge soon, get rid of all the alcohol and carrion before it gets into my system and makes the Pack shy away from me.

Dean watches Thea walk away. Then he turns back to me.

"So…squash?"

I hate squash. Dean loves it because he is a thin man with long arms and a small turn radius and doesn't have so far to go to get the damn ball when it bobbles along the floor. He knows he will win. But I have to deal with him on the Jaxed contract, so we set up a date for two weeks from Tuesday.

"I presume I'll be seeing you at L-Cubed?"

"Of course."

"With…" He nods to Thea's empty chair, his eyebrows up and inquisitive.

"With her? Nooo." I hear a disdainful voice that can't be mine but is say, "She's just a friend."

And, of course, because fate won't let me get away with being a shit in private, I smell the fragrance of cold earth and loam, and Thea's soft cheek slides next to mine, and her whispered voice cuts sharply through all the babble in the restaurant.

"You did what you needed to, Elijah. Trust me to take care of myself."

As she picks up her coat and her backpack from her chair and heads toward the door, my mind slows, as if it's just along for the ride and has no responsibility for the mess it's gotten me into. The only thing it seems to notice is that once again, one leg of her jeans is stuck in her mud-spattered boot.

The revolving door turns, and when a laughing group comes in, I don't see her anymore.

My hand slides along the cheek where she touched me.

"Hmm," someone says with a derisive snort. "Not sure *she* knew she was just a friend."

Who are you?

Blood starts to rush back into my brain, and I jump up, the origami chair skidding like shrapnel across the floor. I push Dean out of my way.

The coat-check girl blocks the door. Trying to be helpful, she doesn't toss me my overcoat as she would to a normal patron. Because I am a Big Swinging Dick, she holds it up, fitting one sleeve over the hand outstretched for the revolving door. I keep pushing through, and the rest of my coat trailing behind me jams the edge, trapping me in a glass cage.

Then, with one furious push, I shred the coat and break the hinges.

"*THEA!*"

I don't see her anywhere.

Pushing the door backward and breaking it again, I

scream at the blank faces around me, begging them to tell me where the woman I was with went. The coat-check girl shakes her head frantically, holding out the tattered, filth-stained half of my coat from the floor.

Unthinking, I shrug out of the other half and hand it to her.

The little humans are all pressed against the copper cladding like paper silhouettes. Alia looks at me apprehensively; the manager hides behind her, his phone at the ready.

"Mr. Sorensson?" Alia asks, plucking at my sleeve. "Is there anything we can do to help?"

I turn on her, and she flinches. But then I do what I always do when dealing with humans: I fumble for my wallet. "Put the cost of repairs on that when they come in." I hand Alia the black card with the subtle platinum writing. "And dinner, of course."

"Mr. Sorensson, thank you. But your friend already paid and left a generous 15 percent tip."

How human. To say "a generous 15 percent tip" when you mean exactly the opposite. When you mean that in a place like this, 15 percent is an insult. That 15 percent might fly at, say, Applebee's, but not here.

"Then put an additional three hundred on and distribute it however you see fit. And I can't tell you how sorry I am...for everything."

Leaning out the broken door, I search for the tall woman with the hair streaming down her back like flames.

"Excuse me?" Alia stands at my elbow with my card in one hand and a copper-clad tablet awaiting my signature in the other. I scribble an approximation of my mark with my finger.

"Thank you, Mr. Sorensson." Alia leans against me, her tight breast against the back of my hand. "We're always happy to see you here. You've always been one of my personal..."

I head outside to wait for the HST car service and call Thea, but it goes directly to her voicemail. "You have reached Thea Villalobos's personal number. If this is an emergency, please call..."

It is *a fucking emergency. I need to tell you something. You were open to me, vulnerable, and I betrayed you.* But how...how do I explain to the only person I care about in the chaos of Offland that I said what I said because, for one stupid minute, I was worried about what Dean Latham, international commerce at Sarnath & Keene, thought about the pilling at the shoulder of your turtleneck?

I lean over the gutter, fighting the need to purge.

The driver waited patiently as I ran coatless through the cold, first to Penn Station. Port Authority. Grand Central. The place near Javits where the blue buses gather.

Then my big Pack-size hands tremble and hit those tiny human-size buttons. With a sound like a breath exhaled, the message is sent into the ether.

Please, Thea.

Leaning forward to the front seat, I ask the driver how much time he has.

"Excuse me?"

"Do you have someone waiting for you at home? Another pickup?"

"Not if you book me."

"Then go north on 87 until I tell you to turn."

The driver dials someone and starts talking. Because

it's not in a language I understand, I don't know if it's his wife, his child, or his dispatcher.

Twice a month, every month, I have driven through the Bronx and Yonkers, rattling along next to the concrete barrier, lulled by the seams of the road. Past sound walls and billboards and retail centers and office complexes. I do it again now, listening but not watching.

Why didn't I just say *No, I'm not going with Thea because she turned me down*?

Or *No, I'm not going with Thea because she recognizes this shiny shit show for what it is*?

Or just simply *No*?

But instead, I had to say *With her? Nooo*, lengthening the *o* like I was offended by the suggestion. *She's just a friend.*

The phone buzzes against my sternum.

"Thea? Thank God. I'll be there in two hours. I need to explain—"

"Sorry, Sorensson. I was calling about that squash game. It turns out I—"

Without a word, I hang up on Dean Latham (international commerce, Sarnath & Keene) and text Thea again to tell her I'm on my way to the cabin.

I stare out the window.

She never comes. I sit there for three hours in the damn car, but she never comes.

The phone in my hand slumps heavily onto my lap.

"You can head back."

The driver takes out his earbuds. "Excuse me?"

"You can turn around. I'm not going anywhere."

When we drive past CU, the door has already been repaired, though there is some blue tape at the top of the glass. The last of the clients are leaving. Men in suits hold the side door open for women in high heels with red lacquered soles and lacquered nails and lacquered faces.

At the apartment, I open up the medicine chest, taking out the bottle of ipecac. I lean my head back, gulp down a big swig, and wait.

A few minutes later, my stomach starts to rumble, and I lurch over to the toilet, vomiting up nothing but a foamy, pale-yellow liquid.

It's too late.

The carrion is part of me now.

Chapter 22

Hāmweard, ðu londadl hǽðstapa, IN *18* DAYS
Homeward, you landsick heath-wanderer, IN *18* DAYS

"YOU'VE GOT TO PULL YOURSELF TOGETHER, ELIJAH," Max hisses, carefully patting the wisps of hair to cover his bald spot. "Jesus. This whole evening, you've just been sitting there like you don't care."

He shakes his hand, and one furtive strand makes a bid for freedom and falls to the floor of the steel-clad bathroom of the trending midtown branch of Roan.

He's right. I don't care. I didn't want to be here. I brought the plastics industry to HST. I came up with their new branding: Americans for Progressive Packaging. I should not have to be here for this. I don't care that they like me and admire me. This is like watching sausage being made, and I don't have the stomach for it.

I don't want to watch HST's lobbying arm decide where to place advertising. How to distribute campaign contributions. Which laws to block and how to slip their agenda through local and national legislatures like a virus. Which nonprofits might give APP moral credibility in return for cold, hard cash.

It's all so that no one will question the extravagantly disposable status quo.

The Pack would be appalled if they knew I'd had anything to do with this.

Shoving the cuff links into my jacket, I hang my jacket over a coat hook and roll up my shirtsleeves.

"Well, Elijah?" he snaps. "Do I have to remind you who these people are?"

"No, I know perfectly well." I put my hand on the latch to the stall. "Now, if you'll excuse me, I need to vomit."

I've lost all hand in my frantic attempts to contact Thea. She's put me on her call block list.

In the dull light of the taxi, I lift my chin, checking what is left of my injuries. We heal quickly, and the swelling is gone—the bruising too—and as I move my face from side to side, all that's left of the hole made by Tiberius's canine is a slight indentation below the inner corner of my eye. The cab stops and I untangle my legs, dropping my feet heavily to the street in front of Testa's dark-green door.

On second thought, I adjust my tie, loosening it so that I look more like a busy, serious man taking some well-deserved time off, rather than a desperate, lonely wolf, trying to pretend that the only woman who has ever mattered to him doesn't matter anymore.

"Excuse me?" A woman looks at my hand on the knob. She turns her head up and to the side, as women often do when they're about to take a selfie. She is perfectly beautiful. Brown hair dyed with reddish-purple stripes curls in layers around an oval face of fine symmetry. She has a tight ass that yields almost indistinguishably into her finely chiseled waist before finally conceding to a slight curve at her pert breasts. "Will you be my escort?" She looks at me from under her lowered lids. Then she bites her lower lip.

I try to imagine taking her to the hotel and closing my eyes and feeling her hands roam across my skin, loving my body. Her ironwood eyes not coy or dissembling, just fierce and joyous. Her long, black hair creating a cocoon of silence that only ends when she makes that sound deep in her chest, a sound that tears through me with something between ecstasy and despair. And when our bodies finally unwind, my soul is left twined around hers like ivy around an oak as she lies next to me, her hand on my gentled cock, and lets me breathe in the smell of cold earth.

Letting me just be.

"Well?" she asks irritably. "What's it going to be?"

I step back from the green door.

And to make matters worse, Janine comes back on Monday. She makes no mention of our last interaction. She is wearing an icy smile and a new dress (Alberta Ferretti), and she smells of Barneys and Bergdorf's. My senses in skin are not very good, but they are at least good enough to tell me when I've stepped in trouble.

In my drawer behind two pens and a highlighter and a stylus is the little box with the fisher skull. I stare at the box and the address, my thumb brushing against the scrawled *Fragile*. The pine needles inside scatter across my desk when I dig the fisher skull out of its box. I set it right in the middle, facing me, with its ghoulish, sharp-toothed smile.

Janine comes almost instantly, using one hand to

sweep the dried pine needles into the palm of the other. Then she reaches for the box. I strike first, covering it. Her French manicure scratches the top of my hand.

"I was going to throw it away for you," she says without letting go.

"Just leave it. And close the door behind you."

After a moment's hesitation, she stalks out.

I turn the skull around and around, admiring its delicacy and ferocity. Then I rub the little thing against my jaw.

"Leave the fishers alone," Gran Tito had said. "Sharp teeth, fierce tempers, superfast." Then he grimaced and sucked at his tongue. "The meat's nasty too. Like mink, and there isn't near enough of it."

He told me to stick with rabbit or squirrel or possum or raccoon. But I didn't want the easy frog or weed or nut eaters. I wanted the fisher, sleek and fierce and wild.

It had the grace of a water snake. I'd tried hunting it before but always ended up with my paws on the tree trunk, barking futilely while the fisher laughed a mile above.

Or maybe not a laugh but a cry like a ghost woman, like a banshee.

I haunted their territory, watching them. My hunts always ended the same way, with me clambering down from some rock or tree, while my prey just swam away through the air. I was earthbound, while they seemed to operate in some extra dimension.

The one I finally caught, I got because I threw myself into space right after him. Grabbing hold, we both tumbled to earth, which hurt me a lot more than it did him. Not as much as the chunk of fur and flesh he would rip from my leg.

But I held on. He really was pretty foul-tasting, but I had been so proud to limp into Nils's office and watch as he placed that skull among all the timid bunnies.

I sweep the handful of pine needles from my desk and return them to the little box. It doesn't take me long to find the number for Susannah Marks in Southampton. The woman who answers tells me there is no Villalobos there and hangs up. When I call back and ask to speak to the gardener, she recognizes my voice and hangs up again.

There's nothing for it but to launch myself into space.

Chapter 23

Hāmweard, ðu londadl hǽðstapa, IN *15* DAYS
Homeward, you landsick heath-wanderer, IN *15* DAYS

DURING THE SUMMER, SUSANNAH MARKS, THE EX-WIFE of hedge fund manager and HST client Tony Marks, lives in a rambling, gray, cedar-shingled house with white trim. The main building is two stories with a gently sloping roof, surrounded by an elaborate wood pergola threaded by neatly trimmed vines that are still wintering.

There is also a pool house, and through the break in the hedge, another small house fronted by cold frames. The whole complex is protected by a solid, six-foot, white wooden fence with sharp points that is supposed to keep the idly curious hoi polloi at bay. It barely comes up to my chin.

"Hello?" I call over the fence to a man who is on his knees in front of the cold frames, but before he can turn around, a huge mastiff comes howling around the corner of the pergola.

"Brutus! Here," he says.

Brutus stops, alert and silent beside him.

The man struggles to his feet and hobbles a little as he moves through the hedge and approaches the fence. The gate squeaks slightly as he opens it. Evidently, the squeak is new.

"What do you want?" the man asks, swinging the gate again, trying to pinpoint the squeak.

"Mr. Villalobos?"

Now I've got his attention. "The name is Colina, Vasco Colina."

"Are you Thea's uncle?"

"Depends on why you're asking."

The whole way out here, I'd rehearsed one story after another about misunderstandings, mishearings, misinterpretations. Each one more stale and nonsensical and bogus than the last. The only thing that didn't sound ridiculous was the truth. So what if it made me sound weak? Thea was strong enough to be vulnerable. I need to be at least that strong.

"I messed up. I said something I didn't mean, and now Thea won't talk to me. I didn't know what else to do, so here I am."

"Was this Friday?"

"Did she say something?"

He shakes his head. "No, but she seemed..." He doesn't finish, just touches the gate hinge, then looks at his thumb. "Want to tell me exactly how you messed up?"

"I pretended she didn't matter to me, but she does. She really does." For some reason, Brutus pulls forward, the muscles at his chest tightening. Colina scratches behind the dog's ear.

"What happened to your face?"

"Car accident."

"Drunk?" he asks, his voice cooling.

"Not me. Can't speak for the deer though."

He seems to relax at that. "You live in the city?"

I nod.

"But you drove all the way out here to talk about my niece?"

"Yes."

"Well then, I'll get my coat, and let's talk about my niece."

The town isn't empty, exactly, but it's like all the color has been sucked out. It's so geared toward summer—bright sun and sand and wealthy children in colorful swimsuits and coconut-scented sunscreen and teen-age flirtation and ocean water and sandy shoes and ice cream—that in the winter when all that is gone, it becomes oddly sepia.

I follow Vasco Colina's truck past the shops that are closed until May and those that have limited hours. There's no trouble finding parking and then a seat in the Sip 'n' Soda.

"Afternoon, Vasco." A guy wiping down the beige-and-chrome counter seating nods at Colina.

Vasco nods back and says something that sounds like "Tone" before heading to a booth across from the counter. He drops to the bench and, with the help of his hands and one shoe, pushes his body farther in. Then he pivots around.

The waitress is a slim, pretty woman, if a little life-worn. She's older, but the smudged dark swoop of liner above one eye makes her seem strangely innocent. She puts her hand on Vasco's shoulder, and he brightens immediately.

"Hey, Krissie," he says and orders a triple-decker with bacon and grilled chicken, extra mayo, and an egg cream. I get a veggie burger and a coffee.

There is some family resemblance, though Colina's face is narrower, craggier than his niece's, but they both have the same ironwood eyes. They also share the same bluntness, though Vasco Colina has none of Thea's reserve.

Maybe it's because he's spent the winter in an empty beach house and an empty beach town, but he seems happy to talk to someone. Anyone.

"So how'd a rich guy from the City end up meeting my niece?" he asks, moving his thin paper napkin to the side and arranging the knife and fork on top of it.

"You, actually. You got in touch with Tony, and he contacted—"

"Ah! So you're the lawyer? The one who warned the police about that pervert? Well, good for you. All those disgusting messages on her phone."

First I'd heard of any messages. Leaning back, I drape my arm over the back of the chair and signal the waitress. She moves in close, pot of coffee steaming in her hand and a smile warm on her lips. "Could I bother you for some milk? Just a glass. For the coffee?"

She glances at the huge bowl of aseptic plastic creamers.

"Please," I say, holding her eyes for an extra fraction of a second. "I really don't like those."

She smiles and shrugs one shoulder before sauntering toward the back. She returns with a small carafe.

"I brought a pitcher," Krissie says. "Thought that might be better."

I thank her with a big smile before I turn back. She raises her eyebrows at Vasco, and when she leaves, she has a strut to her walk.

"Did she call the police?"

"No. She figured she could take care of it."

"Because she has a gun."

"Because she knows how to shoot. Thanks, Krissie," he says when she sets his egg cream in front of him. "Do you know where Thea's father and I met?"

Pouring in milk, I shake my head.

"Fort Benning. Hector and I were at sniper school together. Hector was very…a man's man. Macho, I guess, but he really had no idea how to act around women. Not Lenna, my sister… I know for a fact he was a virgin when he met her. And not Thea either."

He peels the paper from his straw and stirs up the chocolate syrup at the bottom of the glass.

"When Thea's big brother, Paul, went to college, my sister went back to work. She had to work weekends, and Hector was left with Thea. She was twelve at the time and kept herself to herself. Lenna told him to just leave her alone, but Hector, he thinks she should be getting out. Doing whatever girls that age were supposed to be doing. He called her *la chica taciturna*." Vasco chuckles to himself. "He took her to the mall once, and Thea sat on one of those husband chairs reading until Hector yelled at her to go fucking buy something already. That's what he told me he said, anyway. So she goes off, and three minutes later, she hands him a pack of tissues and sits back in her chair. Not a word."

Taking a long draft of chocolate and soda, he settles back with a contented sigh.

"Do you know what the most important thing is to being a sniper, Mr. Sorensson?"

"Elijah, please. Just call me Elijah. Good aim?"

He snorts. "There are thousands of marksmen in this country. So no. The best snipers have self-control, but they also have something else. They have to be like a rock inside. Kind of hard to explain. But there's a kind of stillness to them.

"Anyway, Hector was good. He had self-control, but he had too much extraneous crap. You know: being better than anyone else. Making sure no one disrespected him. That he was living up to his expectations of what it meant to be a man. Like I said, the basic alpha-male stuff."

If these people had any idea of what it takes to be an Alpha, they would know that a Y chromosome was the least of it.

"But I got to give him credit; he saw that something in his daughter. Started taking her to the shooting range. And he was right. *That girl.*" Vasco jabs the air with two stiff fingers, emphasizing each word. "She could empty herself out until she just was. She wasn't bored or nervous or proud or competitive or anything. *She just was*. You had to see it. But it was like she pared down so far, she was part of the landscape."

"Chicken bacon," Krissie says, laying down Vasco's plate. "And a veggie burger." She gives me another smile.

"Krissie?" Vasco calls to her retreating back. "Extra mayo?"

Krissie raises her hand without turning around.

"Where was I?"

"That Thea just was?"

"Oh right. You know, Hector had tried to teach Paul, thought it would man him up, but Paul hated it. Hated the sound, the recoil, the idea. Bored him *to tears*. Thea got Hector's old M24 when he died. I doubt she's looked at it since, but I think she's probably still got it."

Colina smears the extra mayonnaise on his sandwich and tilts his head to the side to take a bite.

In the corner of my eye, I catch the swirl of a bright scarf falling to the floor behind me. I pick it up and hand it to the young woman in the booth behind me. She smiles and then lowers her eyes, her fingers brushing my hand.

When I turn around, Colina is studying me, and I feel the reflexive smile I wore for the young woman fade. Wiping his hands on his napkin, he slowly and purposefully moves his leg out from under the table, making sure that I am watching. Then he pulls up the hem of his Carhartts, revealing the metal joint of a prosthetic. "The army gave me this, but not all parts can be replaced. Thea is as close to a child as I'm ever going to get. From where I'm sitting, you could have any woman you want. So why my niece? She's too independent to be any man's little woman, but that doesn't mean she can't be hurt."

"I know that. I know I hurt her. And I know I don't deserve a second chance, but I also know that while she may not need me, I need her." I peel the pickles off my veggie burger. "Have you ever pretended to be something you're not?"

"Sure, who hasn't? Look at me, pretending I have two legs."

I chuckle at that. I can't help but like Thea's uncle. "Yeah, but here's the thing. I'd been doing it so long that I really couldn't tell anymore when I was real and when I was just pretending. And for years, nobody ever noticed that I was faking it. But Thea did. Immediately. Maybe it's because, like you said, she *just is*, so she can tell when someone else *isn't*."

I take a bite of the veggie burger and stare out the window toward the street.

A man blocks the window and cups his hands on either side of his eyes, looking for someone. He waves to a woman sitting at the counter and comes in. As soon as he opens the door, a metal bell rings.

"I realize that I'm not explaining this well, but I just know that when I'm with her, I remember who I really am."

Vasco drops his napkin on his empty plate.

"I'm going to get some ice cream. It's good here. You want some?"

I'm not focused on what Vasco says. "Okay, yes."

"Cone or cup?"

"Doesn't matter."

"And what flavor do you want?"

"Anything." *I don't care about the fucking ice cream.*

"Hey, Tone," he says, waving over his shoulder toward the man at the counter. "Two cups of Death by Chocolate?"

The man behind the counter nods and taps his scoop against the warm water bath, just about to dig in when I signal him. "Actually," I say, "make mine butter pecan."

Unlike Tarzan, my wolves warned me about chocolate.

"Can I ask you something?" I ask Vasco. "Do you know what happened in Austin?"

"Austin? How do you know about that? She tell you?"

"Google. There's a little story in the *Austin Beacon*. Not much, but there's a picture and one line about her."

I head to the counter as soon as Tone signals that our ice cream is ready.

"I honestly don't know what happened in Austin," Vasco says when I put his bowl in front of him. "Like I said, she was never the most social of girls. I can still hear Hector yelling down the hall, '*Venga, Thea. Saludastes a todos.*' 'Come say hello to everyone.' She'd come down the hall looking like she was heading for the firing squad. '*Que te pasa?*' Hector would always say. 'What is wrong with you?'

"But then she gets a scholarship to Austin, and she changes like a lot of kids do. She got this boyfriend Hector really liked—prelaw, as a matter of fact. He got her to join a sorority. Hector was thrilled. When she called me to tell me, she was all bouncy. 'Can you believe it?' she says. I remember thinking even the way she talked was different. Like everything was so exciting. Perky. It just didn't seem like her. And because I loved her the way she was, it made me sad. I felt like I was losing her.

"And then something happened. A girl died. It wasn't Thea's fault. No one ever said it was. But next year, she moves up to Syracuse. Enrolls in environmental studies or some such thing. 'Earth crap,' Hector said. She slept with men who weren't going anywhere and then broke up with them a year later. Hector was furious. She was the smart one. She was supposed to become a doctor or a lawyer or an engineer. She was supposed to get married and have grandkids and come back to Tucson.

"I didn't say anything, but I was so happy. I had my *chica taciturna* back."

His spoon scrapes along the side of the metal bowl, the metal on metal that sends a shiver along my croup.

"Her parents are dead?"

He wipes his mouth, considering me.

"She told me," I say. "Didn't say how though."

Then he leans back. "It was almost exactly five years ago. DUI. Two years to the day after Paul put his mouth around the barrel of that M24 and his toe to the trigger. He never could be the man his father wanted him to be.

"I think—Thea does too—that Hector just decided that he was done with sadness. But neither of us could forgive him for making that decision for Lenna too. My sister had always made so many compromises and concessions to keep the peace in the family that I think Hector forgot she had a mind of her own."

Vasco waves to Krissie and wiggles his finger in the air, signaling for the check.

"I can't imagine ever forgetting that Thea has a mind of her own."

"Good thing. Because I think she's done with changing for other people. Anyway, I moved east so I could be here if Thea needed me. Though what with one thing and another, I need her more than the other way around."

Krissie walks toward us, her pencil flowing across the pad. Vasco smiles as he watches her.

"Me too, Mr. Colina. And that's why I'm here."

With a perforated rip, Krissie puts the check on the table. I reach for it quickly, pressing my black card into her hand.

"Cash only," Colina says as he counts out the bills. There's no resentment or accusation, just a one-legged gardener who recognizes the primacy of no man.

"I can't make any promises, but I'll see what I can do."

Chapter 24

Hāmweard, ðu londadl hǽðstapa, IN *9* DAYS
Homeward, you landsick heath-wanderer, IN *9* DAYS

THERE'S A MAN IN ANOTHER MIGHTY BUILDING A BLOCK away. I've see him before. Well-dressed, fit, and successful, he stares out toward me. I would have said he was master of all he surveys, but increasingly, I think he's waiting for something.

Then yesterday, I nodded to him and he nodded back, and I realized that this wasn't a man at all, just a broken wolf reflected in the crystalline plate-glass windows when the light is low.

Is this what happened to Aldrich, all those years ago, before he drove into the lamppost?

"Mr. Sorensson? I couldn't reach Janine," screeches Dahlia's voice over the intercom on my phone, an agony in my sensitive ears. "That man from Great North is here again."

Given that our lives are ruled by the calendar, you'd think the Pack would have figured out how to use iCal.

"Send him in. And Dahlia, could you arrange for someone to fix my intercom?"

A minute later, the door closes.

"No hard feelings?" says the low, cool voice.

"Of course not. Have a seat."

Tiberius shakes his head. "As soon as we finish here, I'm going straight home."

Leaning back in my chair behind the barricade of my desk, I cross my ankle to my knee.

"Can I just ask why the Great North no longer uses the phone?"

"Because the Great North has been betrayed once and has become cautious. We will not be betrayed again."

We?

"I'm going to repeat: *The Great North* is getting paranoid."

Tiberius turns, scanning the halls through the glass door. "You know Maxim Trianoff contacted the Alpha."

"Did he? And what did he want?"

"Wanted to tell the CEO of Great North that you were coming unhinged, spinning out of control. Said you'd had an accident on your way back from your last trip up there. Thought maybe you'd been drinking. You look better, by the way."

"It was just a flesh wound."

"Mmm. He seemed especially upset about the time and resources and goodwill you wasted on something about protecting wolves. *Wolves*." He smiles and says quietly, "The Alpha commends your hard work."

"And how did she leave things with Max?"

"She just said that you enjoyed the full confidence of the Great North, and she expected to hear nothing more on the subject. She did it in that way a good Alpha does, and he couldn't wait to get off the phone." Tiberius picks up the skull from my desk. "What's this?"

It's everything I can do to stop from launching myself across the polished oak to snatch it back.

"Fisher." The thing looks so small and vulnerable in his big hand. "Be careful with it."

He lowers his head a little and sniffs. "You marked it?"

"Don't be ridiculous. I touched it, that's all."

"You know as well as I do that there is a difference between marking and touching." He takes another sniff. "Did you mark the woman who gave it to you as well?"

"And *she* is certainly none of your fucking business." With a quick sweep of my forearm, the fisher skull is settled into the drawer next to the box of pine needles it came in. Then I jam the drawer shut, holding it closed with my thigh. "Now, why don't you tell me *your* business."

Tiberius touches his hand to his nose and draws in a slow, deep breath. His senses in skin are better than ours are as wolves. With every breath he takes, I feel exposed, my defenses stripped away.

He nods once as though confirming something to himself. "We will be having a lying-in soon, and the Alpha asks that you bring the necessary signature addenda with room for four new names."

"Four? Tristan and Gabi always cull if there are over three. They—"

"There will be," Tiberius insists tightly, "*four*."

"And who are the parents?"

"Just bring the papers next moon."

"It doesn't work that way. I need the names of the adults who will be signing on their behalf."

He stares out the window for a long time.

"Quicksilver Nilsdottir," he says with a crack in his voice. "Tiberius Malasson."

And for the first time, I see feeling in the Shifter's

dark face. It's not anticipation or nervousness or joy. It's nothing small or light. It's pain and dread and guilt. He clamps his lips between his teeth, and the room reeks of salt and old leather. The unmistakable smell of fear.

I don't know what to say to him. I can't promise that his mate will make it. We use every bit of medical technology we can get our claws on, but we still lose females during the lying-in. Powerful females. Viable females. Females bearing only two. "Silver is strong of marrow," I say, feeling the smallness of the comfort even as I say it. "And the whole of the Great North will be there for her. For you too, if it comes to that."

Tiberius doesn't pretend not to understand. He just slumps against the wall, his arms wrapped around his waist. He shakes his head and stares at the floor for a long time.

"I remember..." he finally says. "I remember when all I'd worry about was how to get rid of them. Women. How to get through those miserable morning hours before I could kick them out and start over. A clean slate."

He rubs at his clipped beard, and I catch a glimpse of those freakish fangs that I've only heard about before.

"God, I miss it." His shattered hand drops briefly to the braid at his neck, the sign of a mated wolf. "I miss the not caring."

"Tiberius?"

He stops, his hand on the door, his head turned just a fraction.

"There will be room for four."

Chapter 25

Hāmweard, ðu londadl hǽðstapa, IN *4* DAYS
Homeward, you landsick heath-wanderer, IN *4* DAYS

VASCO COLINA'S TEXT WAS CRYPTIC TO SAY THE LEAST, but after double- and triple-checking the address, I am in Hell's Kitchen at nine like he said. The address he gave me is for a dive that was once called McCarran's Lounge, but time and flaking paint has transformed the old neon into Carmen's Lung.

He told me to wait outside. B SUBTLE, he said in capitals.

Not sure why I need to be subtle. In the half hour I've been here, only one man has come out. I try to look inside, but the diamond-shaped, mesh-reinforced window is covered with ancient stickers. ZAGAT RATED, 2002 NIGHTLIFE GUIDE.

Another reads THE HAPPIEST PLACE ON EARTH, though someone has scribbled a circle with a line through it in red ballpoint.

I wasn't subtle enough to avoid a lackluster offer of a hand job. I smile my thanks and give the woman forty dollars anyway.

Then the door opens a crack. "Thanks," says that voice, and my devastated wild bounds into the air. "I've got him."

The door to the bar opens inward and stays open. There's a lot of shuffling and rearranging. Thea's clearly struggling with something unwieldy. I lean forward, pushing at a doorknob that is dark and sticky with the buildup of sweat and sugary drinks.

That voice starts to thank me but trails off.

"Elijah?"

"Thea?" Because she is the person who is struggling. And the unwieldy burden is her uncle. Vasco is wobbling and stinks of liquor. But I know what liquor in the body smells like. It smells sickly sweet, not smoky and bitter like this. This is the smell of liquor *on* the body, not in it. Vasco is wearing his bourbon like a cologne.

I stutter a moment, partly because I am processing and partly because it seems appropriate to such a crazy coincidence.

"Here, let me help you."

"Thanks," Thea says, trying hard to take care of it herself. "I've got him now. It was just the door."

"Are you sure?"

Thea nods, scanning the street for a cab, and Vasco's eyebrows jump twice, shooting me a sly grin, before he starts to slide down.

I love you, you mad fox.

"Thea, let me at least help you get him into a cab."

I take Vasco's arm from around her shoulder, pretending to support him. Pretending, because as soon as he is not inconveniencing his niece, he holds himself up.

"Jesus, *tío*," she mutters. "Why didn't you wait for me?"

It takes some doing to get Vasco folded up into the cab. He makes it as difficult as physically possible for the two of us, and twice, he almost topples to the ground. Thea crawls in next to him, and while she buckles him in, he stares at me standing on the curb like a dolt.

I run around to the front passenger seat.

"Where are you going, Thea?"

"Penn Station? I've got to get him home. He lives in Southampton."

I open the door and slide next to the driver, who is not happy to be moving his coat, his coffee, his Tupperware, and his *Post* to accommodate my oversize frame. I drag my legs in and fold them up.

"There's a lever on the side of the seat," the driver says. "To push it back."

"Thanks, I'm good." I click my own seat belt into place and bend low over my knees, unwilling to crush Vasco sprawled awkwardly behind me, his metal leg stretched across the hump.

"Penn Station," I say before Thea's hand pushes through the divider.

"You don't have to do this."

"I know. I'm just going to help you get him on the train. Then it's an easy subway ride back to the apartment."

The driver checks his rearview mirror and whispers harshly, "He's not going to hurl back there, is he?"

"No." I catch a glimpse of my shrewd ally in the mirror. "I think I can safely promise you that."

Between the two of us, the wolf and the fox, we manage to make things just difficult enough for Thea to require my assistance all the way to the Montauk-bound train from Jamaica.

"I don't know what to say. He doesn't drink. Not really," Thea says. "But thank you, Elijah."

"It was nothing." I stall, unsure what to do. "It was

really, really nice to see you again." I should be getting off now. "Maybe we—"

Then Vasco leans forward, gagging. We both leap to help him, but I get there first. "Take me to the bathroom," he mutters softly.

Brilliant! The bathroom!

Vasco refuses to go in but stays in a corner where Thea can't see him until the train pulls out of the station. Then we jerk back to the four seats facing each other.

Thea is mortified and so apologetic.

For my part, I check my reflection in the dark window just to be absolutely sure that I'm not grinning like a fool.

"Don't worry." I look at my phone. "I didn't have anything tomorrow morning anyway." With a few jabs of my finger, I make it true and slide my phone back into my breast pocket. "I'll help you get him into a car and hop the late train back."

She looks tired and disheartened. She balls up her coat against the cold of the train window and stares out into the night. The lights inside the train are so bright that Queens and Nassau are invisible, except for the glare of the occasional high-intensity halide streetlights.

Leaning my own head back, I pretend to sleep, but there's no way I could. Instead, I revel in her nearness. In the smell of damp earth, in the anorak, the worn backpack, the black untamed hair slipping over her shoulder, the lines decorating the corners of her eyes like fine lace.

When she falls asleep under the bright lights, surrounded by vinyl and the smells of stale coffee and old doughnuts left from a million morning commuters,

I move my leg so when she relaxes, her knee touches mine. I hold it there.

A couple of hours into the trip, a train passes us going the other direction. The stone-cold sober Vasco opens an eye and jerks his thumb toward the New York–bound track.

Last train, he mouths.

Somewhere inside me, my wild sits, head up, ears perked, legs taut.

"Thea?"

The train is almost empty by the time we reach the South Fork. In three months, it will be crowded. In five, it will be unendurable.

"Thea?" This time, I stroke the back of her hand. "We're here."

She jolts upright, craning to look out the window. Vasco makes a commendable show of looking sick and bleary as the wooden overhang and the sign for Southampton creep into view.

We steer his deadweight toward the parking lot, a long, narrow strip of asphalt populated by three cars: a slightly shabby, salt-eaten Mercedes, a rusted Fiat Spider, and that well-tended GMC truck of a vintage that requires a metal key that fits into a metal lock.

While Thea goes around to the driver's side, I plant my feet, ready to lift Vasco into the high cab. "Clear off," he hisses. And with a stuttering leap, he gains the seat, then lifts his metal leg with both hands, fitting it into place.

His niece is barely in the driver's seat before I vault over the side panel and lean against the back of the cab. Thea bumps over the low curb and onto the road while I stretch out my legs and breathe in the grass clippings and wood chippings and motor oil and damp salt air. I listen to the waves crashing on a distant beach and stare at the stars. Ecstatic.

At the big wooden fence belonging to the absent Susannah Marks, Vasco continues to pretend to need my support while Thea fumbles with yet another key. As soon as she scrapes it against the lock, a dog starts barking furiously.

"Oh, shut up, Brutus," Thea mutters. The door finally opens, and once again, Brutus comes running around the corner.

"*Tío*?" Thea says worriedly.

We are slightly stuck here. With Vasco playing at being unconscious with drink, Brutus may assume we have harmed the man. He slavers through the last few feet and then is caught short by a harsh growl and an Alpha stare. The mastiff skitters to a stop, his legs flailing as he tries to turn. What's left of his tail droops, and with a low whimper, he twirls away.

"Allergies." I bark out a cough and ostentatiously clear my throat. "Where are we going?"

Thea keeps looking toward the break in the hedge where Brutus disappeared, but Vasco starts to topple again, and she motions toward the small building beyond the cold frames.

A motion sensor turns on the light, a sure sign that Southampton is largely stripped of animal life. If we had motion sensors controlling lights at the Homelands, they'd be blinking on all night, every night, forever.

Vasco's home is divided into two parts: one half is

windowless and looks more like a large toolshed, and the other half is a tidy house.

It's small like Thea's place, but it has two doors leading to what I can only assume are a bedroom and a bathroom. It has a TV and a sofa and a microwave. And it is not a cabin in Buttfuck, New York. It is an open-concept bungalow in the Hamptons.

Thea whispers something to her uncle. He stumbles toward what smells like artificial lemons and hence is clearly the bathroom. She pauses and looks my way. A moment later, I'm there leaning over to hear her voice. "Can you stay here for a second? Just listen. In case he needs help," she says. "I'll be right back."

As soon as she goes through to what I assume is the bedroom, the door cracks open. "She tell you to stand there?" asks Colina.

"Hmm."

"Well, don't. Don't need someone listening to me in the john."

I stand back, not that it does anything. I can hear him in the bathroom from the living room.

"So," he says, checking for Thea's whereabouts, "now you owe me, right?"

"Absolutely. Anything."

"If she's still talking to you by the end, don't you go screwing my niece on my sofa bed."

A drawer closes, followed by the creak of floorboards under Thea's feet.

"Did you hear me?"

"I heard you. She's coming."

The bathroom door closes softly.

"I think he's okay. I mean, I haven't heard anything."

"Thanks, Elijah. Really. I've got it now."

Please, Thea.

"*Tío*?" She waits until he opens the door.

Unsure what to do now, I head toward Colina's refrigerator and the Montauk schedule attached to the front by a magnetized bottle opener. Running my finger down the list confirms that the last train is long gone. Next to it are phone numbers for the Long Island Veterans Center and the Northport VA Medical Center.

Thea leaves the bathroom, holding something that looks like a truncated rubber windsock.

"Is he okay?"

Please, Thea.

"He'll be fine in the morning." She turns on the faucet and pulls the sock inside out, squeezing soap on it.

"The last train is already gone."

Please, Thea.

Her eyes flick to the schedule, and she makes a little *tsk* of disgust. "I'm so sorry. I forgot the last one is so early off-season. I could drive you back—"

"Of course not. I've got nothing in the morning, and it's nice out here this time of year. I'll just find a hotel."

Please, Thea.

She suds up the sock. Then, without lifting her head, she says quietly, "Or you could stay here." She hangs the clean sock from a clamp on the backsplash. "Just...friends."

She turns around, leaning against the counter so we are both facing in the same direction, next to each other.

I rub the corners of my mouth and then hold my hands in front of me looking at the tile floor. "I know what I said, but here's the thing: I really, *really* don't want to be just friends."

The door to the bathroom opens, and Thea stops for a moment, then pushes herself off from the counter.

"Could you make up the sofa? The sheets are in the footstool," she says and heads toward her uncle. "I'll be in as soon as I'm done here."

The Boathouse at Home Pond has a bed that you pull out, but it has rope handles. You just give them a yank, and it turns into a bed. This has no rope handles. It has no handles whatsoever. So I am reduced to getting down on my hands and knees and scenting.

I finally find the smell of Thea's hand on a metal bar under the seat cushions. I don't know how long I'd been there on my hands and knees, my mouth slightly open in a dull-witted smile, my eyes unfocused.

"Are you okay?"

"Dropped a cuff link," I say, jumping up. She nods, then leans into the refrigerator.

Everything in the Homelands is strong and heavy and tough. Made to withstand wolves. Everything Offland is light and flimsy, and if you tug at it just a little, it flies across the room.

Looking to make sure that the door to Vasco's room is closed, I lift the sofa under my arm and tiptoe across the creaky floor until I get it back to the place marked by indentations in the carpet. Then, using only my pinkie finger, I pull it up and open and put on the sheets. After finger scrubbing my teeth with a dollop of Vasco's toothpaste, I lie fully dressed on top of blankets and sheets and the thin mattress with a bar crammed an inch deep into my floating rib.

The discord of anticipation and anxiety is making me feel sick.

Chapter 26

THEA TURNS OUT THE LIGHT AND BEGINS TO FEEL HER way toward me. The Hamptons off-season is dark, but nothing like the Homelands. In the dim light, I watch her creep along, her fingers sweeping the back of a chair, the television, feeling the landscape.

She bumps her toe with a sharp intake of breath.

"Here, Thea," I call to her, my voice breaking slightly. "Over here."

The mattress gives a little as her hands find and search out the shape of the bed, and she pulls back the blankets. She settles in and stares up into the dark. The sheets rustle as her legs move.

I pray she can't smell the nervous dog smell that is so strong in my nose.

"My uncle's a good man," she finally says. "A really good man, but this is the anniversary of my parents' death, and he takes it hard. My father was his best friend. My mother was his sister. Our family was never big, but it got very small very quickly."

"I know."

There's no sound except the slight creak of the ceiling fan turning slowly in the draft from the heat vent.

"How could you?"

"He told me." I take a deep breath before it all comes out in a rush. "You weren't answering, and I didn't know what to do so I came out here to find your uncle, because I knew Susannah's address on Long Island from the divorce papers. I told him I'd messed up and you weren't talking to me and that I needed to talk to someone who knew you, and so we went out to lunch and we talked and he told me that your parents had died in a DUI."

I wait for the inevitable recriminations for having invaded her privacy, but they don't come.

"Did you go to the Sip 'n' Serve?"

"Mmm-hmm?"

"Krissie there?"

"Mmm-hmm."

"I wish he would just ask her out already."

"Mmm-hmm?"

She falls quiet again.

"So I'm guessing you didn't just happen to be at McCarran's this evening."

"No."

"He call you or something?"

"Text."

"Jesus, *Tío*," she says with an exasperated chuff. "What did you tell him that made him like you this much?"

"Nothing. Everything. The truth. I just told him the truth. I told him how much you matter to me." There's an itch at the base of my arch. I scratch it against the big toe of my other foot. "That thing?" I say quietly. "That stupid party. I'm going by myself."

"You go with whoever you want. Don't do it for me."

"I'm not doing it for you. *Because* of you, maybe, but not for you." I turn my head so I can see her more clearly. "Can I tell you a secret?"

"A secret or a confidence?"

"Is there a difference?"

"A confidence is yours to tell. A secret isn't."

"Well, a confidence then." My hand slides along the sheets until I feel the aura of warmth in the tips of her fingers. "That thing I said about…" My tongue stumbles over the words. "Well, you know what I said. I said it because I've been playing a role for so long that I couldn't see that the theater lights were off and everyone had gone home."

She turns on her side, pulling the blanket over her shoulder. "But who are you when the lights are off?"

My mind teeters under the weight of a cataract of memories. Marble, bronze, disinfectant, the tinkle of a piano no one listens to, the crackle of words no one means. Ice fog. Air tinged with pepperberry or wintergreen or wild rose. Smoked goose liver foam on a leaf-shaped malachite plate. The fading life in the eyes of a buck as the blood runs so warm and rich over my tongue. My legs tiring in the fast-moving stream, the shore receding. Collapsing in trust and exhaustion into the indescribable comfort of powerful jaws that take my little shoulders so gently. The endless marking of my Pack. Maxim's sweaty handshake. Seduction. Cunning. Adulation. Sacrifice. Preening. Secrets.

"I don't know."

Me. *Us*. Terrible, beautiful, monstrous, divine.

"But I am trying. I am trying to remember."

I turn over on my side, looking at her strong profile in the dim light.

I love her deep-set eyes.

"It's hard," she says.

I love her long, slim nose.

"When you forget who you are."

I love the very real but very sad smile.

"Thea?"

"Hmm?"

"What happened in Austin? Or is that a secret?"

"Did Vasco tell you?"

"No, Google."

"Well, if it can be Googled, you already know the whole story. Hardly seems like either a confidence *or* a secret."

I love her defiant chin.

"I know what happened, but that doesn't mean I know the story."

John was always very clear: A handful of events with a meaning is a story. A handful of events without meaning is nothing.

"Will you tell me?"

"Well, 'story' makes it sound a whole lot more interesting than it was. It was just...was just *stupid*, was what it was." She runs her fingers back and forth across her torso. "I didn't have much experience when I got to college. None, actually. I wasn't popular or pretty—"

I start to protest, but she shakes it off. "Please, Elijah."

Because I'd recited all that *never wear anything but silk* crap, she has a right to be dismissive. I really wish I hadn't, because now I am being absolutely, soul-wrenchingly honest.

You are so beautiful.

Please, Thea.

"Anyway, I'd had no experience when I got to college and then this guy, Devin"—she says the name quickly, like she wants to get it over—"starts paying attention to me. I was so grateful and so eager to please him. So desperate to be the kind of person who wouldn't embarrass him at parties."

Then I hear that disdainful voice, my voice, pinging around my head. *With her? Nooo. She's just a friend.*

"I joined a sorority, because that's what he expected. God, I was tired. Anyway, at one of these parties, a girl died. We'd all drunk too much, and Devin dared us to cross a wooden board to get to the other roof. 'Walking the plank,' he called it." She stops for a moment and turns to me. "Her name was Linda Thurman, by the way. I feel like it's important to remember that."

I understand that she wants this girl not to have disappeared unmarked. We have the same impulse. It's why every wolf's name is incised with a stone at the *Gemyndstow*. From Ælfrida to little Hannah, Evie and John's stillborn.

"But it wasn't your fault."

"That's the point," she says. "The police interviewed us and determined it was an accident and no one was responsible. All my 'friends' were so relieved, Devin most of all, because he was prelaw, and it'd look bad on his grad school applications if he was implicated in the death of 'that girl.' Linda Thurman was dead, and they were all high-fiving each other. Like I said, I was so tired, so maybe I wasn't thinking straight, but at the moment, it seemed very clear that I had to get rid of everything—Devin, the school, these friends, everything—and start over again."

She stretches her hand up into the air, her wrist extended, just like I do when I trigger my change.

"Even got rid of my clothes. Campus security didn't

quite understand what I was doing in my underwear and took me to the psychiatrist. She said it was shock and not to make any big decisions. Six months later, I had a new state, a new school, a new life, but the old me. And for the first time in a long time, I wasn't tired anymore." She rubs her face and then yawns a little. "Well, I'm tired now."

I love the fullness of her face beneath her high cheekbones.

"Can I lie with you? Just hold you?"

A rough hum from the back of her throat is the only answer.

It isn't yes, but it isn't no either.

I curl around her, smoothing her hair down her back, so I can share her pillow.

She relaxes into me, breathing contentedly at the weight of my arm.

"To me," I whisper, "you are the most beautiful. And I don't want to change anything except the way you think about me."

Then she slips her hand over mine.

Please let me not fuck this up.

Her body slowly relaxes, then jerks, then goes slack in my arms.

Please let me not fuck this up.

I kiss her hair and bury my nose in the spot behind her ear and breathe in that scent of black earth.

Please let me not fuck this up.

I whisper as softly as I can.

"I love you, Thea."

Please let me not fuck this up.

Chapter 27

Hāmweard, ðu londadl hǽðstapa, IN 2 DAYS
Homeward, you landsick heath-wanderer, IN 2 DAYS

HST IS DARK WHEN I GET IN. THE CARPETS ARE MARKED with the long curves plowed by maintenance after eleven when the last of the bullpen has finally gone home. Early in the morning, the smell of cleanser is at its strongest, the smell of coffee at its weakest.

I head toward my office, flicking on the lights as I go. Over my shoulder is my black-tie kit safely stowed in the travel bag.

My closet opens smoothly on the extra suit, two shirts, tie, and handheld clothes steamer I keep at the office. Undoing the snap, I give the travel bag a little shake and push it in. My shoes go on the floor.

I will get to L-Cubed early, meet and greet, and then at the first plausible moment, I will bow out and race for Thea's cabin.

Twirling around in my Titan until my head goes giddy, I jam my feet into the carpet, then fall to my knees in front of the safe. Inside the big letter box containing the trust is a small pocket with a thumb drive holding certain basic forms, such as the necessary signature addendum and power of attorney we use for our children. Because of the complicated structure of the trust, I need seventeen pages to accommodate the four additional signatures at all their necessary places.

I put Tiberius Malasson first because despite what I said to the Shifter, I know there is only a slim chance that Quicksilver will survive her lying-in, and if there is going to be just one signature in each place, maybe it's easier if he doesn't have to remind himself each time to leave that first space empty.

I barely know Silver, but I saw the terror in Tiberius's face as he told me she was pregnant. I try to imagine Thea in her place, imagine some part of me taking root inside her and killing her, imagine the sickening ache that Tiberius must feel. The pointless guilt.

Because partners' offices should not be cluttered with the noise and mess of printers and faxes and shredders, the mechanics are all in the assistants' offices, which is why I'm standing at Janine's desk, waiting while the printer spits out these extra pages, when she arrives, her coat over one arm.

"You're here early," she says.

"Got a little backed up yesterday," I say. *Eleven pages.*

She reaches for the printer. "Why don't I just bring these in to you as soon as they're ready?"

"It's okay. I've got it. You should just get settled in." *Thirteen pages.* "Get your coffee."

"Have one," she says, pointing to a plastic glass filled with iced eddies of pink and blue and topped with an equally garish swirl of sparkly whipped cream. If that's a coffee, then these are the final days of the Roman Empire.

She reaches over to hang her coat on the hook at the back of her door, but as she does, the hem drags across the printer and all the pages go flying.

"I'm sorry, Mr. Sorensson," she says primly and instantly drops to the floor.

I crouch down too, holding my hand out to keep her away. "*I've got it, Janine*."

Standing up quickly, she tucks her shirt into her waistband. The printer is done now, and I straighten the pages before heading back to the letter box I stupidly left on my desk. As I count the signature addenda, a bubble begins to form behind my heart.

One of the pages is missing. The little printer icon promises that seventeen pages were printed, but there are only sixteen here. As soon as Janine heads to the bathroom for her early-morning makeup check, I go back into her office. There's plenty of paper and ink. I look everywhere for the missing page containing the four new spaces for the four new lives. Tiberius's offspring. August Leveraux's grandchildren.

I've just set the file cabinet back in place when she returns in a cloud of paraben and titanium and that artificial vanilla scent that instills a desire for chewy liver. When I ask her if she has seen one of my pages, she shrugs. "These printers mess up all the time," she says, sliding on her high heels. "Just print another."

With my door open, I keep a close eye on Janine. I've never paid much attention to what she does. *Candy Crush* mostly. Occasionally expenses or answering email. She sits straight-backed and cool when she answers the phone. "HST? Elijah Sorensson's office?" she says with a clipped and melodious voice.

But then a call comes through and she slumps forward, her left hand holding the phone and her right hand, the one facing me, twisting her hair around her mouth.

Even my acute hearing can't make out what she's saying, but it lasts a minute and she doesn't take a message.

Half an hour later, she leaves. Nothing but a text—*a text*—saying something about an emergency. I stare at the home screen of my computer, in case she suddenly realizes she's forgotten her umbrella or her gym shoes. When she doesn't come back, I head over to her office and pick up her phone, looking for the one-minute call at 11:39 a.m. from Out of Area: Private Caller.

Moving quietly through the halls, I check the conference room and the associates' offices for stragglers. Most of the staff on this side of HST will be out for lunch, but there are usually a few who eat at their desks.

There's nothing unusual in any of Janine's drawers: files, paper clips, staplers, shoes, walking shoes, jewelry, evening bag. One drawer is empty though.

"Do you need any help, Mr. Sorensson?" Lori, Max's assistant, stands in the door, her coat in one hand, a bag that smells like salade Niçoise in the other.

"Janine was supposed to make some copies for me, but I don't see them."

"Do you want me to look?"

"It's nothing that can't hold until she gets back. Wait, Lori? You have one of these, don't you?" I point to Janine's printer.

"We all do."

"And do you have problems with it printing fewer copies than it's supposed to?"

"Not unless it's run out of paper."

Leaning against the wall in my office, I close my eyes and listen, waiting until the soft snick of her shoes against the carpeting has turned the corner.

I check the halls again before going back to Janine's desk. This time, I kneel in front of the empty drawer, pushing my truncated human excuse for a muzzle deep into it, and suck in a long breath scented with the slight hint of lavender breeze and the off-gassing of polypropylene carpets.

Over the next hour, I wait with my rage building because I was so certain that I'd been careful and that I couldn't be the one who'd been played. That Tiberius was wrong and that the Great North had not been sold out by this self-indulgent, infantile excuse for a woman at whose dragon-bitten nipple I have suckled.

"*Where were you?*"

"I had an emergency," she says nervously, pulling her coat tighter around her neck. "I texted you. Didn't you get it?"

"Where is the other page, Janine?" I stand close, my forearm pushing her shoulder into the wall.

"I told you," she whines. "It doesn't always print everything."

"I don't believe that's what happened. I think you took it. I think you gave it to someone." My body looms over her, shoving her against the wall. The stink of salt and old leather pierces her scented camouflage. Lavender breeze and the off-gassing of polypropylene carpets.

"Please, Elijah," she babbles. "It's just a friend. It was an emergency. He needed help."

"*What did he want with it?*"

"A friend needed *help*," she repeats, emphasizing the last word. Even with my back to the hall, I can tell by the scents of pepperoni and steak frites and hops and vodka that the humans have returned from their carrion-and-alcohol lunches and are gathering behind me. It makes Janine bolder. "Anyway, what do you care who I'm seeing?"

"How much did he give you?"

"Elijah, what's going on here?" I recognize in the faint fragrance of sandalwood on papery skin that someone has gotten Max.

I bend over her head. "Spread your legs for whoever you want," I whisper, "but betray the Great North, and I will make sure you regret it."

"Get away from me," she yells, pushing her purse against my chest as Max makes his way to the front of the crowd.

"Elijah, that's enough. Janine, I'm so sorry." He puts his arm on my arm, trying to pull me away. "Are you all right? Why don't you take the day off."

"Who did you see, Janine?"

"A friend! I told you he's been weird, Mr. Trianoff. I went to see a friend who was in trouble—"

"*Don't lie, Janine. I can smell him on you.*"

Maxim yells for Lori to find out what's taking them so long. Just then, three security guards rush out of the elevators. "Took you long enough," Maxim says, patting Janine's hand with a kind of awkward paternalism. "I'm sorry about this, Janine. You should take some time off. HST will—"

"Make me whole?" she says with the sly smile of someone who's spent her life around lawyers.

Maxim's only answer is a strained smile.

"Jesus Christ, Elijah," he says as soon as the door to my office closes. "'Make me whole.' Wil is going to make sure this costs us a fucking fortune. *Costs you.* I begged you to keep your hands off the office staff. I'm calling Ms. Katana—"

"*It's Kitwana, Max.*"

He slides back between the two remaining guards. "I'm calling her now. Telling her you need time off. Real time. So just pick up your stuff—"

"Does this mean I can skip L-Cubed?"

I can see Maxim's mind running through some sordid calculation of reputation and clients and competitors. He doesn't want me there, but he wants the gossip and speculation even less. HST already lost one partner in sad circumstances, and he can't afford to lose another.

"No," he says. "But then take off. Get a—"

"Don't say 'get a fucking boat.'"

"*Get a fucking boat.*"

On a green metal bench surrounded by rows of palm trees, the sky held back by glass and steel, the earth covered by patterned marble, there is a homeless man sitting with everything he owns in a bag at his feet.

One bench over, my garment bag slung over one arm, the pink bag with my seax, two degrees, the trust, and that fisher skull held tightly between my feet, I call Tiberius.

"Who is this?" he asks over the cacophony of hammering and sawing wolves pushing to get the Great Hall finished before the rains start in earnest.

"Elijah Sorensson."

"*Who?*"

"*Elijah Sorensson. Alpha of the 9th.*"

The homeless man looks at me warily before moving himself and his belongings far away.

"Hold on. Let me go somewhere quieter. Sil, just leave the top ones for me. I'll be right back."

I can't hear her answer.

"Wildfire. *Please*."

He takes the stairs down two at a time. There must be walls now, because there are doors. I know there are doors because they close with a solid thud behind him.

"Elijah?"

"I think you were right. My assistant saw something when I was printing out the signature addendum for the trust."

"You did it *with* her?"

"I did not do it *with her*. She came in early. It doesn't matter. I'm pretty sure she took one copy."

"It had our names?"

"Of course. But, Tiberius, she left a few hours later, and when she came back from lunch, she smelled like that stuff, the industrial smoke remover, that you said Shifters… Tiberius?"

"Tiberius?"

Lifting my head, I shave the vulnerable column of my throat. Left side. Right side. Rinse, warm water, then cool. Suck in my upper lip, feel the ticklish scrape along it. Quick rinse. Lower lip and chin. Quick rinse. Left cheek. Quick rinse. Right cheek. Thorough rinse. After combing my hair, I muss it in just the right way.

Then I unzip the garment bag and begin the intricate mummery of evening wear. Formal shirt (Royal Oxford, forward point). Shirt studs (mother-of-pearl). Pants (tapered, grosgrain ribbon). Waistcoat (never cummerbund; black, three-button). I raise my chin, staring down at the reflection of my fingers flying over my tie (textured silk, semi-butterfly). I carefully fold the collar back in place.

Pulling my sleeves into place, I pick up first one platinum-chain cuff link from the silver Tiffany tray (*With Gratitude from Americans for Progressive Packaging*). Then I shrug into my jacket (ventless, single-button, grosgrain facing, peaked collar). Socks (silk, black). Shoes (cap-toe Balmorals, high shine but not patent). Pocket square (silk, square fold, the red of human blood).

"Hello, Elijah," says the bone-thin woman in the tweed pencil skirt and dark-gray silk shirt. She kisses the air near my right cheek and then near my left. Victoria Cideley has handled PR for L-Cubed for the past six years. "I'm afraid there may be a mistake. We have you down"—she looks up quizzically from the guest list on her iPad—"as one?"

"No mistake." I slip the card with my table number into my waistcoat pocket. "I am"—and for some reason, I say the last word with a grin and a note of triumph—"*alone*."

She raises her eyebrows and smiles too. Her dark hair and pale skin and dark-red lips all look the same as when I first met her and told her gray was her color and that she should never wear anything but silk. But her smile has changed, the way human women's smiles do as they move from the confidence of youth, when every man wants their untried bodies and untried souls, to the more tentative smile of someone who hopes to be forgiven for the crime of creeping toward middle age.

I move out of the way of a pretty, little arm candy whose bright eyes devour the cards with recognizable names—Michael Bloomberg, Derek Jeter, Matt Damon!—while she waits for Daniel Tillmann, the Speaker's chief of staff, to claim his table and prance her around, thereby advertising both his success and the potency of his member.

There's something so freeing. I'm not showing off, worrying about where I fit in the hierarchy. I am proving nothing. I make no introductions. Suffer no invidious comparisons. I have no reservations at boutique hotels. I have no names to remember. No notes to write. No gray silk bathrobes to gift.

I am Elijah Sorensson. That's all, and for the first time since I left home, that's enough.

Some of the men hold their dates a little tighter when I approach, showing the visceral mistrust of a lone wolf, but aside from a polite smile at our introduction, I don't notice a single one, because the Goddess of the City of Wolves is waiting for me.

"Sorensson," says Dean Latham (international commerce, Sarnath & Keene). "I'd like you to meet Monique."

Monique turns so that her hips are angled at best advantage. She shifts her shoulder back, revealing breasts that are large and oddly round and I suspect feel like ziplock bags crammed with pudding. She shakes her hair and lowers her chin, looking up at me from under her hooded eyes. Her sex is all surface irritant, like a red cape that the bull charges just to get it to stop.

He doesn't introduce me to her. "And you're with…?"

"Nobody," I say with a half nod toward Monique. "And it's a pleasure."

He frowns a little, worrying about what game I'm playing.

Maxim, seeing me with a confused and concerned Latham, decides it is a politic moment to pretend that all is well between the partners at HST, so that no one will think we are getting slack and sloppy and it's a good time to try to take us down. He pats me congenially on the back and introduces me to his brother-in-law.

"Elijah is interested in buying a boat," he says with a bright fake smile before separating me from Latham and leading him away. He will have replaced me on the Jaxed contract by the end of the night.

It takes me a beat to return my attention to Max's brother-in-law, a man wearing suspenders but neither cummerbund nor waistcoat. "No offense to your hobby, but I've got no interest in getting a boat."

His eyes slide over my hands, and he shrugs.

"You married?"

"No."

"Then why would you bother?" He smiles brightly at his wife, Tatiana, Maxim's sister. "The only reason to have one is if you need a place to store a girlfriend."

"Darling," he sings out as Tatiana comes closer. "I presume you know Elijah Sorensson?"

"My brother's partner? I should hope so. How are you, Elijah?"

"Well. We were just talking about boats."

"Really?" says Tatiana. Her husband kisses her lightly on the cheek before shuffling off to greet the deputy mayor.

"I don't know why he bothers with the boat," she

says, her smile hardening. "The insurance on that thing is ridiculous. If he needs a place for his whores, why doesn't he just get a fucking apartment?"

I drink only water and eat only salad. Several men look at the untouched pâté and steak, but I am done eating carrion so that humans will think I'm a real man.

As soon as the raspberry cocotte is served and the last of the awards for hard work or money are given, I drink two cups of coffee and run for my car.

I nod toward Maxim, who, with a single tight wave of his hand, mouths the word *Boat*.

Chapter 28

Four hours and something later, I squeeze the latch on the cabin door. Once inside, I close it, giving the little extra push until it clicks. Then I sag heavily on the side of Thea's bed.

She turns over, her fingers feeling the fine black wool of my tuxedo. I look over my shoulder.

She must have showered not long ago. Her hair is still damp, fusing together in sharp, black flames that lick against her naked skin. Silently, she pulls her legs from under the covers and kneels in front of me. She unties my laces and tosses my shoes (cap-toe Balmorals, high shine, not patent) to the side. Her hands slide up my calf until she touches skin, then she rolls down my socks (black, silk) and throws them to the side too. Leaning between my knees, she unbuttons my jacket (single-button, no vents, grosgrain facing, peaked collar). She pushes it from my shoulders. I shrug once, and it falls first to the bed, then slithers to the floor.

With a twist, her long, strong fingers open one button on my waistcoat (three-button, black). Then another. Then one more.

She feels around for the end of my tie (textured silk, semi-butterfly) and pulls. Inserting a finger in the loosened knot, she drags it down until the ends hang around the collar of my shirt (Royal Oxford, forward point). Without a second thought, I tilt my head back, my eyes closed, giving her free access to my neck. The cool air hits my skin as she works each shirt stud (mother-of-pearl) free. She disentangles the platinum chains from my cuffs, setting them on her table next to the studs. Then she pulls off my waistcoat, my shirt.

She unbuttons my pants (tapered, grosgrain ribbon).

"Up?" she says.

Holding on to the finial of her footboard, I lift my hips, allowing her to slide everything off to join the rest of my kit puddled on the floor.

Thea wedges between my legs, pushing them wider. She leans forward, inhaling my most secret scent, and, with each breath, leaves a whorled caress that makes me whimper. Her hands trace the outline of my shoulders and the sloping curves of my arms and my chest and continue down, taking my already heavy cock. My hand touches her hair, spreading it over her shoulders and my thighs until I feel her kiss, warm and fierce.

She kisses it, not lasciviously or like it's a tool. She kisses it tenderly, like it is not an "it" at all. Like "it" is me.

I jerk when she takes me deep and long, exciting me with her mouth and gentling me with her hand along the tightening seam below, using a restrained rhythm that builds slowly until each new stroke makes me ache to come home inside this woman who has reminded me how to be untamed and immoderate. How to be real.

My hands slide and explore, reveling in each centimeter of her skin, the furrows of her ribs, the soft curve of her breasts with their taut tips. The slope to her belly and further until I twine one hand around her waist and cup her sex with the other and pull her up, feeling the pressure and dampness on my hand and the way her hips undulate against my palm in her need for more. No matter how tightly I hold my hand against her, her body twists against me, looking for more.

When I lift her up, her knees part on either side of my thighs and my thick crown pushes against her. She shudders, her head shaking fiercely as she puts her hands to my chest and pushes me away. "We need to stop," she says, and straightening one leg, she reaches for her nightstand.

"You took me already, Thea." I pull her back to me, kissing her lips and tasting the trace of salty muskiness there. She took me already.

"*That's* because I believed you when you said you were very careful," she says, pressing her forehead against mine. "No man with that many condoms and an apartment that OCD is going to play fast and loose with his body. But it doesn't mean I can't get pregnant."

She starts to reach for her nightstand again, but I hold her one second longer. "Supposing it did. Supposing I told you that's exactly what it meant. That I can't get you pregnant. What then?"

That stops her.

She hesitates for a moment and then settles back on my lap, her legs wrapped around my hips, her arm crossed in front of her chest. "You're…?"

"Sterile." Which isn't true, but it might as well be.

She looks me over carefully, as if she's trying to gauge how the end of my bloodline makes me feel.

The answer is…elated. I can't tell her how overwhelmingly grateful I am that she will never have to suffer through a lying-in—that *I* will never have to suffer through her lying-in—but she must see it in my eyes.

"And you're okay with it?"

"Me? Absolutely. But the reason I told you has nothing to do with me and nothing to do with whether we use a condom tonight. It's about the next night and the next and a whole lifetime of days and nights. It's about a future with you. I need to be with you, but there are things I can't give you. Not just children. I have...obligations, so while you would always have my heart and soul, you wouldn't always have my bod... I mean, nobody else would have my body, because it doesn't even work with anyone else anymore, but I couldn't live here—"

"You're rambling," she says, putting her fingers to my lips. "I was seeing a guy before—"

"Doug?"

She frowns a little, trying, I suppose, to figure out how I know.

"He tried to warn me off. After Liebling died. Told me I wouldn't be able to domesticate you."

She offers a half smile and reaches behind her for a blanket. Of course she's cold. She's human. They get cold. I help her pull it over her back. I'll have to get used to this.

"I'm not sure he was clear on what 'domesticating' meant. For him, it meant getting a television, a 'real' refrigerator, a sofa, and a couple of children. He always said it in the same sentence as though children and refrigerator and television and sofa were all part of a set. Like patio furniture."

She pushes my hair back from my forehead. "He didn't understand that I didn't need any of it. I like children when they come on field trips. They ask strange questions with no answers and questions so simple that I've never thought to ask. But I've never wanted to *have* a child. Like I could own another human being."

I pull her hand to my lips and kiss her palm. I don't want to *have* her either. I don't want to mold her or domesticate her or change her, because she is my compass, and if she lost her way, I would be lost too.

Then she kisses my palm and presses our hands together. Our bodies together. Our mouths together.

She isn't saying no.

Then she moves her hips in gentle waves over my erection, making me jerk uncontrollably.

She isn't saying no.

I hold tight to her calves, keeping them spread wide. She lowers herself on me, slowly surrounding me with every soft, tough, liquid part of her until we are fully joined. I push her hips down, reveling in the fierce grip of her body and the teasing rhythm that mirrors the tiny pulsing of her finger that first day I met her, but now it is playing out on my cracking cock that can't help twitching inside her. Carefully, so that I will not lose this connection, I turn her over, and only then, when she is splayed in front of me, do I pull myself most of the way out. Her hands push down on my lower back, right where my spine is going soft and spongy, and I slam home.

Home. Again and again and again, until it is impossible to be any deeper. And having tightened so far, there's nothing left for it but to release everything I have into her body.

In the end, she falls asleep in my arms, swollen and saturated with me.

And I am home.

As the fire dies down, cool air is sucked into the chimney, bringing with it the faintest whiff of creosote. I hold Thea tighter. At the end of this moon, I will do whatever needs to be done to make sure the 9th is secure. When I leave, Celia will be Alpha, and I will be just another low-ranked Offlander.

Hearing the change in Thea's breath, I whisper her name. She turns to me, her hand finding my chest in the cold dark.

"I'm taking some time off. Going home."

"Nnng?" she says sleepily. "Not 'the apartment'?" She gives the words a special emphasis, because of course she has noticed that I never call that stasis chamber close to work *home*.

"No. My real home. It's time for me to make it right."

Her hand slides along my sternum up to my collarbone. "How long will you be gone?"

"I'm not sure. A week? A month? God, I hope not that long."

She pokes her head over the blankets, looking toward the dying fire. Then she pulls the throw from the foot of the bed and crouches in front of the stove.

"Where is it?" The door creaks as she opens it. "Home, I mean?"

I watch her feed the fire, swift and sure. Watch the slight movements of the bones of her spine that seem so delicate under the gold skin brushed with tiny upright hairs, that paltry excuse for fur. Every detail of her reminds me that things Offland are fragile and break easily. It makes me ache to shield her.

"Not so far away. A little south of Canada. I wish I could take you there, let you see you how special it is. Let them see how special you are, but my people… They're very wary. They really don't trust strangers."

The sheets are cold again when she crawls in.

"Sort of like the Amish?"

I rub her back and shoulders and pull her close to the furnace of my body.

No, Thea Villalobos, Goddess of the City of Wolves, not Amish.

Werewolves.

"Yeah, just like that."

Chapter 29

Wilcume, ðu londadl hǽðstapa
Welcome, you landsick heath-wanderer

How is it that after years of wanting nothing more than to come home, I have an unscratchable itch to leave?

But I can't, not until the loose ends are knit up. Like Sarah and Adam, the loosest of those loose ends. For three moons, they have stayed close to Home Pond. Thin and uncommunicative, they seem to have lost the will to hunt. Textbook lupine depression.

Curled in the roots of an old white cedar not far from the water, Sarah licks her paw, not bothering to lift her head when Celia appears with fresh raccoon. Adam sniffs once, but he takes his cues from his mate's lack of interest and quickly puts his head back down.

I disagree with Celia. Feeding them is pointless. They don't need nutrition; they need a purpose. They need to hunt again, to be a part of something. I think Adam might do it, but not without Sarah. She has to remember the way her heart beats when the warm scent of prey hits the back of her throat. She has to remember the way her lungs expand when the earth talks to her. She has to remember the tingling of her skin when she races through the cold air of the Homelands.

Celia nudges the still-warm raccoon closer with her nose, but Sarah just keeps picking at her pads with her teeth, refusing to notice her worried mate, the offering of her echelon, the slowly quickening land.

Me.

Pick. Pick. Pick.

By god, *she will notice me*.

I bite her, my jaws tightening on her withers until she yelps in pain. With my jaws still clenched around the loose skin and fur, I lift. She is light and I am strong, and even if she doesn't want to, she will stand. She wobbles uncertainly. Then I lean forward over her, my chest at her muzzle, my jaw resting on the top of her head. The snarl reverberates through my body and surrounds her.

Stand up, Sarah. *Stand the fuck up*.

A wolf may be wounded, exhausted beyond bearing, but they will still respond to the hard-wired debt of obedience that they owe their Alpha. Sarah's legs begin to tighten. I do it again and again and again, getting fiercer each time. Harrying her until she stumbles away and moves.

Then I start off at a steady loping pace that is both quiet and easy. Celia makes sure that Sarah is surrounded by the echelon, leaving her no choice but to keep up.

At the frosty edges of the bog and spruce flats, I scent a bear. He's just out of torpor, so his prints drag slightly and are not as deep as they will be later in the season when he's eaten his fill. I parallel him, going backward, going toward where he *had been*. The scent grows incrementally weaker. Celia butts my head. It's what we do when we don't have words and means *What* are *you doing?*

I shake her off, because I have no words to offer her, no explanation, just trust and the duty of leadership.

But then Sarah slows down and whines at my retreating back.

I look back along my flanks and wait. It's up to her to decide if anything matters anymore. Does hunting matter? Does eating matter? Does living matter? If it does, she will survive. If not, then the coyotes will have her before summer.

Sarah crouches down on her forelegs and rubs her face on something, then she runs toward me, thrusting her bear-stink head into my face.

I stare at her. *What are you going to do about it?*

What are you *going to do about it?*

She hesitates, looking for Adam, but I make sure my massive body blocks her view. I don't want her to see him, see her own sadness reflected in his eyes. I want Sarah to decide and Sarah to act.

I lean in closer.

What are you going to do *about it?*

Then, with a leap, her thin body twists in the air and the damp crusty dirt churns, and Sarah turns around and tears after that bear.

Any other time of year, we would have given him a pass. Our claws are no match, our strength just barely. Fang for fang, we are evenly matched, but a bear's jaws pack twice the force. What we have is speed, agility, cunning, and teamwork. Plus our metabolisms are working on all cylinders, as opposed to the bear, who, following the winter cold, is stumbling around like a human after a huge meal of red wine and turkey.

Sarah takes over hounding the bear from the rear along with the other subordinates. I keep the bear's claws and jaws busy while they corral him toward the bog. Celia holds back the rest of the echelon, because too many wolves hunting in a bog is simply messy. With several wolves behind, he has no choice but to face the one in the front. Smartly, Sarah makes several swipes at his left hind leg: nothing deadly, but once he is in the bog, his weight works against him. Unable to rear up on his damaged leg, his front paws sticking in the soft mud, every move requires laborious effort that wouldn't be a problem in summer but is hard now.

I grab his nose in my jaws. His sharp claws slice through the back of my neck, and while it is painful, it failed to damage my organs or bones or major arteries. A flesh wound.

The death is as good as we can make it. The echelon springs toward the carcass, though I force them back with a snarl. This is Sarah's kill, and she has the first choice. Burrowing through the thick fur of his underside, she snaps through the ribs and digs out his liver.

Then Sarah snaps at a subordinate wolf wheedling for a bite, and I know she will live.

At Home Pond, we pick up two pups. Every echelon does. It's part of the rhythm of the Iron Moon. We hunt first for food, then to teach. There's a logic to it, because teaching the pups has its own rhythm: patient tracking—*squirrel!*—patient tracking—*jay!*—patient tracking, and so on.

Humans say *Don't shop when you're hungry*. Same principle.

When the change comes back and we've cleaned away the remnants of fur and blood and mud and plant litter, we assemble for the Iron Moon Table at the Meeting House. This is the last time this important observance will be celebrated with stale bagels and four-day-old boxes of Munchkins. Wolves are crammed in, some standing, most on the floor.

A pup races by, her whiskery chin completely covered with butter. A turbid mass of fur races after her.

Then Evie stands at the front of the room and makes the pronouncement that marks the official start of the Iron Moon Table.

"In our laws are we protected."

"And in lawlessness are we destroyed," the Great North responds with a roar.

I stand with the 9th, close but not too close to my two wolves, so they can feel the presence of echelon and Alpha when the announcement is made that Quicksilver Nilsdottir, a runt just recently graduated into adulthood, will be having her lying-in.

It's just not fair.

When Evie announces that Silver is carrying four, the Pack goes silent. Most of the faces have the solemn look of hearing that a member of the pack has received a death sentence, as carrying four almost inevitably is. But Victor seethes. He looks toward some of the younger Alphas, who seethe likewise.

What are you up to, Victor?

It is the thin, red-haired wolf in front of me who breaks the silence with a loud "*Anhydig hama, Seolfer!*"

Sarah yells it again, louder this time and joined by Adam and me and Evie, and by the third time, like thunder rolling down from the mountain, the Pack joins in.

Anhydig hama.

Stalwart birthing.

Tiberius stands behind his mate, his arms reaching

around her ribs, just under her breasts like he doesn't want to feel her swollen belly. Doesn't want to feel the place where his seed has taken root with such fatal consequence.

Silver rubs her cheek along her mate's thick arms. After John died, Evie could not bring herself to look at Tiberius, but that has passed. Now she looks at him sadly, because she suspects as I do that he will not survive the loss of his silver wolf.

The rest of Table is taken up with reports on the rebuilding of the Great Hall and a few minor housekeeping matters. The 5th's Alpha bites William for not refilling the ice-cube trays. Because the 11th has been leaving towels to molder on the floor of the Bathhouse, their Bathhouse privileges have been revoked. This is the second time the 8th took a car out and brought it back almost empty, so now their Alpha will have to walk to and from the gas station with a jerrican because, ultimately, the responsibility is his. Punishment will then be meted out within the privacy of the echelon, but it's a good guess that whoever is hemorrhaging at dinner was the culprit.

As soon as the official business is over, Tara whispers that Evie wants to see me in the back room. She then moves on to Tiberius, though she motions for Silver to stay. Celia looks at me quizzically, but all I can do is shrug.

The back room is too small to serve as a proper office, so it houses little but the central phone for the Great North LLC and the main Wi-Fi array. Evie stands in front of the phone, waiting.

"We got a message yesterday," she says. Then she pushes the button.

A mechanized voice gives out details of the date and

time before being replaced by another voice, one that is even more monotone and artificial. In the background is a low, regular buzzing.

"Hello, Great North LLC." A long hollow breath interrupts the buzzing. "Tiberius, is it true? That your bitch conceived?" Another long, labored breath, and the chair back under Tiberius's hands disintegrates.

Evie raises her hand. "Listen."

"If so…this changes everything." August gasps one more time and clears something from his throat. "*Anhydig hama*," he says.

Click.

"*What* changes?" Tara looks at Tiberius, who stares blankly at the wooden shard in his hand and the blood dripping from his palm.

"*What. Changes?*"

"*I don't know*," Tiberius snaps. "I don't know what he means." Then he looks at Evie. "I shot him," he says, beseeching Evie. "I shot him *in the throat*."

Evie waves him off. Wolves do not have time for regret and recrimination. Instead, she looks at me.

"Elijah, the woman in your office clearly did tell him. You are to go back and find out anything you can. What her instructions were, what she told them, what the reaction was. Anything."

"It won't be easy," Tiberius says. "She will be afraid of my father."

"I know her, Tiberius. She's just a spoiled child. I can handle her," I say.

"I don't think you understand. Shifters are bound to my father by loyalty. But humans are bound to him by money and terror. He has a lot of secrets, and fear is what keeps them. You're not going to get anything out of her unless you make her understand that you are more vicious—"

"*Tiberius!*" Something hits the wood of the little table with a *thunk*.

Evie leans forward, her seax shivering in the wood. "We are Pack. We do *not* aspire to human brutality. Elijah, after preparations are completed for Silver's lying-in, you will return to New York. Find this woman. Question her, but do not forget that your Alpha will not tolerate torture."

Silver stops her pacing when her mate returns and lunges toward him. She stills as he whispers urgently. When he is finished, she murmurs something to the huge Shifter and pulls his bleeding hand to her mouth. He hunches still lower, curling himself against her and hiding his face in the thickness of her silver hair. A shudder runs through his massive back.

Last fall, looking at the two of them, I would never have suspected which one needed shielding—which one was strong and which was vulnerable—but I've learned a lot recently about the nature of strength.

She takes his hand and leads him out, probably to spend the last few hours alone before the beginning of the lying-in when they will have no privacy and her body will no longer be her own.

It seems like a lifetime ago that we prepared the Meeting House for John and Evie. But now John's gone. The Great Hall was burned and the Meeting House is occupied, so this lying-in will take place in the Boathouse.

As they walk past me, the Shifter mutters something about "Ice...on the *inside* of the windows."

"Because I am Alpha," spits out Lorcan, "and you're not. That's why."

From the top of the ladder, I yell for Lorcan to treat Celia as Alpha. Extending the broom, I push at an empty wasp's nest.

"I'm not treating her as Alpha because she's not an Alpha. She's just your *shielder*."

Then, to my utter amazement, he leans over to smell if she's receptive. Receptive? Have wolves always been this dense? Maybe it's all my years Offland, but I can *see* that she's not. I don't have to smell her to know that if Lorcan exhales in her direction, he will inhale with one fewer lung.

The wasp's nest falls from the eaves, landing next to the rocking chair. Lorcan startles as it explodes into gray dust and paper and mummified pupae.

In the moment of silence that follows, a tall, rangy female who's busily scrubbing down the sink turns and almost imperceptibly nods. Immediately, wolves from the 12th swoop down on the nest with brushes and sponges, and before I am at the bottom of the ladder, every last mote is gone.

For years, I have come home, changed, run with the 9th, changed again, brushed my teeth, grabbed a muffin, marked my echelon, and headed back to the hierarchy of New York. In that time, I have lost track of the power structures of the Great North.

The 9th has been assigned to clean the Boathouse in preparation for Silver's lying-in. Helping us is the 12th, the largest echelon in the Great North.

It is also the most disciplined, and that is clearly not because of overfed and oversexed Lorcan. The real power of the 12th and the reason Lorcan is so snappish about position is his shielder, Varya Timursdottir. Some juvenile werewolf armed with an SAT prep book and no goddamn common sense at all dubbed her Varya the Indurate. The name stuck, though no one who prized their hide would say it within earshot.

Her dark-brown hair is pulled back from her broad face with high cheekbones and dark, slanted eyes beneath black brows that fly up like crow's wings. She looks exactly like what she is: the least affable wolf I've ever met, even given the high standard for humorlessness set by Pack.

With one more nod of her head, Lorcan's rocking chair joins the lamp with the faded shade and the thin red-and-white-striped carpet in a procession out so that there will be room when other echelons bring in the medical equipment and blackout curtains and soft carpets and a huge bed and a small refrigerator and food and new lights.

And when it's all clean and stocked, the Alphas head out to the Meeting House to retrieve Silver herself. I link elbows with Eudemos to my left. Across from me, Tristan takes my hands. Altogether twelve of us, with Evie at the head, join hands and arms, linked together in this unbreakable chain of responsibility. Silver's slight body will be laid across our arms, and we will carry her to the Boathouse.

Silver may be the weakest member of the Pack, but she is about to fight the hardest battle a wolf can face. Up until now, the little beings inside her have changed in response to their mother's hormones. Soon, they will start responding to each other, and for the next month, Silver will be forced to follow the whims of the four tiny tyrants as they change from skin to wild and back again. If she doesn't change when they do, if she gives up, her body will see them as aliens and destroy them. The pups will die, but so will Silver.

Every Alpha, the whole Pack, owes her its support, but Victor and a small group of sullen Alphas stand back, gathering around the edges.

Tiberius is already in the large chair, waiting anxiously when we carry Silver in and lay her down. Pillows are fluffed. Blankets are tucked. Then one by one, the Alphas bend over her. Most mark her, though some do not touch her skin. Evie does it last, of course. She squeezes Silver's hand tightly and whispers something to her. Silver nods.

She seems so small in the middle of the huge mattress built to handle a more viable female.

Everyone looks expectantly at Victor standing at the foot of Silver's bed, waiting for our Deemer to give the traditional blessing that marks the end of the ceremony and the official beginning of Silver's lying-in. But Victor says nothing. Because he is standing in front of me, I can't see his face, but I see the slight movement of his head as he scans the gathered Alphas. Lorcan nods slightly. So do two other younger Alphas. Not Eudemos though. The burly Alpha of the 14th steps forward, positioning himself behind Silver and Tiberius.

Evie's eyes narrow, burning like fire and ice, with a warning to her Deemer.

The thing I thought I saw when I fought Tiberius is

real. Victor doesn't like change, doesn't like what's happening to the Great North. He wants it to go back to the way it was, when we were all, at the very least, wolves.

Because I am descended from the wolves of Mercia, he thinks I am an ally. I know how to speak our tongue. I know our laws. I studied them for years at the feet of the ancient Sigeburg, our previous Deemer. What he doesn't know is that I am an abomination much more terrible than a half Shifter. I am a monster beyond his worst imaginings.

I am a wolf who loves a human.

"Say it, Deemer." I bow my head and whisper softly in his ear. He suddenly lurches to his toes. I squeeze tighter on the vulnerable sac in my left hand. "Say it."

"*Wes þu gebledsod*," he starts with a squeak.

Be thou blessed. Be thy body as strong as the tree. Be thy will as hard as the mountain. Be thy young as wild as the storm. Be thy land as plentiful and untouched as the stars. Be the lead of men as soft as snow upon thy fur. Be thou blessed.

I let go, my left hand covering my right, my head still lowered. *Wes þu gebledsod*, I murmur with the rest.

Victor whips around to face me. "You," he whispers, shaking the crimp out of his clenched scrotum, "have made a *fatal* mistake."

"Fatal? Is that what you really mean? Are you challenging me, Deemer? Please, I will not lose."

"You lost once," he spits out. "When you needed to win."

"I have never lost when I *needed* to win."

He stomps away, followed by Lorcan and those two other young Alphas.

Had he been any other Pack, I would have challenged him in the paddock, but I can't. I am a lawyer. I understand the need to protect judges from intimidation and influence, but that doesn't mean I wouldn't dearly love to tear his miserable hide to shreds.

The room has cleared, leaving only Gabi, the ob-gyn, who has once again taken time off from her Offland practice, and Alex, the radiologist who is fitting Silver with an ultrasound holster so that he can give her as much warning as possible that her progeny are switching species.

At the door, I watch Tiberius hold her hand. He looks momentarily at the four little bodies in her body, but then his eyes go careening around the Boathouse, searching for something solid and real and comforting that isn't the woman who is both the source of his strength and his ultimate weakness.

Then I lope back. Leaning down, I mark Tiberius, first along one cheek, then along the other.

As I leave, Silver gives me a sad, hopeful smile full of sharp teeth.

I'd always dismissed the 14th's remaining Alpha as an awkward, oversize child. But I was wrong. His speech and movement may be crude and slow, but Eudemos is surprisingly thoughtful. When I warned him about Victor, he nodded once. He already has a rotation set up to watch the Boathouse, making sure that Tiberius and Silver, members of his echelon, are not disturbed during this already difficult time.

"The Alpha needs me to return Offland. It won't be

long, but Celia knows that the 9th is also at your disposal, if you should need it."

Back once more in my car, I turn my phone on and slip it into the mount. I wrap my arm around the passenger seat and begin to back up.

Hāmweard, ðu londadl hǽðstapa IN 27 DAYS.

Homeward has reset.

Chapter 30

Whether it is because of my run-in with Janine on Friday, or because Maxim has somehow let them know that I am on enforced vacation or simply because I am not dressed in my usual suit and tie, when I arrive in the cold, antiseptic lobby, the nervous security guards do not let me in.

"Just call Dahlia at reception."

There is a lot of whispered conversation behind the front desk. Blocked by the turnstile, I am, for once, too far away to hear what they're saying.

"Or just call my office." I give them Janine's extension. "Janine's actually the one I need to talk to."

The guard shoots a worried look at the head of the morning security detail.

"Mr. Trianoff is coming down," says the head of security. He's usually friendly, but now he does nothing but stare at the big screen divided into many tiny screens, one of which must show an elevator coming down from HST.

"*Where have you been?*" Maxim says, grabbing my arm.

"You told me to take time off. I'm taking time off. See?" I pull my arm from his grasp, readjusting my stand-collar jacket over my T-shirt, making sure to cover the marks of the bear's claws at my neck. "I wouldn't be here at all, but there's a personal matter I need to take care of."

"Well, you better come upstairs with me." Maxim turns to the guards and nods once. This time when I approach the turnstile, it opens.

A young man who smells like meatball subs and an internship starts to follow us into the elevator.

"Take the next one," Max says, blocking the doors, his finger jammed hard into the DOOR CLOSE button.

"Are you going to tell me what's is going on here, Max?"

"Janine's dead."

"*What?*"

"Dead. Murdered. I'm not supposed to tell you anything, but I need you to promise me that you didn't have anything to do with this. HST does not need this kind of publicity."

"Thank you for your very touching concern, Max. But of course I didn't have anything to do with it! I haven't seen her since—"

The elevator door opens on a man in a sapphire-blue tie, hurriedly knotted so that the narrow end is backward and sticks out beneath the front.

"So this," he says, "is the elusive Elijah Sorensson?"

He has pale borders around his receding hairline and a stray piece of pink glitter at his temple.

"Elijah, this is Detective Conradi. He is directing the—"

"Mr. Sorensson, perhaps we could talk in your office?"

He smells like steel and eggplant pizza and hostility.

I have a very bad feeling about this.

"Elijah," Maxim says, trying his level best to play the Alpha, "HST is doing everything it can to cooperate in the face of this tragic loss of one of its prized employees."

Distracted, I lead Conradi past the waiting area with its bottled water and potted plants and twigs bent into unnatural shapes. The hall between my large, light office and Janine's smaller windowless one is littered with cards and LED candles and balloons and bodega flowers and drugstore teddy bears.

Conradi shakes his head when I point him toward my supersize chairs. Instead, he stands, feeling for something inside his jacket pocket. He holds his hand there.

"Ms. Unger's family is apparently on vacation, so we have not been able to reach them, but since you were closest to the victim..." He pulls his hand out and slides a photograph over to me. "I'm wondering if you can make a positive identification."

I look at the picture and back at Conradi. I can't possibly make an identification, and he knows it. He just wanted to see how I reacted to this skull without a face.

I am Pack, and we know death, honor it. Death doesn't shock me, but torture, that uniquely human activity, always does.

This was not a good death, and Janine, that spoiled child, suffered.

"Of course I can't."

"How about this?" With one finger, he slides a picture of Janine's torso framed by the cold metal of the autopsy table. The dragon with its jaws at either side of her perfect apple-seed nipple seems especially garish against the paleness of her bled-out skin.

"Mr. Sorensson?"

I push the picture back to him. "Yes." It's pointless to lie. "That's her."

"So can I take it from your reaction that you two have been intimate?"

I say nothing.

"Maybe I'm not being clear enough. Can I take it from your reaction that you had sex with your *assistant*?"

God, that sounds pathetic. I can't deny it; enough people knew already. Janine was hardly discreet. There's no way to explain to him that it wasn't lust, that I wouldn't have done it at all, except for that crippling hunger for castorine liver.

"A few times, and not for weeks. Months. It was stupid and utterly meaningless."

"Meaningless? It's interesting that you would say it was meaningless. According to several of your coworkers, you two fought about who she had gone to lunch with on Friday."

It's not a question, so I don't answer.

"Mr. Sorensson?"

"I'm afraid I didn't understand the question."

Conradi slides both pictures into his pocket. "What did you two fight about on Friday?" The corner must have gotten stuck, because he opens his jacket, shuffling the photographs around.

Almost everyone on this side of reception must have heard us arguing, so again, it is pointless to deny it. "I was angry because I had reason to believe she had betrayed confidential communications."

"Are you saying this was about attorney-client privilege?"

"Exactly."

"Yet several of your coworkers said that during your fight, you yelled that you 'smelled him' on her. That doesn't really sound like a question of attorney-client privilege. I want you to understand, I'm not making any judgments—these things happen all the time—I'm just trying to get your side of the story."

Please. Do not try to play a player.

"Whatever it sounded like, I certainly wasn't jealous. I'm not lying to you. I did have sex with her, and I regretted it almost immediately. I would have been relieved if she'd found someone else."

"Do you know who she was meeting that afternoon?"

"No idea. She sent me a text around eleven thirty saying she had an emergency and then left the office."

"She sits there?" He motions to Janine's office. I nod. "Is that normal for her to text you from her office?"

"No. She didn't usually text me from her desk."

"And do you still have it? The text?"

"Possibly, I don't know." I pull my phone from my jacket pocket. Unlocking it, I find her text and pass it to him.

He stares at my phone.

"Why do you have her listed as Janine (Dragon)?" he asks, holding the screen up to me.

Taking it back, I go to my contacts to show him that Janine (Dragon) is followed by Janine (Redhead).

"Now you know. But being a sleazy shit does not make me a sadist or a murderer."

"No need to be defensive. I'll say it again: I'm not trying to imply anything. I'm simply trying to find information. Where were you Friday night?"

"I was at the Plaza. There was a charity event there."

"What was it called?"

"Its name?"

"Yes. What was the name of the charity event you went to on Friday?"

"I don't know the real name. Everyone calls it L-Cubed."

"I don't call it 'L-Cubed.'"

"Well, your chief of police certainly does." It is a basic part of establishing one's self within the human hierarchy. See? Here are the people I know. Here are the people who will return my phone calls, send me invitations, greet me on the street. All of them human variations of Pack markings but without real meaning. None of these people would protect me if I needed it.

And mentioning the chief of police only seems to make Conradi pricklier.

"There are people who can vouch for you?"

"Dozens."

He slides a piece of paper over to me. "If you could give me some names. I don't need dozens. Maybe five."

I start to write down names. Lawyers in good standing mostly. The deputy mayor. I leave the chief out of it.

"And did you go home alone?"

I'd love to be able to say I had, but I can't. With the doormen and security cameras in my building, it would be too easy to confirm.

"No, I didn't go home. I went Upstate for a long weekend. I really needed some time off. You can check my E-ZPass." I lean back in my chair. "So you see, Mr. Conradi—"

"Detective," he says sharply.

"*Detective* Conradi, I wasn't even in the city."

His expression, never warm, had gotten noticeably colder. Now it has turned frigid.

"Seeing that Ms. Unger was murdered in Hudson—*in Upstate*—I think we will be taking a look at your E-ZPass."

I slide the list of names who saw me at L-Cubed over to him and toss the pen back into the drawer. "Why is the NYPD handling this if it happened in Hudson?"

"Hudson's a small department; she was last seen alive in Manhattan. It makes sense to work both ends. More so now."

Now. Because *now* Conradi has set his sights on me. I know what he sees. He sees a man who makes a fortune circumventing the laws he puts his life on the line to enforce. A man with bespoke outerwear who disdains his crummy off-the-rack affair that gaps awkwardly at his neck. A man with no wedding ring and so many women that he needs mnemonics to remember which Janine is which. A man who doesn't understand the fearful responsibility that goes with being the father of a little girl whose pink sparkle he unknowingly wears. A little girl like Janine (Dragon) once was.

There's nothing I can say to change his mind about me. I have too many secrets that aren't mine to share, and my single confidence, the thing that is mine alone, involves the woman I love. I cannot, will not, expose her to him. I will not let him poison her against me. Thea and my wild. I will protect them both.

I reach for the door. "I think we're finished here."

One by one, he pops his knuckles. "Those are some nasty-looking scratches on your neck, Sorensson. How'd you get them?"

Shit. I tug at my jacket again, pulling the collar against my neck. "Fight with a bear."

I'm tired and pissed off, but the second the words are out of my mouth, I know I've made a mistake. I try to play nonchalant, pulling a tissue from the box that Janine always put on my desk to wipe the screen of my phone.

"Listen to me, asshole," he says, his eyes narrowing. "Don't think I haven't seen plenty of people like you. People who think they're invulnerable, untouchable. And you know what? You people always, *always* fuck up, and when you do, I'm going to be there, because from now on, I am going to be on you like shit on a shoe."

With a quick flick of my wrist, the balled-up tissue goes dead into the middle of the trash can.

"You have no idea what I'm *thinking*, so let me tell you what I *know*. I *know* that you have nothing but circumstantial evidence. I *know* that if I had anything to do with Janine's death, I would have come up with a better alibi. And I *know* that every day you waste hassling me cuts your chances of finding her actual killer in half."

He follows me into the hall. Clearly, the details of Janine's death are not generally known, because in a tragic miscalculation, someone has added a bright-red helium balloon to the pile at her office that says I MISS YOUR FACE ALREADY.

It bumps into Conradi's head, and he bats at it irritably.

"Don't leave town, Sorensson."

"Are you detaining me?"

"I'm asking you to stick around. In case I have more questions."

"If you're not arresting me, you can't tell me what to do." I start to walk away.

"You *want* me to arrest you?" Conradi says to my back.

"You can't. You don't have enough to make it stick."

"Maybe, maybe not," he says, following me through the door to the reception area. "But forty-eight hours in a holding cell has a way of making people a lot more cooperative. It's a dog-eat-dog world in there."

I push the button for the elevator.

"Good thing," I say, staring straight ahead, "that I am a wolf."

As cool as I tried to seem, I am not. Zigzagging through the streets around the courts, I quickly find one of the many stores that sell burner phones.

"So you did not kill her?" Evie says when I reach her.

"*No!* It was not good. She suffered. Did Tiberius—"

"Tiberius has not left Silver's side for more than a minute at a time. Hold on." I hear a wolf's voice and the cadence of a question but not the question itself. "Call this number, and ask for Mary Jean," she says to the questioner. Then the dull click of a pencil into a cup before she returns to me.

"How is Quicksilver doing?"

"As well as can be expected. I had a hard enough time with just two. With four, she is getting no rest at all. She is strong of marrow, and it was her choice not to cull. Tiberius, though, has no control. There is nothing for him to do but watch her fight for what he has planted inside her. If she does not survive, he will die. Yes?"

Her murmured voice blurs through her hand over the mouthpiece. I cannot hear the words, but her tone is severe.

"I have to get off. I'm presuming you understand that this needs to be kept Offland?"

It's not enough that Evie has to deal with the daily running of the Pack. She has recovered her strength now, but that doesn't mean that there aren't wolves willing to test a new leader. She has a lying-in, the rebuilding. Victor. She does not need the police following my fuckups to the Homelands.

"Yes, Alpha. I understand."

Chapter 31

Hāmweard, ðu londadl hǽðstapa, IN 22 DAYS
Homeward, you landsick heath-wanderer, IN 22 DAYS

AFTER FOUR DAYS, CONRADI CALLS ME OVER TO THE first precinct for an interview. I wait, but he is nowhere to be found. Maybe the officer sitting at the high desk legitimately doesn't know where he is. Maybe this is some new kind of human game that I have not yet learned. Officer Buton simply nods me toward the row of upholstered chairs decorated with dark ellipses of old gum.

If there is anywhere in the world where humanity in all its excess and misery and general meatiness is more pungently represented, I don't ever want to go there.

I sit next to a thin, bruised woman who smells like pepperoni and methamphetamine and fear. Another person of interest who is of interest to no one.

Half an hour later, I tell Officer Buton that I can't wait anymore.

"Don't leave town," he says without looking up from his newspaper.

A few days later, I am called in for a repeat performance. This time, Conradi manages to show up. He sits across from me at a narrow table covered with faux-wood contact paper meant to cover up the chips and gouges in the previous surface. He has a map and a complex calculation that allowed him to reconcile my E-ZPass record with Janine's murder.

"Why wouldn't I have just driven up the Taconic? No tolls, no records. Leaves me on the east side of the Hudson?"

"And without an alibi."

I push down a bubble under the contact paper with my thumb. It springs back up. Nothing I say is going to do anything to change his mind. He continues to focus on questions he has already asked. I continue to give him the answers I have already delivered.

Another detective I recognize as Hernandez sticks his head in the room. "Sam?" he says.

Samuel Conradi, I repeat to myself while peeling off the excess contact paper sticking over the edge of the table.

"Don't do that," Conradi says irritably.

The other detective looks briefly at me. "He's leaving now," he says. "I told him not to go anywhere."

Popular refrain. I look at my watch. I've wasted two hours here already.

The other detective starts to close the door, but as he does, I am hit by the unmistakable stench of lavender breeze and the off-gassing of polypropylene carpets. I leap up, my chair flying behind me, and run to the door, loping after the scent, following it toward the door. Conradi yells behind me.

Tiberius is a Shifter-Pack mix. Larger than Pack and much larger than the typical Shifter, but any Shifter—because that's who it must be—will still be larger than a human.

There's no one here but two uniforms and a handful

of humans. Two women talking to each other and a white-haired man in a neat suit halfway out the door, fishing for something in his pocket.

"Did you see a big man?" I yell at the policemen. They look at me skeptically. "I'm looking for a big man."

"Me too, honey," one of the women says. "Me too."

Her friend and the two uniforms start to laugh.

Disgusted, I turn back toward the interview room. Conradi watches me from his perch against the doorjamb, his arms crossed in front of his chest. "Sorensson? How well do you know Daniel Leary?"

"Who?"

"Leary. Daniel Leary."

"Never heard of him. What is he? An Irish poet?"

Conradi looks at me, trying to decide something.

"Don't leave town," he says.

Hāmweard, ðu londadl hǽðstapa, IN 12 DAYS
Homeward, you landsick heath-wanderer, IN 12 DAYS

I've been sleeping badly again, and the dream comes back to me almost as soon as I fall asleep. This time, I am in the interview room when the change hits. This time, instead of my legs changing, only my head does, but Conradi doesn't seem to notice. He keeps yelling at me to tell him what I did with Janine. I feel my mouth's high, narrow roof and its frilled black lips and sharp teeth. I try to respond, try to tell him that I am not the monster, that when I kill, I eat.

But all that comes is a howl.

The buzz of Thea's text wakes me up, my heart

pounding. I press on my chest with the heel of my hand. My fingers shake as I dial her number back, but the moment I hear her, my wild reaches his head up for the soothing stroke of her voice.

I make up excuses to keep her talking. I miss her so much. I miss her body and her voice and the times between when she isn't speaking. I tell her I'm not sleeping well and that I need to listen to her. Just please tell me about what's happening in the forest around her. How it's waking up to spring.

Thea puts her phone on her little unfinished pine table with the charger so that I can hear her.

With my wolfish senses, I listen as she makes her dinner and washes her dishes. She tells me about the first wail of the loon and the *gruk-gruk* of the mergansers and the almost living sound of ice as it twangs and cracks. She's seen newts, she says, sunning in black water, and ground bees and partridgeberry and liverwort and speedwell. A clutch of eggs. The promise of peepers.

She says she misses me too. Then against the soft crumple of pages turning, I fall well and truly asleep and do not dream.

Hāmweard, ðu londadl hǣðstapa, IN 7 DAYS
Homeward, you landsick heath-wanderer, IN 7 DAYS

"The mail's in, Mr. Sorensson," says Gregori, the doorman.

I've become one of those people. The people for whom the arrival of mail gives rhythm to otherwise rhythmless days. Because my bills are all paid electronically, I used to gather it once a week and run it through the shredder in the mail room. For the first time, I look at the offers for credit cards and the Dear Valued Customer notices.

One postcard sports a photograph of a peaceful glade with overhanging willows.

Dear Neighbor, it says in ostentatious lettering. *Have you thought about where your final resting place will be?*

I feed it into the shredder, because I *know* where my final resting place will be. I've always known. *My final resting place will be in the descending colon of a coyote.*

"Elijah?"

Oh shit. Mutton.

And sure enough, Alana stands at the mailboxes in that raw wool poncho. But it no longer has any power over me. Except for the salivating; that simply can't be helped.

"Hello, Alana."

"What are you doing home at this hour? Did you lose your job?"

"Nope, just taking some time off."

"Is this about the...you know? Transience?"

Oh god.

"No, just some time off. Actually, though, I've got an appointment coming up—"

"Did you know there's a *rat* in the *laundry* room?"

"What were you doing in the laundry room?"

"Inez found a lump and took the day off? I saw it? It ran right between the dryers?"

"Have you thought about taking Tarzan downstairs and letting him have a crack at it?"

She cocks her hip and rolls her eyes like a juvenile. "Don't be ridiculous. Tarzan's not meant for that kind of thing."

I don't ask what the hell Tarzan's actually *meant* for. Nor do I ask what exactly makes her think that I was "meant for that kind of thing." I know. She is still angry with the super over his inability to fix her remote control. Now Luca is unavailable, and because I was stupid enough to sleep with her, I have to play backup husband.

But my downtrodden wild, now woken by mutton, stretches out his front paws, his tongue lolling out the side of his mouth. Whining.

"I'll take care of it."

Thankfully, she doesn't ask how I, Elijah Sorensson (JD, LLM), propose to get rid of the rat.

At 3:00 a.m. when the building is asleep, I pull on my bathrobe and white slippers bearing the name of a hotel I don't remember visiting and head down to the laundry room with a big bag of sheets I don't need to wash but to explain why I'm skulking around in the basement. The laundry room is bright with a warm, tiled floor and a big farm sink. Looking between the dryers, I find the hot-water pipe leading down to the subbasement.

Careful to avoid the cameras, I dart down the stairs into the subbasement, to the big, dark room where the boiler and elevator, HVAC and other mechanicals that support the stage set of the building live. In the middle is a forest of struts from a planned storage area that was abandoned when the subbasement flooded during Hurricane Irene and again during Hurricane Sandy. To the side are mountains of ductwork covered in blue plastic.

The concrete is cold and damp on my now-naked body, but I don't care. I stretch out my arms, the heel of my palm straight and long. My skin starts to tingle and my hands narrow and lengthen and bones become rubbery and bend where the muscle tightens. My nose itches. The boiler growls menacingly and is the last thing I hear as my ears and eyes migrate into their wild form.

When I come out, I bound, tossing myself into the air and down again. I bound without incident along the full length of the subbasement, over rolls of baffling and piles of screens and the low drainage gutters, until one hind foot catches on a pile of tiles left over from some renovation project and they fall over.

I listen to make sure no one heard. Then, with my shoulders low and my nose to the floor, I race among the giant trunks of steel oozing their oily sap into the ground until I light upon the dusty, musky fragrance of rat.

Over the creaking and knocking of steam heat and the burbling of the pump comes a slight *scritching* from somewhere behind a stack of plasterboard propped against one wall. Because the wall got wet and then dried out again, it doesn't take much for me to claw out a hole big enough for my muzzle. I sniff once again to make sure I'm right, and then I wait, legs tense, chest leaning forward.

Half an hour later, the rat risks creeping out.

He is delicious.

When my change is done, I pick up my dirty clothes bag. The super's wife watches me leave the laundry room through a crack in her door.

In the bathroom as I wait for the hot water, the mirror fogs up. I rub my fingers through my hair gray with plaster dust and lick the dried blood dribbling down my chin.

~

"The mail's here, Mr. Sorensson. And I believe you have a package," says Gregori, handing me the thing I've been waiting for: a large box from Great North LLC, Plattsburgh.

As soon as I get back to the apartment, I slice open the tape with my seax, releasing the scent of deer hide and black walnut. There's an envelope inside with the instructions that Gran Jean promised to send. What she sent was a photocopy of the original Old Tongue instructions written out in tiny, archaic script.

Nim þu þæt leðer...

It takes fifteen minutes of migraine-inducing squinting just to get through *Nim þu þæt leðer*... "Take you that leather..." I doubt anyone has actually used these instructions. Gran Jean learned how to make our braids at the knee of Gran Wulfwyn, who learned at the knee of Gran Sæþryþ, who learned at the knee of Gran Dagmar, who probably learned at the knee of whatever Mercian sadist originally wrote this.

"Take you that leather."

Screw it. Leaning over the counter, I rub my finger along the trackpad until I line up the half-dozen YouTube videos I need to take the place of that ancient wolf. It takes me a couple of hours to make a smooth lacing. The deer hide is soft in spots, and I have trouble keeping the pressure consistent, so it is not a single thong, but in the end, I have six lengths. I make three slightly longer.

Just in case my seax was dulled by opening the box, I give it a few more passes on the whetstone before rinsing it, drying it, and slicing it along the length of my sternum. As the blood beads, I lay the first leather thong into the gash, holding it tight with the flat of one hand and dragging it through with the other. It is painful, but the constant abrasion keeps the wound from healing before I can finish with all six. I don't know if blood stains marble, but because of our fund manager's admonitions about resale value, I am careful to lay them out on a piece of plastic from the dry cleaner.

In a proper *Bredung*, the long, single thong would be stained with the blood of the Alpha before being tied around the couple, who would then mount until the leather was stained once more, this time with the results of their coupling. It is all very symbolic: the hide and the oak tannins represent our land; the blood, our pack; the seed, our mates.

Instead, in the shower stall, I close my eyes and imagine that proper *Bredung*, in which Thea's naked body is tied to mine. Under the spruces, where the needles make a soft, fragrant bedding. She rides me hard until her ironwood eyes soften and cloud, and her body clenches around me. A feral howl reverberates through the luxury condominium, and someone bangs against the shared wall. Panting and shaking with one forearm propped against the marble panel, I come to my senses long enough to anoint the six strands.

Why is this so important for me to get right? It's not because Pack will ever acknowledge it. Not because Thea will even know what it means. I want to get it right because this woman who knit back my unraveling heart and body and wild is my mate. Doesn't matter if I'm the only one who ever knows it. She is.

I spend the night braiding and unbraiding until I am

content with the shape and size and smoothness. Each has a loop made of a braid of three, then the two loose ends are braided into a six-strand braid. The larger one I leave on the Tiffany tray (*To Elijah Sorensson with Gratitude from Americans for Progressive Packaging*). The smaller one, the one I braided and rebraided until it was as perfect as I could make it, I coil into the padded overnight envelope with a casual note. *Had some time on my hands, so I made this*, I write as though it was an afterthought. *Hope you like it*.

Two nights later, she sends me a picture of the perfect gold column of her neck, with my braid. It's a little twisted from its day spent coiled in transit, but it will relax soon against the warmth of her skin. Then it will lie flat around the base of my mate's throat.

In my icy, sterile bathroom, I fumble, threading the knot at one end of my own braid through the loop at the other. I slide it around so the fastening is at the back, hidden under my hair. As I put my hands on either side of the marble sink, I flex my shoulders. There are wolves in the Great North who will challenge my right to wear the braid.

But they will do it only once.

Chapter 32

Hāmweard, ðu londadl hǽðstapa, IN *3* DAYS
Homeward, you landsick heath-wanderer, IN *3* DAYS

"MR. SORENSSON, THERE'S A WOMAN HERE. A... WHAT'S your name again?"

"Celia Sorensdottir," enunciates an abrupt voice. "I am Elijah Sorensson's shielder."

What is Celia doing Offland?

"She says she's Ce—"

"Send her up."

In my bare feet, I wait in front of the elevator bank and hit the up button. I don't know the last time Celia went Offland, and I can't imagine that she's ever used an elevator. The first elevator opens with only a single distracted dog walker. I let him go and push the button again. This time when another door slides open, two human men stand awkwardly at the numbered panel. Much-taller Celia has squeezed herself into the opposite corner, her shirt covering her nose and mouth.

"You should come out now, Celia."

"Alpha," she says, her voice muffled by her T-shirt.

One of the men is keeping the door open as they crane their heads, watching us. But Celia, who does not understand the difference between a stare of idle curiosity and a stare of challenge, lunges for them.

I grab her around her waist, pulling her back. "Your Alpha," I whisper, "will not have you biting humans."

Unfortunately, a door opens behind us—not just any door, but Alana's door. Luca yells for the men to hold the elevator, while Alana scoops up Tarzan in his quilted purple jacket.

"*What have you done?*" Celia's horrified expression takes in Tarzan over the hem of her shirt. "*What is that?*"

I'm not sure whether Celia is talking about the quilted purple jacket or the pint-size perversion wearing it, but before she can attract any more attention, I drag my shielder into the apartment and slam the door on their stunned faces.

Cautiously, Celia lowers her T-shirt and sniffs the air before deciding that the smell is more wolf than human and won't poison her. She moves her head toward mine, but I am Offland and I forget and, instead of marking her as I should, I kiss the air near her right ear and then near her left.

She draws back, looking at me quizzically.

The furrows between Celia's brows deepen as she looks around the sterile apartment.

"Can I get you something?"

"What do you have?"

Ahhh. "Water?"

"Do you have anything else?"

"No, just water, really."

"Why did you imply there were options?"

"I wasn't implying anything. I wasn't thinking about it at all. It's just a thing one says."

"Wolves don't say it. I'll take water then."

What is she doing here?

I hand her the glass of water. It sloshes when the phone in my pocket chimes, warning me that I'm due back in the gum-spotted chair.

"I have an appointment soon. Do you want to wait for me here? I'll come back as soon as I can. I can bring something to eat. Falafel, maybe?"

"No. I don't like falafel, and I don't like Offland either. I wouldn't be here at all, but we have been shielders for a long time, so I felt I should do this in person."

"Do what?"

"Elijah Sorensson." She clears her throat, then continues. "By the ancient rites and laws of our ancestors and under the watchful eye of our echelon, our Pack, and our Alpha, I challenge you for primacy of the 9th. With fang and claw, I will attend upon you the last day of the Iron Moon."

Her voice is stiff and formal; her fist is tightening around the glass.

I cup her hand in mine. "Relax, shielder. Things break easily here."

As soon as she does, I put the glass on the countertop and hold her hands again. "I won't fight you. I should have given up primacy years ago. I didn't, but it wasn't because of power. It was because I needed to matter in the only place that ever mattered to me. But what matters to me now is what's best for the Pack and best for the 9th. Evie thinks it's best for the Great North if I stay Offland. And I know that you are what's best for the 9th. Anyway, you've been Alpha in all but name for so long. It's time for that ass Lorcan to treat you like one."

She looks at her hands cupped in mine and then cocks her head to the side.

"I will be proud to call you Alpha, Celia."

And Celia leans forward, not with some meaningless air kiss. Instead, with the slide of her skin against mine, she leaves minute traces of herself and the promise of protection and belonging.

The way a wolf does it.

This time, Conradi tries something new. He shows up, sits me down at the interview table, and pulls out a pack of gum—not the kind with the bubbles, but the old-fashioned kind with the papery aluminum foil. Because the room is covered in acoustic tiles, I can hear every crinkle and bend.

Maybe he has had success with people who are unnerved by silence. Who will start talking just to fill it in, and when they start talking, he starts tying them in knots. People maybe, but not me. So I settle in, waiting like a wolf at a watering hole.

An hour later, he stalks out and slams the door.

A skinny, balding cop with a thick mustache and a distracting hairy mole on his jawline opens the door and tells me that Conradi's gone and they need this room. He drinks noisily from a coffee mug that instructs me to "Be Safe: Sleep with an Officer."

"Don't leave town," he says to my back.

As soon as I leave the interview room, pulling on my jacket, I smell it again. The strong unmistakable scent of lavender breeze cutting through the fug of churros and steel and sweat-stained polyester and beer-saturated livers.

I don't even bother to pretend. With my mouth partly

open, I lower my head, sucking in short, panted breaths to help me focus on the source. I follow it to the door and to a man waiting outside. Last time, I had been confused because I relied like a human on my eyes. I saw the white-haired man and discounted him. This time, I track the scent like Pack.

Underneath his pricey suit is a thin, almost hollow body. The skin at the back of his neck is sallow and papery. He stops and turns to the side, a lighter held in the hollow of his yellow fingers, trying to protect his cigarette from the wind.

Half of his mouth is topped by a pale strip, as though a mustache had once blocked the sun there. The other half… It isn't properly a mouth at all. It's just a slit in a cheek that is bright pink and puffy and smooth like a mushroom. With no lips to keep it in, saliva collects in the corner.

I follow him from the precinct to a bench in the tiny park at Canal and Sixth. He alternates between sucking at his cigarette and dabbing at his leaking mouth with a large handkerchief.

"Why don't we play Twenty Questions," he says without bothering to look at me.

I don't respond.

"You have to say animal or vegetable or mineral."

I don't have to say anything.

"Fine then," he says, taking a deep toke. "Are you a wolf?" Smoke leaks out with each word.

I stand behind him. "If you know what I am, human, you should know to be afraid. What did you want from Janine?"

With the practiced action of his thumb, he flicks ash on the ground.

"What did she tell you? *What did your boss want from her?*"

"Is this the part in the movie where the villain, for unaccountable reasons, reveals in agonizing detail both his motivations and his plans? Though before we assign villainy, can I point out that *you* were the ones who ate my fucking face?"

"And *you* were the ones who invaded our land."

"And *you* were the ones who sent the parricide. Between the two of us, I imagine we could spend a few rollicking hours trading accusations."

"There's a difference between us. We just want to be left alone. *We* are just trying to survive."

"Isn't that all anyone is trying to do? Ensure the continuation of the species?" He pulls out his phone and looks at it briefly; he swipes twice with his thumb. "Their own species, of course. Other species be damned. Like those that cling to their habitats even as those habitats shrink and then—*pop*—the noose pulls tight and there is no room for them at all." Having gotten a response, he turns his phone facedown on his leg. "You, for example. When will you get it through your heads that this world has no room for monsters?"

"*We are not monsters*."

August Leveraux's human pawn laughs, his tongue darting out to lick the fold where his lips should be.

"Shall we test that? I invite you, in the view of all these lovely, lovely people, to turn into a werewolf—"

"*Not a werewolf*."

"Well, whatever you choose to call yourself. I think you would find that the next thing you heard was the sound of every one of said lovely, lovely people slipping off the safeties."

He wipes the inside of his missing mouth.

"Growl all you want," he says. "Yes, you can tear me apart. Physically, maybe, but practically speaking, you can't. Your strength has to be kept secret. Our strength—my employer's strength—does not. In fact, his power is the sort that has no point without people to wield it over. People to buy and frighten and persuade. I am the first to admit that I am not strong, but, Mr. Sorensson, I am *terribly* powerful."

A black car stops in front of us. The tinted window rolls down, and the driver leans his head out, looking back and forth between the two of us. "Daniel Leary?"

"That'd be me," Leary says. He stops for a moment at the door to the car. "Don't you have to be getting home too?" He takes a look at his phone and then stuffs it back in his pocket. "If I'm not mistaken, it will be Alpo time soon."

Then Daniel Leary, the man with the scar-rimmed, bright-pink cheek and yellow fingers and rotting breath and half lips, the man who killed our wolves, who burned our home, who hammered a spike through Tiberius's hand, who peeled off Janine's face, and who has the gall to call *us* monsters, slides into the back of a car and closes the door.

"Penn Station?" asks the driver, looking in the rearview mirror. And my tongue finds the slight point of my canine.

Maybe Leary has been flagged by the IRS. Maybe he has a dodgy passport. Maybe he's just afraid of flying. But whatever the reason, his route "home too" is via Hell's Vestibule.

And that...that is a place with room for monsters.

It takes me no time at all to find him in Penn Station. The stench that disguised his association with Shifters is so strong and so easy to follow. I don't need to see him, making it easy to stay hidden. Mostly hidden. Nothing makes someone more nervous than the feeling of being followed without any tangible proof. Wolves sometimes do it, follow a deer for hours unseen. It makes the deer skittish and unfocused and tired and prone to mistakes.

Like Leary. He whips around and snarls with his misshapen face, "*Get the fuck away from me!*" That was a mistake, yelling into the crowd. Humans really don't like ugliness and insanity and unpredictability and scurry away from him.

This is how wolves hunt: separating the weak and infirm from the protection of the herd.

I know every hidden space and secret passage of this maze. I know how to access platforms without heading up and down crowded escalators. I can cross tracks unseen. I can be nowhere and everywhere. I don't show myself until he is in the broad, brightly lit tunnel that was used to usher delegates away from protestors during some convention before it was soldered up and turned into...

...a dead end.

"Wolves believe in the sanctity of death." My voice echoes down the empty hallway.

He walks quickly, fumbling for his phone. He jabs at it, refusing to believe that there are parts of New York without network coverage.

"They do not kill without reason. They do not torture."

"August Leveraux will flay you alive if you touch me." A dribble of spit flows down the side of his mouth.

"Unfortunately for you, I've spent decades with humans. Thanks to them, I know what it is to be truly monstrous. And when I am done, you will know too."

He starts to scream, but it dissolves quickly into a breathless hacking cough. For his power to work at all, he needs people to buy and terrify and persuade, and there are none here.

I punch the oversize handkerchief through his teeth and drag him to the break in the wall where the rats are.

Chapter 33

I push the last concrete block back in place. On the other side, in the dark, a rat scurries toward the body I left there.

I've got to get home.

Running from the narrow side exit beyond one of the half-dozen pretzel places, I raise my hand for a cab. My phone buzzes. There are three missed calls and a voice message, all from a 518 number I don't recognize.

Sliding into the back, I give the driver my address and check the message.

"Elijah?" There's a long pause, almost like Celia's waiting for my voice to answer her. "Yours is the only number I know by heart." Celia's usually firm, clipped voice sounds tentative and weak. "I think someone followed me from New York. A Shifter and a human. I killed them, but not quickly enough." She begins coughing up something that I know must be blood. "It isn't a flesh wound."

Where are you?

"The man in the gas station is looking at me," she says weakly. "They will not have my body."

Oh, min schildere. Where are you?

I throw money at the cabby and run down the sloping exit to the parking garage, calling the Great North.

It takes nothing for the Pack's wolfish hackers to track the phone number to a body shop near Corinth.

Within minutes, Evie has sent Tristan and four other wolves south. I am racing north at the same time, but Corinth is in the middle, and it will be hours before any of us can get to her—and by then, it will be too late.

Celia is strong and our bodies are resilient, but she will not survive if the man at the gas station calls the EMT. If someone draws blood or listens to her heart or anything, they will realize she is not human, and in the name of science, they will torture her. They will cage her, and they will find out what she is.

At the stoplight, I pop open the glove compartment and look grimly at the contents. Aside from the usual proof of insurance, maintenance schedules, owner's manuals, registrations, and ice scrapers, all Pack cars carry a lighter and a WD-40 Big Blast, because Offland, we cannot simply die: we must immolate.

I do the only thing I can think of to save Celia.

The moment I call Thea, she begins to move. There's the swish of her coat, the jingle of her keys, the dull thwack of that emergency backpack. Her boots.

At first, I couldn't remember the word that would make a human understand why Celia was so important to me. She is within the prohibited degrees of consanguinity that is family. A female littermate. I finally remember.

"Sister. She's my sister." What a bloodless word. An accident of birth and parentage, carrying none of the sense of shared responsibility of a shielder.

Thea pulls her door closed with a dull click and runs for her car. The door slams, and I tell her where my "sister" is.

Her car engine comes to life, and she shifts into Reverse.

I tell her that my sister does not trust strangers. "Do you have the braid I gave you?"

"Yes."

"Show it to her. It will be enough."

The Pack is already there by the time I pull in behind Thea's Wrangler. Tristan has brought the kitted-out long-bed truck he uses on the rare occasion when he has to retrieve a wounded wolf. There's another Land Rover as well. We're not very imaginative when it comes to cars.

Thea is outside, running toward me before I close the car door. I pull her to me, my face buried into her hair, drawing one desperate breath after another.

"They're here," she whispers. "*Your people*."

Thea opens the door to her cabin where *my people* crowd around like a family of giants in a dollhouse.

My blood runs cold. Standing beside the bed, one hand hooked around the broad main beam is Varya the Indurate. Her blood is pouring through a tube the size of a garden hose into pale-faced Celia.

On the other side, Tristan kneels on the floor, working on Celia under a surgical lighthead, its beam being directed by Marco. Two younger wolves are assisting.

"Alpha," Varya says with a discernible accent and a freight load of scorn.

Thea's phone chirps in her pocket. She puts her hand on my chest. "I better take this outside," she whispers.

Varya stares silently at the place where a human hand had been until Thea gives the door that extra pull.

"What are you doing, Alpha?"

"Celia didn't have hours to wait for us. She wasn't going to be conscious much longer. She's a good wolf and would have burned first, but she deserved better than that."

I lean over the bed, my hand gentle against her cold forehead.

"There is a human here. A human *who wears your braid*?"

"She is not your concern."

"You have made her my concern. You have made her the concern of the entire Great North."

I keep looking at Celia, brushing back her hair. Her closed eyes look like bruises in her pale face. "Celia? *Min scildere*? *Lada mec*."

"She can't hear you. And it's not her forgiveness you are going to need. It is the Alpha's, and she will never forgive you for letting the humans know about us."

"Stop being melodramatic. Thea doesn't *know* anything."

"She will certainly suspect something. Look around you, Alpha. Look at *us*." She waves her hand at the outlandish bodies crammed into Thea's cabin. As though to make her point, Marco cracks his head into the sloping roof with a resounding *clomp* and a muffled curse.

"The law is clear. Either you do it, or I will, but..."

The sticky latch on the door clicks. Thea looks at me, her phone in her hand.

"*Se westend sceal forþferan*."

Se westend. The waster, the destroyer. It is the word wolves once used for humans. *Se westend sceal forþferan:* The human must die.

I jerk Thea to me and kiss her slowly and deliberately, making sure that Varya is watching me. Watching me mark Thea's face and her neck and her body until she is thick with my scent.

"*Wiðsæcest þu min fæstnung*?"

Do you deny my bond, my protection?

Our laws are both remarkably exact and remarkably vague. They are exact in that there are prescriptions and proscriptions for every interaction: sex, mating, protecting, hunting, eating. They are vague in their assumption that all those interactions take place between Pack. *The one so marked*, it says, *shall be under said Alpha's protection even unto death*.

It doesn't say *the wolf* or *the Pack member* or *the half Shifter*. No, all it says is *the one*.

"This is not over," Varya says, her already rigid face hardening. "You have only delayed the inevitable. The Deemer will know the law."

Before I can answer, Thea tugs on my arm, pulling me down until her lips are against my ear, in the mistaken notion that she can't be heard. "They have to go."

"As soon as—"

"No, they have to go *now*. That was Doug. He called to say that an arrest warrant has come up from the city for you. I said I hadn't seen you for weeks, but I could tell he didn't believe me."

Had the cabin been filled with humans, no one would have heard anything, but as it is, Varya is already pulling the tube from her arm. "Henry," she says to the younger wolf. "You take over. I will drive."

Varya continues barking orders. Henry plugs the garden hose into his own vein, and as the four wolves carefully take Celia out, he holds his arm high, finally folding himself into the back of Tristan's truck. Marco and the remaining wolf are sent to retrieve Celia's car.

"As for you," Varya says as she starts the ignition, "do *not* let this mess follow you home."

The door slams and the wheels jounce and I head back into the cabin. They even removed Thea's sheets, in case they were stained by a drop of Celia's alien blood.

"We need to talk," she says.

"I know. I said they were *like* the Amish—"

"That's later. What I want to know is why no one ever interviewed me about where you were the last night we saw each other."

"What?"

"Doug told me. The warrant is for the murder of a woman who was killed that Saturday, but you were *with me* the entire time."

"It's..." I smooth out her mattress. "I'll get you some new sheets."

"*Stop it. Just...stop it.*" She takes my chin in her hand, forcing me to look her in the ironwood eye. "You were *with me*. I'm not asking about what just happened here with those people who are not even *remotely* like the Amish. I am asking you *why* you didn't tell anyone that you had an alibi."

My wolfish ears pick up the sound of tires hitting the forest track that leads to Thea's cabin. Doug will be here in five minutes.

"You want to know why? It's because that girl who was killed was my assistant, and I had slept with her. I was a shit, and I slept with a lot of women. Then I met you, and I thought I was done with that other me. I never wanted to have anything to do with him again. But I couldn't get away from him, and I knew if the police interviewed you, they would make sure you knew every horrible thing about me." I push her hair behind her ear.

"And I would lose whatever chance I had that you would love me like I love you."

It's coming closer, the sound of wheels spinning against the loose stones.

"He's coming," Thea says, grabbing some clothes from the drawers under the bed and stuffing them into her backpack. She comes from the bathroom with a small bag and adds that as well. Then she starts to lace up her boots.

"What are you doing?"

"Coming with you. Going to clear this up."

"I don't—"

"I told you to trust me to take care of myself. Well, I do love you. So taking care of myself means taking care of you too." A car door slams. She looks toward the window. "He's here."

Doug's footsteps crunch along the small stones. He takes a picture of the license plate of my Land Rover.

"I'll follow you in my car," she says.

The heavy tread creaks on her porch. Doug looks through the window. Then he knocks on the door.

"Take mine. It's got a parking sticker, and..." I fish in my pocket for my keys. "This is for my apartment."

"Thea," says Doug's muffled voice. "I know he's in there."

"Is there anything else you want me to hold on to so it doesn't end up with the property clerk?" she whispers. "Hold on a second," she calls out. "We're coming."

I hand her my phone and my watch and my wallet, taking only my driver's license.

Thea opens the door to Doug standing with his hand to the back of his belt.

"He doesn't need handcuffs, Doug. He's not resisting."

"He's a *fugitive*, The."

"I'm not a fugitive. I was only a person of interest."

"You were told to *stay put*. Hands behind your back."

I put my hands behind my back, palms out.

Thea's ironwood eyes narrow, and she slips back into her cabin.

"So you're just her lawyer, eh?" Doug says, opening the handcuffs. "You should have known better."

"I wasn't under arrest," I say again.

"Well, now you are." He begins reading me my rights while he tries to close the cuffs, but the hinge pinches tight against my wrist bone and won't close. "Dammit," he says and slips the metal cuffs back into his belt, fishing out plastic restraints instead.

"It's a long drive. At least let me have my hands in front."

He puts my hands behind my back, tightens the restraints, and then covers my head with his hand as I tumble awkwardly into the back of his car. Through the rear window, I watch Thea pull herself up into my car and adjust the seat forward. She reaches over to put something into the glove compartment and buckles herself in.

My fierce female.

"What are you smiling about?" Doug asks when I face forward again.

"Nothing."

He looks suspiciously into his rearview mirror.

Thea waves.

I wave back, the ripped remnants of the plastic shackle swinging from my wrist.

Chapter 34

Hāmweard, ðu londadl hǽðstapa, IN *1* DAY
Homeward, you landsick heath-wanderer, IN *1* DAY

IF I'D KNOWN MORE ABOUT THE REALITIES OF CRIMINAL court, I wouldn't have smiled. I'd counted on the absence of any evidence against me, on Thea's testimony, *on my innocence* to spring me by midafternoon.

My lawyer said to be patient. Thea had given a strong interview, and more importantly, another suspect seemed to have fled the country. But the law is slow, he said, adding that Conradi *really* seemed to have taken a dislike to me.

But time is the one thing I don't have, because in thirty hours, I will no longer be human.

In a windowless holding cell deep underground, surrounded by white walls, two low metal benches, bars, a broken telephone, and a metal divider barely disguising the shit-covered toilet, I wait with a revolving cast of twenty-five men who are not yet guilty.

No one has a phone or a watch in the Tombs. There are no windows, and if there were, there would be no light. I try counting one Mississippi, two Mississippi, three Mississippi, but when I get to 2,759 Mississippi, I realize that my grasp of time has stretched and contorted like Silly Putty.

The corrections officer told us that chow is at seven and noon and six. Lights out at nine thirty.

I ask every CO and every man who comes into our bullpen for the time, excepting only a man with one shoe who curls into a ball on the floor near the toilet. He smells of diabetes and frostbite and barely moves.

A CO passes out sandwiches. I don't know whether that means it's noon or six. Several of the men flock to him, calling out their preferences, usually steak and lobster, which, as jokes go, is stale from the beginning. I get a sandwich of processed halal meat. When I tell the CO I am vegetarian, he snorts, and my little corner of hell becomes darker.

Because I've been so preoccupied with time, I haven't been paying attention to the emerging trade in strength and weakness that has been taking place around me. Someone has been made the top dog, the shot-caller. He is a thick man with elaborate tattoos starting at his wrist and creeping up the side of his arm under the ripped sleeves of his sweatshirt and up to his cropped skull. He has a long scar along his jaw and a teardrop tattooed on his face.

He looks at me. I do not look away.

The men are not entirely sure who is the alpha here: I am the bigger man by far, but I have a Kiton jacket and a double-twill Egyptian cotton shirt and am wearing driving shoes. Aside from the faded bear-claw scars at my neck, I have no body art. I wear a braided necklace. The men are more familiar with the signals sent by the man with the teardrop, and most congregate around him. Only the very lowest, like the man with one shoe, stay near me, mostly because there is space.

Teardrop's eyes get harder, and he nods toward my little pack without shifting his eyes from mine. A man with deep pits in his face yells at the sick man for smelling bad, then kicks his bare foot.

It is meant as a challenge, and as tedious as it is, I know that challenges must be met. I ignore the man with the deep pits. It is never worth interacting with subordinates. Instead, I go to the shot-caller himself, who has reserved one entire bench for himself.

I ask him what time it is.

He asks me if he looks like a fucking clock.

I take his wrist as if to check the watch he doesn't have, and when I press with my thumb, it bends, then breaks.

And I sit back down. By the time the CO has come to see why the man is screaming, everyone else is seated too, looking at the floor. Now many of them are congregated in my corner. They leave the sick man alone.

At chow time, I easily trade my processed halal meat sandwich for peanut butter.

At nine thirty, the lights go out. Most of the men try to carve out a piece on the floor and get a little sleep. I can't. I stare at the now-dark lights and try to decide if it is possible to stand with my bare feet on the metal bench, stick my tongue into the light socket, and immolate.

Hāmweard, ðu londadl hǽðstapa.
Homeward, you landsick heath-wanderer.

It is sometime after the arrival of the corn flakes and tiny cartons of icy milk that the CO finally calls my name. I pick up the thin plastic bag with my driver's license and follow the police officer to the door, blinking at the sight of the bilious yellow sky. At first, I think it's the afterburn of exhaustion and all those yellow walls, but then I realize there's a storm coming.

A hand touches my arm right above my elbow. "Elijah? Hey, I'm—"

"What time is it?" My throat is dry, and my voice is cracked.

"What?"

"*What time is it? Please, Thea.*"

She hesitates for a moment, then checks her watch. "It's eleven forty. What's up? Are you okay?"

I hold on to her wrist and look at her watch myself, like it's some kind of talisman. "I have to be home in six hours. I'm not sure I can make it."

"Not the apartment?" she asks, looking alarmed. She raises her hand for a cab.

"No, not the apartment. *Home*. I have to get to my car. I have to leave *now*."

From the cab, I stumble down the ramp toward the garage. Where's my car? Where are my keys? I slam my fist into a sign that reads MAXIMUM CLEARANCE 6'9". Thea's voice bounces around the cement. I can't pinpoint it.

"Elijah! The car's over here."

"Where are the keys?"

"I've got them, love. I've got them."

Love. My mind is swimming. *Bleep*. *Bleep*. Door open. Door close. Seat belt. Cell phone in cradle. Homeward. Passenger door opens, then closes.

"You can't come with me. I have to do this on my own." I reach across to push her door open again, but she holds it locked.

"I don't know what's going on, but I do know you're in no shape to drive."

"I can drive jes find," I say.

There's a sudden jerk and crunch of metal. Thea falls forward sharply, her hands bracing against the dashboard. I look in the rearview mirror for the jackass idiot driver.

It's a cement column.

"Let me drive," Thea says softly.

"I need to go home."

"I hear you. You're going home." She unfastens my seat belt. "Just tell me how to get there."

We trade places, and I show her the blurred directions toward the Great North that are now on the Homeward app. I rub it against my shirt. "I've got it," she says, disengaging from the column. "Seat belt."

"Promise me. Promise. Soon's we get there. You churn around and go back home. Promise me, please?"

"S'okay. I promise." She takes the belt buckle from my shaking hand and snicks it into place. "I'll take care of it."

I wake up with a jerk, my muscles cramping and my mouth like the bottom of a birdcage. The last thing I remember is a sign for the West Side Highway.

It's dark, and I can't see anything. Just two red blurs of taillights through the rain-drenched windshield. Thea shakes me again. "It keeps saying something I don't understand."

Then the voice of Homeward's Offland wolf reverberates through the cocoon of the car.

Ond swa gegæþ þin endedogor.

And so passes your final day.

Thea's hands are tight on the wheel and her eyes on the road. "What was that?"

"Nothing. An alarm."

She strokes my arm. "Do you feel better?"

"Yeah, I guess so."

"We'll be there in forty-five minutes. Maybe a little less if the rain lets up."

Doesn't matter if we fly there. It's too late. *And so ends my final day*.

Not quite. There's one more thing I have to do. Inside the glove compartment, the bag with the WD-40 and the lighter has been shoved to the side to make room for something that wasn't there before. I feel around, my fingers finding an unfamiliar shape.

"You brought your gun?"

She frowns a little and shrugs. "You were in handcuffs. Wasn't sure what we were up against."

We.

I close the glove compartment. I can't do it. This woman who is so fiercely *I* has joined herself to me in an even fiercer *we*. I can't do this. I can't jump out of the car, set myself on fire, and leave her to wonder what the hell happened and how she was to blame.

I'd rather have her know exactly what the hell happened. Let her see the truth. Let her fear me. Let her hate me.

Kill me.

And let her feel the relief of knowing she's rid the world of a monster.

I unzip my jacket and toss it into the back. Then I peel off my shirt, followed by my shoes and socks.

She checks the rearview mirror and then hits the turn signal. "What are you doing?"

Lifting my hips, I tug down my pants. I don't want my last moments to be sealed inside. "Do you mind if I open the window?" The heat of the change starts to hit, and I peel off my boxers, sitting beside her naked while the rain needles my bare shoulders.

I take out the gun and put it in the cup holder and then slam the glove compartment closed.

"Elijah? What—?"

"I'm sorry, Thea. I really am." I pull her hand to me. "I didn't want—" Even as my lips are pressed against her hand, my mouth begins to change, pushing out, the teeth grinding in my jaw. The hand that is holding hers elongates, the fingers shrinking and bending.

There's a jerk on the steering wheel, a car horn sounds. We swerve, and I don't hear anything anymore.

My body churns and swerves, and my knees find the floor as I slither out of the seat belt, my elbow banging painfully against the side panel. My eyes see nothing but a pale, opalescent haze and my ears hear nothing but a dull roar interrupted by the thump of my heart.

Then my muzzle bangs awkwardly in the tight space at the foot of the passenger seat. Something bounces against my head. I know what I look like now. Even Pack, for whom the change is revered, normal, still find this midpoint, when we are neither one thing nor the other, grotesque.

I keep waiting for it, wondering what the bullet will feel like. Will it be hot like fire? Or cold like steel?

Or like rain splashing through the window. My senses are starting to return. My sensitive nose smells the tart mineral rain and Thea's fragrance, more pungent now and thick with salt and old leather, the smell of fear. And my eyes see her, staring straight ahead, her hands clenching the wheel, her knuckles straining against her skin, her gun on her lap.

She refuses to look at me.
She didn't kill me.
Shit. She didn't kill me.

Chapter 35

Now what?

I hadn't planned for this. I'd been so sure she would kill me that I hadn't given a single thought to what would happen if she didn't. If she just kept driving to the Homelands. As soon as we leave the smooth asphalt, I recognize every bump and turn and gully and root and rock of the road to home.

At the top of the path, the car comes to a stop, headlights shining brightly on the raindrops, making them glow white like snow. What she can't see, what she doesn't know to look for, is farther under the canopy of the trees. The pale-green distant reflection of hundreds of eyes.

Thea reaches across me, her arm just brushing my fur, and opens the door, letting in the rush of air that's cold and damp and fragrant.

I rub my muzzle against her arm one last time. There are so many things I wish I could tell her. Most of all, I wish she knew that of all the humans and wolves I've known, she was the one who saved me. Not my body; that's forfeit now.

But my wild soul.

I hop out and, putting my weight against the door, make sure it shuts properly so no wolf can get in and she is safe.

Then I trot toward the line of eyes. With Thea, I have

brought Offland home, which is a crime punishable by death. No, *punished* by death. *Punishable* makes it sound like there is an alternative.

There isn't.

Joelle, Gamma of the 10th, is the first to reach me, her teeth bared. I could kill her easily, but I won't. I know what I am; I am strong enough to be vulnerable. Strong enough to love. And strong enough to die for it.

I won't fight them, but I will stand as long as I can, because it's important that they remember I never submitted.

Joelle's claws rip through my flank, her jaws on my neck holding me while the rest of the Pack descends. I lock my legs, refusing to crumble under the weight of a dozen wolves. It's like when we were pups, all this roiling fur and warm wolf breath. Except now it hurts.

Above the growled anger is a dull thud and rapid footsteps and a deafening shot. The Pack freezes as Thea pushes her way through the crowd of giant wolves, firing again. The Pack retreats, confused. The headlights blazing behind her cast an oversize shadow of a woman beside a wolf. My legs wobble as blood trickles down.

Joelle moves forward tentatively, testing Thea, who, with a slow breath, takes aim. Then there is a bang and the 10th's Gamma jumps, but the bang isn't from a gun; it's from a door slamming shut near Home Pond. Heavy human footsteps pound along the damp ground.

"*Stop! Alpha, I need her*." Tiberius slides to a halt in front of the black wolf standing front and center. Then the proud man falls to his knees in front of her, his eyes lowered, his chin to his chest. Rain gathers in his short, black hair and starts to stream down his dark face. "Please, Alpha, please. *She's dying. I can't do this alone.*" He lifts his head, his ringed eyes staring frantically at Thea. "*I need help. Please. I need...help.*"

Evie looks from the Shifter to the human to me. I am *felasynnig*, and Thea is the collateral damage of my sin. By law, she must die to protect the Pack's secrets.

But this is what it means to be Alpha. Making the hard decisions, the unpopular ones, and with a sharp bark, Evie turns to her Pack and orders them back. A few wolves waver, but Evie is fully recovered from her lying-in. She is wicked strong and fearsomely fast, and with a growl, she darts forward. A young male who hesitated a moment too long loses a chunk of his hide at the shoulder. It is a bloody and painful flesh wound, a warning. Evie widens her chest, drops her head slightly. Her thighs are tense; her eyes scan for dissenters.

The glowing green dots back away and then slide into the darkness.

Tiberius grabs Thea's arm. "Come now!"

"No!" she shouts, pulling out of his grasp. She points to me. "You don't understand. They tried to kill him. He's not like them. He's human. He's... I don't know. He *was*...human. He was *human*."

Tiberius is too strong, and Thea's heels drag through the muck and snow. I shake off the pain of my wounded body and run after them.

"He is many things," Tiberius says, pulling her harder, "but never human. Around the back."

I run beside her so she knows I'm here.

At the glass french doors at the back of the Boathouse, Tiberius hesitates. The inside doesn't look like it did at the start of Silver's lying-in when everything was clean and neatly organized. The cot on the side has been raised so Tiberius can lie level with his mate. There are the packets of protein bars and nuts and high-calorie snacks that he was evidently trying to feed Silver when she was in skin during those last agonizing days.

A bottle of vanilla Ensure spilled, and with the Iron Moon, no one is around to clean it up. There's only the exhausted Tiberius and a skeletal silver wolf in the middle of the floor. She is licking at the tiniest excuse for a pup I've ever seen. It is stiff and still and clearly dead, but she won't stop; it's like a mania has taken hold of her. Tiberius kneels beside her and tries to extricate the pup. Tries to push her to drink water. Three surviving pups wobble against her abdomen, mewling.

"Leave it, Wildfire. Please, leave it." The water drips from his hair and his face and his eyes as he pleads with her, but she bares her teeth and keeps licking at the little black dot with her bone-dry tongue.

Thea stands back, taking in Tiberius, Silver, the pups, and me. She shakes her head, takes a deep breath, then putting her gun into her pocket, hangs her jacket on a hook.

"Can I take a look at it?" she says to Tiberius.

"Him. He's dead. I need Silver—"

"I worked at a veterinary clinic for a while. I might be able to help."

Tiberius bristles. I growl beside Thea, but she just pats the air behind her.

"Look, I'd love to say that I'm an expert in werewolf neonatology, but I can't. I did, however, *work at a veterinary clinic*." She grabs a clean sweatshirt from a pile of clothes. "Now, is there a suction bulb?"

"*Not* werewolves," Tiberius mutters, but he is already rummaging through medical supplies in the metal drawers.

Silver looks at Tiberius for one delirious moment. She whimpers when Thea takes the tiny black thing in her hands but doesn't bite her.

Thea holds his stiff body with the head slanted down. "Where's that bulb?"

As soon as Tiberius hands it to her, Thea squeezes it and slides it into the pup's mouth, where she carefully releases the pressure. The bulb slucks up something fluid. Thea squirts it onto the floor and then does it again.

She fits her mouth over his nose and gently blows in. His tiny chest rises. Thea begins to rub him hard, too hard it seems to Silver, who snarls and tries to lift herself up. Tiberius keeps his hand on her, watching Thea with bloodshot eyes.

Thea turns the pup over, still rubbing briskly, almost like she's trying to get a fire started.

"She's got to drink," she says, pointing her chin toward Silver.

"I've been telling her that."

"When you talk to her…she can understand?"

"She's not *deaf*."

She looks at me without stopping the friction of her hands against the pup. "Can he understand too?"

"Hmm."

The pup's body seems looser now, and Thea kneels down in front of Silver. "I can't believe I'm doing this," she mutters. Then she leans in, speaking stiffly, the way humans do to foreigners or the infirm. "You have to drink," she says. "If you don't, they are *all* going to die."

Bleary-eyed with exhaustion, Silver still manages to curl her lip back, revealing her fangs and her irritation at being spoken to like a child. But when Tiberius holds the water to her, the thin wolf drinks.

I pace back and forth, helpless. Shaking the sticky liquid that smells like beaver castor from my paws. Talk about useless. All these human supplements are poison to a wolf. Usually, Silver's mate would hunt for her, but Tiberius is pathetic at hunting anything except humans…

With a quick bow of my head, I rub my muzzle against Silver's thin head, marking her, making her my responsibility, and sprint away.

The Pack does not have doors with knobs. The Pack has doors with levers so no matter what form we find ourselves in, we will not be trapped inside.

Outside, the Pack has dispersed. They're all out running or hunting except for two wolves that Evie has set to guard the Boathouse. They ignore me. Clearly, their concern is the human with the gun.

The overcast sky has opened up, and the retreating edge of the clouds is silvered by moonlight as it draws back like a curtain from a screen of a million stars.

It's like what will happen in the Homelands soon. The snow and ice will retreat like a curtain from a screen of trillium and spring beauty and leatherwood and bloodroot and vireos and warblers and kinglets and goldeneyes and grebes.

Peepers.

None of it is exotic or rare, but it is as much a part of me as my blood and bone. There is a reason that exiles always end up dead in a puddle of blood or vomit, or both.

Because this is my home, I know that the best place to look for deer after the rain is the hemlock grove overshadowed by huge white pines. The soil is acid, so nothing much grows up from the thick carpet of needles. It is less chaotic here and more peaceful, and deer huddle here for protection when the rain is fierce and the hardwoods are bare. Or when they are old and sick and done. An old bull bedded down during the storm is still struggling to get up when I come upon him. It is a good death, and he does not suffer.

Two juvenile wolves come almost immediately when I announce a fresh kill but stand back respectfully, waiting for me to carve out the big, nutritious liver. As soon as I go, they snarl and fight and gorge.

I can't see Thea when I return to the Boathouse—the chair is turned with its back toward the dock and the french doors. Silver is lying where I left her, her eyes closed, three pups trembling at her belly. Tiberius has his face buried in his big hands. Having three survive is miracle enough, but I feel a deep sadness for the death of that little black dot everyone was trying so hard to save.

Then the Shifter moves his head side to side, and a skinny little tail pops up like a flag above his hands. The dot isn't dead. He's just tiny and blends into his father's cropped black beard. Once Tiberius has finished marking him, he nestles the dot next to his littermates at Silver's abdomen.

As soon as I open the door, the chair turns around. Thea is dwarfed in this high-backed seat meant to accommodate a Pack doctor. Her mouth is open like she was going to say something, but whatever it is freezes on her lips. She looks away from me and my muzzle filled with dripping-fresh organ meat.

The deer liver drops to the floor with a squelchy plop. I don't try to disguise it, because nothing I do now is going to make me seem like feasible boyfriend material.

Silver's nose twitches and her eyes flutter open. Then Tiberius pushes it closer and she lunges at it, beyond caring that the pups are complaining.

"Elijah?"

I stop without facing her so she will know I hear her, but she won't have to look at the bloody gobs on my fur.

"I am trying," she says.

Chapter 36

And I leave.

At the spruce flats, I run for the bull carcass, in case there's still a little meat on it, though wolves eat everything and quickly, so I don't hold out much hope.

A coyote call nearby means that there's another kill with some meat on it. More coyotes gather, going silent as I pass them in the woods.

Near a tiny stream that is only just forming from winter melt, a sable wolf with a dark saddle limps along, looking for where the little trickle of water may have pooled enough for a drink.

Min schildere. Lada mec.

My shielder. Forgive me.

Celia's hackles are up, an instinct so she'll look like she's not weak, though the smell of blood advertises her coming death on the wind. Coyotes are opportunistic: they scavenge what's left of our kills and will pick off an unprotected pup, but there is a reason we call them *wulfbyrgenna*. Wolf tombs.

Celia licks at the blood dripping from her nose. We are strong, and most other times of the month, Tristan could have saved her. But an injury this bad, so close to the Iron Moon, is almost always fatal. Because when the change comes, her wound will be pulled and stretched and reopened and torn. And even if there was someone who could stitch her back up, it would all come unraveled again at the end, when she takes on skin.

Still, if there's nothing I can do to keep Celia alive, she will not die alone, ripped apart by carrion eaters. I snap at them, and the coyotes back away, settling in a circle just out of reach.

There is the occasional tussle and bark, letting us know that they are still here, but mostly they are patient. I mark Celia again, then lick the wound that will not heal.

When we were little, we slept piled one on top of one another, a belching, yawning, tumbling, complaining hillock of fur. Despite all the belching, yawning, and tumbling and complaining, there was a contentment that we'll never know again. I curl my body around hers, trying to pull her back to that hillock, trying to give her as much of that warmth and contentment as a dying wolf can have.

Her lungs are filling with blood. She coughs, but she can't clear them. Her breathing changes, and she begins to pant in short uneven gasps. Celia turns to me, her eyes pleading, then she lifts her chin toward the stars, revealing the long, vulnerable column of her throat, asking me for this final service as her shielder.

Asking me for a better death than slowly drowning in her own blood.

I am an Alpha and her shielder, and I don't hesitate to put my jaws on either side of her throat. It's what we do when we can't speak, and it means *trust me*. It means *I see you at your most vulnerable*.

With one powerful bite, I tear through her neck. She fights, just because we are wolves and we fight to the last, but her claws barely scrape across my hide. Then she coughs and gags and shivers and stops. I hold on tight, until I am sure that the last pulse of her blood and the last beat of her heart are over.

Even then, I can't leave her. Instinct pulls me to clean her fur and debride her and care for her even though her body is already cooling.

When I am done, I tell the Pack what we have lost. My howl starts low, then floats up, cracking at the middle before falling away in a muddled moan. Almost immediately, wolves respond, mourning with me the loss of one of us. The lessening of the wild in a world that already has so little of it.

I bolt, running as hard as I can, trying to get away before the inevitable. But the coyotes were close, and they call to one another immediately. I am not far enough away before they fall on her body, snarling.

At an edge of Home Pond, I hit the dark water that has been freed by the trickling streams heading down from the High Pines. The eroded edges break away as I let myself sink until the stiff bristles of deer blood and wolf blood dissolve from my fur.

In the dark and cold, with my lungs starting to burn, the water closes over me like everything I have lost: Celia and Thea and John and Nils and the Great North, because the best I can hope for is exile. I sink down, down, down until the cold outside and the burning inside meet and I feel nothing.

The moon shines through the black waters, and just like that last time at Thea's mountain, the moon speaks to me with Gran Sigeburg's impatient voice. *What are you doing down there? Waiting for death like a human? Pffft*, she barks dismissively. *Wolves don't die like that.*

Wolves die hunting.

My legs churn frantically, pushing up through the slush just before my final breath gives out. Torquing my body this way and that, I shake off spray after spray of dark water and gray ice. Every few yards, I do it again so that by the time I get back to the Boathouse, my coat is cold but mostly dry.

I ignore the two new guards and lie down by the front door. Silver is sleeping. The pups are too, even the tiny black dot.

Except for a dark stain near sleeping Silver, there is no trace of the deer liver.

The Boathouse is not winterized, and enough sound leaks out. Thea is still sitting in that big chair once occupied by Alex, but now she is talking to Tiberius.

The Shifter doesn't know a lot, but what he knows, he has learned from Silver, who was always Gran Sigeburg's favorite, long after she was no longer Deemer.

Victor has been Deemer for maybe twenty years, and all the younger echelons have learned the law from him. I learned from Gran Sigeburg, who taught law but always in the context of our legends. For Victor, those legends are pointless fiction, but for Sigeburg, those stories were what gave flesh to the bones of our law.

"You cannot understand the law," she said, "unless you enter the minds that created it. Stories are the keys that give you entrance."

So Tiberius tells Thea stories. He tells her how millennia ago, humans accepted our miraculous transformation in the way that they accepted that a caterpillar could turn into a butterfly or a tadpole could turn into a frog or an egg could turn into a bird.

It worked well enough, until humans decided they

needed a god with a plan, and that god and that plan required them to codify their thinking, to divide the world into good and not good. Things that served them were good. Even things that were innocuous—birds and butterflies and frogs—were acceptable components of this benevolent god's plan.

But things that did not serve them—anything wild or inedible—were not. Our transformation was the worst of both, and they could not imagine a god who would allow a man to turn into something as untamed as a wolf. *Monstrum*, Gran Sigeburg said, originally meant a disruption in the natural order, a sign of divine displeasure.

Something that did not fit the plan. Something wild. Something evil.

That's when we became monsters, moving from the heath to the forests, hiding in the shadows.

The emaciated runt sighs under the weight of Tiberius's hand.

"I look forward to meeting Silver," Thea says. "You know, when she's...herself again."

Tiberius blinks twice and rubs the bridge of his nose.

"She is herself *now*. Don't make the mistake of thinking this is something they have to go through to become human again. This is who Silver is. *This* is her truest form.

"*That*"—he points through the french doors directly at me—"is who Elijah really is."

He yawns. "There's food in the refrigerator. The bathroom is through that door. You'll be safe here. No wolf would ever disrupt a lying-in. Now, I'm going to change for bed."

Then Tiberius pulls off his long-sleeved T-shirt and, in one move, slides off his sweats and boxers.

Thea turns her head, her eyes searching every whorl of the wood-paneled wall rather than look at the huge, scarred, and very naked man lying on the floor.

I don't think she completely grasped what he meant by "change for bed."

Arching his back, Tiberius triggers his shift. Thea's eyes stay glued to the wall, her fingers touching the rough texture of the planking. At least in the beginning. But as the lengthy process continues with its stretchings and grindings and twangings, she shoots the occasional glance his way: How much longer is he going to be? Her finger taps slowly on the arm of the chair, and she cocks her head to the side as if deciding something. Finally, she swivels around, coming to a stop facing Tiberius writhing on the floor, his eyes moving around in his face, his ears changing and migrating to the top of his skull, his mouth widening until his fangs are surrounded by the frilled lips.

His hips and shoulders constrict, his chest deepens, his feet and shins narrow—and this is all before the fur comes.

When he is done, the huge, black wolf circles around and around until he lies down, curled like a closing parenthesis in front of his mate and the four pups.

Thea sits staring at the floor, her elbows on her knees. Then, with a sigh, she pushes herself up, reaching for her coat. As soon as she opens the big glass doors, one of the guard wolves growls. I snap at the wolf over my shoulder, and she barks back but doesn't come any closer.

"Elijah?" Thea asks, peering toward the three of us standing at attention on the dock. It's not her fault, I tell myself. It's not her fault that she can't distinguish the wolf who loves her, who would do anything to feel the still surety at her core, from two utterly random females who just happen to be on rotation.

I follow her to one of the Adirondack chairs at the end of the dock. Holding her sleeve down over her hand, she sweeps away the sludgy remains of snow and rain and folds herself up, her thighs against her chest, her arms around her shins and her cheek on her knees. She stares over Home Pond. The moon picks out the shards of snow floating across like clouds along the water.

"It's been," she says, holding herself close, "a long day."

My only response is a chuffed breath into the cool night. Then I sink to the weathered wood, my head on my paws.

~

Over the next two days, I hunt for Silver, Thea uses the skills she learned at "the clinic," and Tiberius tries to help her understand what we are and what we aren't.

But he doesn't tell her the only thing I need him to. He doesn't tell her to run. He doesn't tell her to move quietly and downwind, and when the Pack discovers her, as it will, she needs to start firing. It's a long shot and many wolves will die, but a *westend* does not simply walk out of the Homelands.

Thea watches Tiberius caress Silver's thin body through the closed window. "I just can't do it. I can't pet you or scratch behind your ears," she says to me, returning to her seat at the end of the dock.

After a winter of standing up to the burden of snow, the branch from a long-drowned spruce cracks and falls into the water.

"You were," she says, pulling her braid up so that it touches her lower lip, "my lover."

From the opposite shore comes the beating of wings, and geese—a mated pair—land on Home Pond. It takes a long time for me to breathe again.

Chapter 37

THE LAST NIGHT OF THE IRON MOON, I REPEATEDLY SCAN the still-dark sky. But try as I might, I can't get back into skin. I stretch out my paws, roll my shoulders, arch my back, bend deep into my haunches. Pushing my body to light the spark that will start the change, but the Iron Moon is done with us when she's done with us and not a minute before.

The storm and the slowly thawing earth have given rise to a dense mist. It would give us cover from humans who rely so heavily on their eyes, but not from wolves.

After one large twang, the world goes silent and blank, and my skin begins to prickle. My bones feel like rubber, and my organs torque inside my body.

The larger the wolf, the longer the change takes to complete; I've always been one of the last to finish. My feet haven't fully formed yet when I jump up, crushing the little pine table beneath me. Quicksilver, who is small and already fully in skin, says something that I can't make out.

In a curdled voice that is half howl, half human, I call for Thea to come. She is barely awake, her hair knotted around her like a dark halo. I throw her coat around her shoulders and grab her hand, pulling her toward the woods at a run.

A fine dusting of fur falls from my skin.

Thea tries to pull away. I stretch my jaw, desperately

popping my ears, trying to hear what she's saying. *What are you saying, Thea?* She holds back, her wet, filthy socks skidding on the ground. Shoes, I forgot shoes. Doesn't matter. We can't stop. We don't have time.

Please, Thea, Please.

Run.

The Pack gathers in front of the Great Hall, and with each passing moment, another huge dirt-spattered body crashes from the forest.

The pups skitter around, leaping up, their feet on the legs of nearby adults, looking for the reassurance that even though we look so alien, we belong with them and love them still.

Thea hisses my name. *Elijah?* I put my hand to her mouth, scenting the currents. We need to go to the forest to the north and east of the Great Hall. Staying deep in the woods, we will trace a broad circle downwind before finally racing for the car.

The rains have saturated the ground above the frozen subsoil, and everything has turned to gray snow and mud, but under the evergreens, I pray the cushioning layer of pine needles will muffle our steps.

I should have known we didn't have a chance. Not with the whole Pack here. Not with every single wolf of the Great North descending from last-minute runs higher up. Not with the sinewy wolf with the auburn hair, the best tracker in the 9th Echelon, standing in front of us.

"No, Sarah, please—"

She calls out for Evie.

Everywhere I look, there are wolves. Wolves I've hunted with. Wolves I've fed. Wolves I've covered. Wolves I've fought. For the first time, I feel the hopelessness of the deer who knows what it is when we emerge from the trees.

I pull Thea tight against my chest as more and more feral giants emerge from the fog-covered forest. Hair bristling, skin covered with mud, many still stained with the blood of their final hunt, they do look like monsters. I murmur comforting nonsense to her. *It's going to be all right*. Loving me wasn't a fatal mistake.

Though, of course, it was.

The Pack makes way for the dark silhouette emerging from just past the birches. Evie shakes once, not from the cold, but because her change is only just finished and she is trying to rid her body of the last remnants of black fur coating her steel-muscled body.

She doesn't hesitate. No doubt she's been seething over this for the three days when she had no words and no thumbs. She strides up to us, then bending down, she plucks at the braid around Thea's neck and sniffs several times in quick succession before letting the scent roll around in her nose.

Thea draws back, and the hard thing in her pocket swings loose, hitting my thigh.

"What were you thinking when you did this? When you braided the gift of our land with your blood and your seed?" She stands back up. "Did you think it meant something? Did you think this made her your mate?"

Evie's fingers go to the braid at her own throat. Every strand is even, and the braid is as neat and perfect as decades of experience can make it.

"The braid, *this braid*, is sacred to us. And you cannot bind this pack and this land with this human, *þes west-end*." She spits out the word and her disgust. Her hand slides once more along the braid that reminds her every day of her mate and her loss. "It was not your *right*, Elijah. What you have done is to make a decoration. It is meaningless."

Victor snorts derisively and pulls his seax from its sheath. I slide my hand toward the heavy thing in Thea's pocket.

"*But it is not meaningless to me.*"

And the second I pull the gun out, an explosion rips through the air. Shards of wood fly from a tree.

I hadn't *meant* to fire her gun, just wave it around, buy us some time. Let my tired lawyer brain think of a way out. But like so many human things, it takes such a little pressure to ruin everything. I stare down at my tingling hand as shocked by the steel object in my grasp as the Pack is.

Thea's fingers slide over my hand, loosening my hold. Numb and dumb, I let her take it. She'll know what to do with it. How to cock it or aim it or make it kill. But she doesn't aim it or cock it or make it kill. Instead, she ejects the magazine.

"*Thea!*"

With one smooth movement, she turns the gun to the side, pulling the slide. A single bullet falls to the ground.

She looks down the barrel before slipping the gun back into her pocket. "Who would you have shot?" she asks me, pointing to Sarah. "Her?" She indicates a wolf from the 11th. "Him?"

A curious pup bolts from between the legs of the adults, intrigued by the tart-smelling metal thing in the dirt. Thea scoops him up, holding him to her neck. "This one?"

The Pack moves as one toward her, Evie with her hands out, pleading for her to be careful with our child.

"That is not who you are," she says. "And it's not who I am either." She rubs her cheek against the pup's muzzle, then hands the cringing, whining bundle of gray fur back to his furious Alpha.

A slow disturbance starts at the far edge of the Pack. In a wave, the enormous bodies move to the side, clearing a path. All I can see is Tiberius, but I know his mate is the one pushing her Packmates out of the way.

Silver is at the rock bottom of the hierarchy, but she knows better than most that the Pack does not coddle weakness, and she shows none as she walks toward us, her back straight and her chin high.

If possible, she looks even worse in skin than she did wild. Her fur at least gave her some bulk, but without it, her pale skin clings tight to her cheekbones, and her gray-green eyes seem almost ghoulish in her gaunt face. She is wearing the kind of long, loose dress our females prefer in the last weeks of pregnancy, though it hangs from the distended joints of her shoulders like a shroud.

Tiberius follows her, a worried look on his face and a sturdy basket, the kind we keep kindling in, on his arm.

"You should be resting, Silver," Evie says as the runt stops in front of the amassed pack.

"I won't stay long." She looks at the seax in Victor's hand. "But before you kill Elijah's human, Deemer, I wanted to raise a point of law."

Victor's sour face turns immediately hostile. There is something about the runt that Victor does not like, and it's not just her choice of mate. Tiberius makes a hard warning sound in the back of his throat, and Victor takes a half step back.

"What is the Fifth Law?"

Victor did not join the rest of the Pack until he was fully cleaned and dressed and armed. He's got no little bits of prickly juniper in his hair or raccoon between his teeth. Always jealous of the dignity of his station, he is clean and well dressed.

"That's ridiculous." He turns to Evie. "Everyone knows the answer. Why should I—?"

"Because she has asked a question, Deemer, and we do not fear questions."

He sucks on his teeth before saying that "the only compensation for a death is a death."

"That's the interpretation, but what does it actually say? *In agenspræc, Dema.*"

In our own language, Deemer.

"Alpha, I object—"

"Answer it," Evie snaps.

"*Eoldor angylde eoldor,*" he says, spitting each word.

"Exactly," Silver says. "A life equals a life." Now she turns, her hand out, and Tiberius moves forward, the basket toward her, his other hand ready at her back where she cannot see it or feel it or force it away. Unfolding two blankets, Silver gently scoops up the tiny black dot, whose fur has dried, making him look slightly less tiny than before. The pup is blind, its ears still folded close, and when he yawns, his mouth is pink and toothless. "This is Theo Tiberiusson. Maybe I would have survived this moon without the human's help. Maybe not. So I do not ask for my own life. But Theo was already dead."

Silver rubs her cheek against the pup's little head. Smelling Silver's scent, he turns to her, hungry again as our nurslings always are.

"Now he's not. He is alive and greedy." Her voice is already fading. Tiberius moves behind her, his massive chest nearly touching. "Our law is clear: *Eoldor angylde eoldor*. A life equals a life."

"*That is not what it means!*" Victor shouts. "The Fifth is meant to punish, not reward."

Silver stumbles. Evie grabs the pup with one hand and the basket with the other. When Tiberius lifts his mate, the soles of her feet and the hem of her dress are dark with blood.

"Tiberius," Evie says, "take Silver to medical. Tristan, go with them." Evie rubs the tiny pup with her cheek, adding her own mark to this new addition, before settling him back among his littermates. "And, Adrian, find the human some shoes."

"Stay, Adrian," Victor barks without bothering to face the nervous juvenile. "You aren't actually taking the runt's argument seriously?" he asks Evie.

Victor is playing a dangerous game. He is questioning Evie, forcing her to make a decision: either back Silver's argument, or appear indecisive in front of the Pack and risk it dissolving into chaos.

Evie strides in front of Victor, her lean, hard body so close that her last loose guard hairs shed onto his clothes. "I take the law seriously, Deemer. I take that *life* seriously. *Deemer*."

Victor backs off just enough to cross his arms above his belly. A handful of wolves who had been arrayed behind him move closer. Others vacillate at the edges.

"It is your *duty* to preserve the Old Ways. And this... this is *not* of the Old Ways."

"No, it is *your* duty to preserve the Old Ways. *Mine* is to preserve the Pack. When Ælfrida left her land, when she took in the wolves of Wessex, she was not keeping with the *Old Ways*. If she had kept with the Old Ways, Pack Mercia would have remained in Mercia and would have died there."

"But it was the *wolves* of Wessex. You can't compare what she did with this. With letting a human live. *Sum westend þe wat*."

A human who knows.

"Look what happened when your mate deviated from our traditions," Victor continues. "Because he allowed the Shifter to join the Pack, we almost lost everything. *Everything*."

Ignoring the unsheathed dagger in his hand, Evie moves toward Victor, her black eyes close to his and very hard. "Careful, Deemer. Fretting over what might have been is a very human thing to do." Her hair blows around her in a halo of tight, black curls specked with dried grasses and burrs. "I can't know what would have happened, and neither can you. The Shifters had already found us. One of our own made sure of that.

"If it is your job to uphold our laws without question, my job—the harder job—is to question them. Adrian," she says, turning to the young wolf, "shoes."

This time, Adrian does not waver. He has been raised to obey both Alpha and Deemer, but he knows where his primary obedience lies. Evie watches the skinny juvenile as he runs off.

In that second, while Evie's attention is distracted, Victor whips around.

My senses in skin aren't strong enough, and I hear him too late. I see him too late. I smell him too late. I twist my back toward him.

Too late.

Thea falters in my arms. Her back arches, and her mouth opens with a soft cry that smells like copper. Something warm runs down my arm.

Then Victor raises his hand, showing the Pack his seax covered with Thea's blood as though he has battled a worthy opponent and won their submission. *As though he hadn't just ambushed my unarmed mate.*

My breath stops, and when it starts again with a huge rush of air and power, the fury of my wild pumps through me with a deafening howl. A howl filled with all the anger and despair over the daily corruptions and the constant soul poisoning that I have put up with for decades in order to preserve this land and this pack. To keep you *you* YOU alive and safe and—

"Let him go, Elijah."

Victor is suspended in midair, his eyes bulging, his hands clawing, his face turning purple.

"Your Alpha would not have you kill him," Evie whispers in my ear. "Not yet, at any rate."

When that ancient duty of obedience looses my fingers, the Deemer collapses to the ground like a sack of lentils. Several wolves break away from the Pack and kneel beside him.

I don't care if he's alive or dead. *Tristan*, I whisper, my throat unaccountably sore. I plead with the Alpha. *I need Tristan.*

Evie squats down beside me. "Gabi is coming," she says. "It's better." Her hand is on my arm. "Tristan doesn't know how they work."

My shielder is dead. I am a pariah to the Great North. And Thea, my lodestone, my axis, is bleeding in my arms. I hold her tighter, rocking slowly, whispering into her hair. Pleading with her not to die. *Please*. I've lost any delusions that we could be together, but I need to know that somewhere she just...*is*.

Please, Thea.

Evie leans forward, her knees in the cold muck, and lifts my chin. She holds my eyes to make sure that I am at least this focused. So that I understand what she's doing when she rubs her cheek slowly and deliberately against mine. First the right, then the left.

Don't worry, she says in our wordless way. *You are not lost. You have a place*.

And then she does the unthinkable.

She marks Thea. She rubs her scent on Thea's pale-gold skin, extending her protection, her grace, to the woman I love.

When she stands, Victor's bloody seax in her hand, she stares at her wolves, daring them to question her judgment. Daring each of the strongest ones to return her gaze. Having made her decision, she is ready to fight for it.

And one by one, they lower their eyes.

Chapter 38

"Elijah, move your arm," a voice says. "I need to listen." Gabi kneels beside me, still naked and covered with bits of fur, but carrying her med kit. She puts the cold metal bell of her stethoscope to Thea's chest—first here, then there—while I watch anxiously, murmuring promises about a future I don't believe in.

"Not a flesh wound," she says, her stethoscope around her neck, "but not fatal either. Let's get her to medical."

"Gabi, you take her. I need to talk to Elijah," Evie says. She hesitates a moment, then calls to Varya Timursdottir. "Shielder, make sure no one tries to hurt the human."

"Yes, Alpha."

I hold the woman I love tighter. "Not her. She's already threatened to kill Thea."

Evie scratches her eyebrow. "And, just to be clear, do not harm her yourself."

"Yes, Alpha," Varya says, lowering her head in submission.

"If you're going to be at the Homelands," Evie says once she is sure we are out of earshot, "you need to relearn the subtleties of the Pack. It is true that Varya hates humans, though I've never seen any sign that she much likes wolves either. But what she really hates is chaos. Disorder. If she says something will happen, it will happen. I trust her." She steps over the tiny gully that serves as a course for the stream that runs past the Alpha's cabin when the ice thaws.

"So I'm not… I'm not exiled?"

"The Pack is vulnerable. There are too many stresses both inside and out. I need strong Alphas to help keep it together. And with Celia dead, I need you to come home."

This is it. It is all I've wanted for so long, but now… Evie holds the storm door open for me.

"And Thea?"

The Alpha's cabin is exactly the same as all the other cabins, except that it is more centrally located and close to the Great Hall. It is crowded with a desk and shelves of documents. The pink bag that I gave Tiberius for the trust hangs over the window latch. Soon, all this will be moved into Evie's new office.

"I took a risk letting your human live. Watch out." She points to a long mattress in the center of the main room that seems like an unnecessary complication in such a cramped space. "I did it because she understood the nature of sacrifice. I need to make sure you do too."

Evie opens a narrow closet under the stairs that lead up to the sleeping loft. "More than strength, sacrifice is what makes an Alpha. Pants," she says, thrusting a pair of extra-large and tall sweatpants at me. They have been washed and do not smell so much like John. I doubt she could have done it if they did. I know I couldn't.

"The greatest Alphas have the same qualities as Ælfrida," she continues, pulling up her own jeans. "The willingness to sacrifice and the ability to make hard decisions. If your human—"

"Her name is Thea Villalobos."

I catch sight of her eyebrows shooting up as she pulls on a pale-gray muscle shirt.

"I am not a believer in any fate I do not make myself, but that is a coincidence. Still, if we have any indication that your Thea Villalobos has betrayed us or simply been indiscreet, then I need to know that *you* can make the hard decision and that *you* will make the sacrifice."

I know what she is asking. She's asking where my loyalties lie. The risk she is taking is not just for herself but for the whole pack. And she needs to know that if there is any doubt about Thea, any doubt at all, I will protect the Great North and rip Thea's throat out.

"If I am wrong, I will do what needs to be done."

Evie nods and heads into the bathroom, coming back with a wide-toothed comb.

"Alpha, there's something you need to know."

While Evie slowly combs through her tight, black curls, removing all the forest duff, I tell her what I learned from Daniel Leary in the minutes before I killed him. That Tiberius was the last live birth. That Shifters are dying out. That Tiberius and Silver's young represent possibility. And that August Leveraux doesn't believe it is a coincidence that the only live Shifter births of recent decades have had Pack mothers.

I didn't know that Celia had already been taken. I doubt Daniel Leary did either, because at the end, he would have told me anything.

Thankfully, Evie doesn't ask how I know any of this.

Her eyes close for a second longer than a blink but not long enough to show hesitation or fear. When she is done combing her hair, she unzips a waxed suit bag. There's no suit inside, just an old, worn flannel shirt that does smell like John. He must have worn it before that last moon, and Evie kept it. She pulls it over her muscle shirt, buttons it up, then stretches her arm high, rubbing her head against the sleeve. There is no one above Evie in the hierarchy, no one to mark her and reassure her when things are falling apart. But that doesn't mean that the instinct for that reassurance disappears. Only that its source has.

There is a slight *scritching* from the sleeping loft above. When I look up, two furry, yawning faces, their noses twitching excitedly, stare back at me from between the railings. Then, with a pop, they disappear again. There is more *scritching* in the loft. "Stand back," Evie says, then she takes a hair tie from her wrist and tames her hair.

Two little brindle bodies come flying from the sleeping loft. They tumble and twist onto the soft mattress before righting themselves and trotting happily over to their mother. Evie lifts one in each hand, marking both of them.

The two pups look up at me expectantly. I smell like their mother. I smell like Pack. For them, I smell like love and home. As soon as I mark them, though, they are done with me and squirm toward freedom.

"The Pack has assembled in the Great Hall," Tara says as soon as we leave Evie's cabin. "I'm sorry to tell you that the human will live, Alpha. Even more disappointing, the Deemer will too."

Evie's mouth quirks with a little smile, but her eyes are solemn. "Tara, I am calling the Pack home."

"*Who?*"

"The Pack. Keep up."

Tara lopes beside her Alpha.

"*All of them?*"

Evie nods and runs up the stairs of the Great Hall. Tara follows behind, her engineer's mind swirling with the endless complications of accommodating full time the appetites and tempers of four hundred wolves, twice the usual number.

I remember my own Year of First Shoes, the time when we start to learn how to function in skin.

We never are before that. In skin. Why would we be? Our bodies are stronger and more agile, our senses more acute, our connections more intense.

But to stay as wolves forever is an invitation to slaughter.

The Year of First Shoes is when we start to wear clothes and use words and hold forks. In skin, the world seems muffled and our bodies alien. It is a horrible, horrible time.

It is also when we begin taking on responsibility, and in the afternoon, our echelon, like every echelon before us, would gather around in the big kitchen. It started with us standing awkwardly in clothes that had been passed from one generation to the next. Inside out, back to front with stretched-out necks and frayed hems and holes the size of cabbage roses, they were stained by years of careless beginning eaters. But they were nonetheless clean and as comfortable as clothing could be to a pup who didn't want to be wearing anything at all.

We would be lined up at the huge trough sink with three faucets and told to wash our hands. Get rid of the bits of prey and one another lodged under our nails. The dirt and blood and butter that inevitably extended halfway up our arms.

Once we'd been washed and dried and inspected, we gathered around a huge, old table of pale wood that had been bleached and scrubbed and dotted with burn marks from pots straight from the stove. Then we were each given a ball of dough to fight and tussle with and to mold and hit and beat, and while we did it, one of the wolves who taught us would read to us.

We called it Knead and Read. And while I know that I hated each component individually—clothes, washing, working, being in skin—melded together and through the lens of memory, it was glorious.

It is hard to finally come home, just when everything has changed.

Even the back door that leads straight into the kitchen is different. It is bigger now, taller and broader and designed to accommodate not the humans who originally built the great camp a hundred years ago, but the wolves who live here now.

Inside is different too. It had been dark—dark wood cabinets, dark tongue-and-groove paneling on every wall and even on the ceiling. Now it is much larger, big enough for two echelons. The ceilings are higher so that a full-grown wolf can stand without feeling oppressed. The walls are white, though there is still dark tongue-and-groove waist-level wainscoting, because white walls and pups do *not* mix. The claw-scratched wine-and-beige-checkered linoleum has been replaced by sturdier tile. The trough sink is new and industrial-strength, the warped wood around it replaced by white tile.

The windows are big and bright and crisscrossed with a dozen shelves holding seedlings.

All the adults are in the main room listening to Evie

explain how we will squeeze muzzle by jowl into the Homelands. And why.

But it is not something she wanted our children to worry about, so the juveniles are here washing dishes, while pups scurry underfoot, being picked up and fed choice bits of leftovers.

And the Year of First Shoes sits around a huge, scraped wooden table banging at dough while Gran Moira reads Harry Potter. They hate Fenrir Greyback, Voldemort's villainous werewolf, just as much as any child does, failing to recognize that *this* is what humans think we are. *This* is why we have to be so secretive. For now, they no more recognize themselves in fictional werewolves than they do in talking spiders or car-crazed toads.

A pup whines at my leg, worried about the secrecy. I lift her to my cheek and mark her. As I set her carefully on the floor, a juvenile at the sink looks nervously over his shoulder. He is at that awkward age when he is young enough to feel anxiety, too old to ask for reassurance, and not old enough to know that reassurance is his right and an Alpha's responsibility.

I mark him without being asked and then, one by one, with a gentle bend of their heads, the juveniles raise the lower lines of their jaws. I mark each and every one of our worried children. For the first time, I truly understand what it means to be Alpha. It means interposing every ounce of my power and strength between our enemies and the pack. To carve a home for them out of the granite of a hostile world.

A phone dings, and the juveniles move quickly to the ovens. Huge trays of orange and cranberry muffins are dumped on cooling trays. I take one that has fallen to pieces on the counter, squeezing the crumbs into a ball before, *pipipop*, it disappears into my mouth.

Then I head quickly across the hall so that I don't distract the Pack listening to Evie and open the door into the medical station.

Tiberius puts his finger to his lips, as though I didn't see that both Silver and Thea were asleep the second I came in. He is reading, with his legs propped up on the foot of the bed, like someone who knows the drill. Someone who knows that constantly replaying the decisions that landed the one you love in the medical station leads nowhere.

But he doesn't have the same problem I do. When Silver wakes up, she will love him. When Thea wakes up, who knows? The only thing I do know is that we will have a discussion consisting of three topics, none of which I want to touch:

(A) I am a monster, and not just in a metaphorical sense.

(B) My particular monstrosity doesn't come with the romantic nihilism of, say, vampires. It comes with the much-less-acceptable suggestion of bestiality.

You were my lover.

(C) And most monstrous of all is the fact that if she should tell anyone anything about us, I will have to hunt her down and eviscerate her.

I'm not sure I have the strength for any part of this conversation, but when I look down at her, her arm thrown back over her head, gold and black against the white pillowcase still stiff from the cold, dry air… When I see her chin tilted slightly up, her long neck exposed, I am not at all sure I could do it.

Before she wakes up and remembers what my mouth

looked like yesterday and we start in on the whole conversation about part B, I bend over to kiss her, catching an unfamiliar wolfish scent from under the blanket. It trembles a little and burps a tiny burst of warm wolf milk. Theo licks his muzzle and stretches out contentedly between the breasts of his soft human godmother.

That's when I know beyond a shadow of a doubt that I could never do it—and even more certainly that I will never have to.

Her braid is on the bedside table. I crumple it in my hand.

Sitting on the hard chair, I lean forward, burying my face into the blankets near her hip. I hold my fist clutching her braid close to my heart.

Please, Thea.

Forgive me for being a monster.

I wake up to a plaintive mewling and Tiberius's arm stretched across my head as he tries to retrieve his son. Theo's tiny paws are tangled in Thea's hair. Thea shushes Tiberius while trying to disengage the pup's claws.

In order to avoid conversation parts A, B, and C, I pretend to be asleep. Through my slitted lids, I watch the little furball wobble around the vast plain of his father's palm, complaining. Tiberius lifts him high, giving him big openmouthed kisses to his ear. Theo's tail wags, and his wobbly legs collapse.

"Elijah," Tiberius says, his hand at the door. Would it have killed him to let me pretend to be asleep? To ignore the change in my heartbeat or the sudden overwhelming stench of my fear?

"Do you want the door open or closed?"

"Closed," we both say.

Then we say nothing.

And yes, it is awkward.

Without looking at Thea, I pluck at the blankets, pulling them up to her shoulders, as though covering her now makes up for all the other ways I failed her.

"So I guess we have to talk."

"I'm so sorry, Thea. About everything. About lying to you most of all."

She shrugs. "Why? Belonging to a pack of werewolves—" I take a big breath, but she taps my arm. "I know, not werewolves, but still belonging to a pack of Pack is hardly your secret to share. Can you help me up? I feel weird lying down like this. I think there's a button on the floor." She points to the opposite side of the bed.

There is a button hanging not far from the rubber tubing that runs from her chest to a bag partly filled with bloody liquid.

"Shh, Elijah," she says, putting her finger to my lips. Then she touches my braid and feels for her own. "What happened to my necklace?" She flinches as she looks around.

"I've got it." I open up my fist. It had been so tightly clenched that the pattern of the braid is imprinted on my skin. The crumpled leather unfolds on my palm.

She holds her hair up with one hand. "I can't...I can't lift my other arm."

She is asking me to help her put my braid back on.

She isn't saying no.

But she's not ready to say yes. Not until she knows what she's saying yes to.

When I pull her hand away, her hair tumbles after,

falling across her shoulders. I cough, trying to clear a sudden tightness in my throat.

"This..." I say, stretching her braid across the bed-cover. "It isn't *just* a necklace any more than you are *just* a friend. I don't want you to wear it if that's all you think it is."

I pull my chair closer to the head of her bed, then take her hand, rubbing her palm with my thumb. "Evie was right. I was pretending before. I wanted you bound to me, so I pretended I could just do it. Ignoring what that meant for the Great North, and most of all, what it meant for you. But I'm done with pretending. I need for you to understand what it means."

"Tiberius had one," she says quietly. "He said all... Well, he said all mated wolves wore them."

"It's not just that. Here's what it means. It means tying yourself to a life of secrecy, because if you ever tell anyone anything about us, because—"

"I would never."

"We have a lot of enemies—humans, mostly, but there are others."

"Shifters."

I think maybe Tiberius was more forthcoming than I could have imagined.

"Exactly, but that's not all. It's a dangerous time. The... Evie..."

"The Alpha. *Your* Alpha."

"Yes, my Alpha. Has asked me to come back. But you can't live here, because the Pack... They don't trust anyone who isn't Pack. Especially not humans, and especially not humans who know what we are."

Sum westend þe wat.

A human who knows.

I hold one end of the braid, turning it around and around into a tight coil.

"I'm going to put this into your pocket."

I slip it into the pocket of her coat that doesn't hold her gun.

When I sit back down, Thea takes my hand. There are a few scrapes and a bite mark near the wrist. About what you'd expect from a meal of muskrat.

"Something I ate," I say. "It's what we are. What *I* am."

She keeps looking at my hand, at the masculine but not bestial smatterings of hair, at the undeniably bestial claw marks left by my dinner.

"Did you brush your teeth?"

"Yes."

"Flossed?"

"Yes."

"Good," she says, and she pulls me to her and tastes my hunter's mouth.

Epilogue

The Pack is home.

We've had over a week of rain. How much over a week, I don't remember, but enough to force prey to higher ground. Enough to make the earth churn under paws and feet into a slippery veneer of mud. Pack tempers are running high. Dominant wolves are constantly fighting dissent. Except for the ones who are fomenting it.

Now a wolf has killed a young, healthy moose, ripped out the best parts, and left the rest for rot and coyotes. I nose the earth around her remains, trying to distinguish the scent of the responsible cur from the random scavengers.

Something is riling the Pack *again*. Ælfrida founded a pack with just fifty wolves. In the 350 years since, we have added to our territory whenever possible, but there simply isn't space for four hundred wolves with too much time on their hands.

Nosing the carcass aside, I try to get underneath where hopefully the rain hasn't washed away the smell of this breaker of laws, this waster of life. Let the dominant wolves closer to the Great Hall deal with the ruckus down below.

Then finally, I get it. A tiny remnant of wolf scent. This is no small crime, and someone is going to pay for it.

Now the call has been taken up by the 9th. The other echelons fall silent as Sarah and Francesca and Adam and Lorin and Dani call for me. I howl back. Enough already, I'm coming. *I'm coming*.

Through an elaborate triangulation, my echelon guides me past mixed woods and spruce swamp and Home Pond and sugarhouse. In the distance, Melanie from the 13th is talking about taxes.

They called me from halfway up the mountain for this?

"No, actually, I'm a tax attorney. We have CPAs who…who do the actual taxes."

I can't see who she's talking to. *About taxes*. She scratches the back of her mud-covered calf with the big toe of the other foot. "Do you…do you have an accountant?" she asks conversationally.

"No, I use the 1040EZ."

I skitter to a stop. It's been six weeks since I heard that voice. Six weeks since I sent her away with a promise to think about what it meant to tie her future to me. To us. To be under attack from a hostile world outside and a prejudiced Pack at home.

To give up any dream that she might have children of her own.

Because this thing of ours… It's not like a marriage. You don't give it a whirl. Try it on for size. It's a fight to the death. That's what I told her. You just keep fighting, and then you die.

I start to run.

"That's good," Melanie is saying. "Though it'd be better if they upped the interest income rate, right?" She raises her nose and sniffs at the air. "He's coming. Well, it was nice to meet you, Thea." She pats her naked hips. "I'd give you my card, but…"

I break through the trees onto the path leading to the gate.

"Another day," Thea says. "When you have pockets."

Melanie twists quickly and jogs toward me. "The Alpha does not believe it is safe for her here…"

I didn't stop to listen, so I don't know what else she had to say.

"Elijah?"

It's not the Iron Moon, so the tall main gate isn't locked, just the low fence that keeps cars from driving up. Sliding through the mud, I race toward the granite boulder that really should be excavated but right now forms a ridge above the eroded dirt—and if you're strong and agile, you can get enough lift from it to clear the gates.

I land stumbling but upright in front of her, my nose to her shoulder and breathing her in. Why have you come? And how can you smell so good? Should I be afraid? I know I wanted you to take some time and really think. But six weeks…

Should I be afraid?

"I wanted to show you something," she says and walks away from the Homelands, downhill and across the access road. Then she starts a steep climb back up, holding on to trees as she drags herself up to the top of the ridge. We walk to the edge of our territory and then to the wolf markings that so clearly delineate the end of the Homelands and the fence and No Trespassing signs aimed at dissuading humans.

With one step, I am Offland again, for the first time in over six weeks.

We head a little farther and then parallel the border with our land. Straight ahead is the fire watchtower. I've never seen it from up here. Didn't know there was a cabin, though I suppose I could have guessed there'd be one.

The porch has been recently patched up. A handful of pale boards among the gray. Thea wipes her feet on a sisal mat before the door. I do too. First front paws, then back. The door isn't locked.

The door opens, and my soul aches as I sniff at each familiar object. The black-and-white chaise, the little table. The narrow shelf with a single cup, a single bowl, a single plate. The books that smell like the Plattsburgh Public Library.

"I offered to switch with the ECO for northern Franklin County," she says, hanging up her anorak. "He leapt at it. Too much nothing up here, he said. Told me I'd never find a man. I said that was fine with me. He said I'd never find a woman either."

She turns around, pulling slightly on her collar. She is wearing her braid.

"I left it at that."

Sitting on the foot of her chaise, she unties her boots, sliding one beside the cast-iron stove. I sniff at the various rust spots, then scrape dismissively with my hind leg.

"Yeah, I'm getting a replacement." She puts the second boot beside the first, then she looks at me. "So… do you maybe want to get changed?"

I nose the door that has a latch tucked into the handle, a space too narrow for anything except a goddamn thumb. That will have to be replaced. Looking along the length of my flanks, I ask Thea for help.

"I'm going to take a shower. Just do it here."

That was not really the answer I wanted. I wait until the bathroom door closes and then throw myself on the floor where the back of the chaise nearly touches the wooden table and stretch out my forepaws. Of course she can't luxuriate in the shower, and of course I am at that half-man, half-wolf, naked, freakish, gargoyle state when I feel her hand on my skin. I can't see, I can't hear, I can't smell, I can't move. But I can feel.

What I feel is a warm, slightly damp hand stroking my changing skin. What I feel is a woman who knows what she is, who knows what I am.

And who loves me anyway.

When my eyes finally are able to focus, they find Thea sitting on the cold floor, her cheek propped on her bended knees. She rubs something between her fingers.

"You're shedding," she says.

"It's... It gets worse in the spring." I cringe as my palm collects a loose coat of sable fur. "Molting."

"Makes sense. Do you want to take a shower? I put in a drain strainer."

With that, I know everything I need to. It's not the romantic declaration of a flightier woman. In her quiet, practical, knowing way, my fierce female has considered what it means to tie herself to me and said yes.

When I am done, Thea slides to the side of her bed, lifts the blankets.

And in the arms of Thea Villalobos, Goddess of the City of Wolves, I am home.

Take a look back at how it all began in

THE LAST WOLF

Book one in the Legend of All Wolves series by Maria Vale

Chapter 1

Upstate New York, 2018

WOLVES WHO DRINK SMELL LIKE BAILEYS AND KIBBLE.

It doesn't matter that Ronan's poison is a 7 and 7 and chimichangas at the casino over at Hogansburg, there's something about our livers that still makes him smell like Baileys and kibble.

He lies slumped partly on his stomach, partly on his side at the edge of the Clearing, the broad expanse of spongy grass and drowned trees that is what remains of an old beaver pond that fell into disrepair when the Pack ate the beavers one lean year. New beavers have established a new pond nearby. Eventually we will eat those too.

And so it goes.

The Clearing is used for ceremonies and rituals because it is open and accommodates larger numbers. Usually the Pack prefers the cool, muffled, fragrant darkness of the forest, treating the Clearing like an anxious Catholic treats the church. We shuffle in on major celebrations and otherwise give it a wide berth.

The *Dæling*, which I suppose translates most conveniently as "Dealing," is one of those celebrations. It marks the transition of our age group, our echelon, from juvenile to adult. Here, we are paired off, not as mates yet, but in practice couplings. We will also have our own Alpha who answers only to the Pack Alpha and is responsible for keeping our echelon in line. The whole hierarchy will be set up. Not that it's permanent or anything, more like the start times assigned before the lengthy competition that is Pack life.

Basically, the *Dæling* is one enormous squabble. There are challenges for the right to pair with a stronger wolf and challenges for a more elevated place in the hierarchy. Our whole youth has been taken up with tussling and posturing, but now it really counts. A wolf who is pinned to the ground in front of the Pack Alpha is the loser. Period. This sorting out of rankings and couples takes a long time, and the others watch it with endless fascination.

Me? Not so much. Born crippled and a runt, I've had to struggle long and hard for my position at the dead bottom of the hierarchy. I've never fought anyone, because there is no honor in making me submit, no rank to be won by beating the runt.

Ronan, on the other hand, is big and was once strong enough to be the presumptive Alpha. But he is, as they say, weak of marrow. With no determination or perseverance, he has become filled with fat and drink and resentful dreams of life as it is lived on Netflix. His nose is cold and wet when he's human and hot and dry when he's not.

"He's not much, our Ronan." That's what Gran Drava said to me. "But he's a male and..."

She gave me one more sniff before leaning back on the sofa in the Meeting House, where the 14th Echelon was gathered for her inspection. Her eyes and back are failing, but her sense of smell and her knowledge of Pack bloodlines are not. "And he isn't within the prohibited degrees of consanguinity."

So because he is weak of marrow and I am weak of body, we find ourselves together at the bottom of the 14th.

When the Pack Alpha eventually turns our way, I nudge Ronan, who doesn't stand until I bite him. Finally, he hobbles up, looking at me mournfully with his greasy eyes. Nobody much pays attention as we approach the Alpha. They're all too busy debriding each other's wounds and sniffing new companions' bodies.

John's paw hangs lazily over the edge of a granite outcropping shot through with mica that shimmers slightly in the moonlight. It seems like a nervous eternity, waiting for John's pro forma nod of approval.

It doesn't come. Instead, he pulls himself up, one leg at a time, until he reaches his full height. The paler fur of his belly shimmers as he shakes himself and jumps down to the damp sod.

His nose flares as he approaches us. Anxiously, I push myself closer to Ronan's flank. John presses his muzzle between us, shoving me away. He sniffs the air around Ronan and starts to slap at Ronan, each hit of his head getting harder until Ronan stumbles backward.

John bares his teeth, snarling.

Ronan blinks a few times as though he is just waking. He wavers unsteadily, trying to comprehend the simple gesture that was all it took to exile him from the protection of our law, our land, our Pack. The sentence that forces him into a life wandering from Pack to Pack searching for a place until he dies in a puddle of blood and/or vomit, like most exiles do.

I scuttle to John, my head and stomach scraping the grass, my tail tucked between my legs, submitting into the earth not because I care about Ronan, but because if he leaves, then I am a lone wolf. There's an old saying that lone wolves are the only ones who always breed, their children being Frustration and Dissent. That's why they are given over to their echelon's Alphas to be their servants, their *nidlings*. A *nidling* has nothing, is nothing. Even at the bottom rank, you're paired with someone who is just as shit a wolf as you are, so at least at home, you don't have to submit. But the *nidling*'s life is one of endless submission.

John snaps at me, then at Ronan. I roll on my back, my eyes averted, whimpering. But since he's made up his mind, no amount of groveling is going to make any difference. John wants Ronan gone. He stands erect, leaning over Ronan's now-shivering body, and a low growl emerges from deep in his chest. Any second now, he will attack.

Ronan backs away, shell-shocked. He stops for a moment, still looking hopefully at John, until the Alpha lunges forward. The exile trips over his own feet as he turns to go.

He doesn't even bother to look at me.

John stays alert, watching until Ronan lurches into the dark forest. He listens a moment more to be sure the exile is truly gone before he howls and signals an end to the *Dæling*. The newly reordered 14th finds their pairs and their places behind John. I'm all the way at the end, where I'm used to being, until our Alpha, Solveig, runs back and, with a growl, reminds me that I am to follow her and her companion, Eudemos, the pairing who now control my life. I take up my place behind them, my tail dragging between my legs.

Stopping suddenly with one paw raised, John focuses on a sharp bark in the night. It is a warning from a perimeter wolf. Probably signaling that a hunter has trespassed on our land. Wolves will be gathering around the interloper now, following the hunter at a silent distance. As there's nothing like an honor guard of seething wolves to scare off prey, hunters usually give up pretty quickly.

John lifts his head, his nose working hard as he looks toward the north woods. I can smell it too. Over the fragrance of fecund grass and swollen water and bog and sphagnum come the subtle scent of a half-dozen Pack and the overwhelming stench of salt and steel and blood and decay.

With a quick snap of his jaws, our Alpha sends our echelon's fastest wolf back to Home Pond for older reinforcements. John runs around to the north flank, closely followed by Solveig and Eudemos and the other newly minted leaders of the 14th. His forefeet are light on the damp grass, his hind legs ready to jump. Hunters don't come this far in. *This* is past the high gates and barbed fences and threatening signs and the trackless tangle of ancient, upended spruce and their young that are the reminders of a violent blowdown ten years ago.

The footsteps are soft and definitely human. Heel, the controlled curve along the outer rim of the foot. The toe barely grazing the grass. It is the footfall of someone used to stealth. I wouldn't have heard it at all, except for the occasional stumble.

Solveig's haunches tighten in front of me.

Finally, a man appears. He blends in with the night, so it is only when he walks into the moonlit clearing that we can see him. Sometimes we say someone has a heart or an ego or an appetite "as big as night."

But this tall, broad-shouldered human is really as big as night.

He pauses for a moment before threading his way through the wolves and lowering his body into the center of the Clearing. He crosses his jeans-clad legs. His feet are bare. Aside from a dark jacket, he has only two things:

A gun and a gaping hole in his stomach.

Chapter 2

"I KNOW WHO YOU ARE, AND I WON'T HURT YOU," THE stranger says in a voice that is cool and hard and perfectly calibrated to reach even to the outer ring of the wolves who were following him. "This." His hand caresses the gun. "This is just for protection."

As soon as John gives a nod, I start forward. When I am wild, I am a strong tracker. More importantly, I am expendable. If the man shoots me, then we will know what he's up to. He is armed and will kill many of us. And though he will eventually die, the careful ordering of our Pack will be undone.

His eyes lock on mine, and he slowly moves his hand to his knee so I can see that he's not touching the gun.

I creep close, starting with the wound. He has been clawed and not by one wolf; I can make out at least three different scents. They circled him and came at him from different directions.

For us, only the most heinous crimes warrant a disemboweling. But the *Slitung*, flesh-tearing, is a solemn ritual, not butchery. Every muzzle must be bloodied, so the tragedy of a life that we have failed is borne by all.

This man may not look it, but he is extraordinarily lucky. There is damage to the fascia and muscles, and while there is blood—and a lot of it—there is not the distinctive smell of a gut wound. Those things are hard to repair and go septic quickly.

Lifting my nose to the spot behind his ear, I almost gag at the overwhelming human smell of steel and death. But before I recoil, I catch the scent of something else. Snorting out air to get a clear hit, I try again. It's faint but it's here—crushed bone and evergreen—and it's wild.

There's only one creature in the world that smells both human and wild, and it is the creature we fear most.

Shifters are like us, but not. We can all of us change. But *we* cannot always change back. We are the children of the Iron Moon, and for three days out of thirty, we must be as we are now. It doesn't matter what you're doing—putting coolant in the backup generator, coming back late on the Grand Isle ferry (retrieving the car required some explaining)—Death and the Iron Moon wait for no wolf.

It is our great strength and our great weakness. We depend on one another. We support one another. Without the Pack, we are feral strays, trapped in a human world without words or opposable thumbs.

Shifters can always shift. They are opportunists. They used to change back and forth as it suited them, but now that humans are top predator, it suits them to be human. Like humans, they are narcissistic, self-delusional, and greedy. But they can scent things that humans can't, and they are dangerous hunters.

They know what we are, and in these past centuries, our numbers have been decimated by Shifters coming upon a Pack during the Iron Moon and slaughtering us with their human weapons.

There is something else, though, about this Shifter's deeply buried wild. Something more familiar than simply wolf. Moving close to where the scent is most concentrated, I suck in a deep breath.

"Found something you like?"

Snarling, I back awkwardly away from his crotch, but moving backward at a crouch makes my bad leg turn under, and the pain tears through my hip. Bone grinds against bone, and I stumble.

"A runt *and* a cripple?"

I flash my fangs at him. I may be a runt *and* a cripple, but I am still a wolf, damn it. John and Solveig and Demos sniff at my muzzle and immediately know what I know. Ears flatten, fur bristles, forefeet are planted, haunches bend under, and a menacing rumble spreads through powerful chests.

"Yes, my father is Shifter, but my mother is…was… Pack-born. Mala Imanisdottir."

I knew it. I knew he smelled familiar. John sniffs my muzzle again, scenting for proof of his ancestry.

"I challenged our leader, and I lost. I escaped his first attempt to kill me, but I won't escape another." His mind seems to wander, and then, with a real effort, he focuses again. "My father told me to escape. Find you. You are my last chance."

John looks out across his Pack, now bolstered with the older echelons. He snaps at the air over one shoulder and orders the Pack home. Mala or no Mala, this is the Great North Pack, not a sanctuary. The enormous Shifter will bleed out, eaten by the coyotes who even now are signaling to each other that there is something big and dying. They won't come near us, but as soon as we are gone, they will move in.

Solveig growls softly, calling me to heel. I hadn't

realized how far ahead they had gotten. I stumble after her with my tail between my legs.

"The runt," the man calls between panted breaths. "She's not mated?"

Without turning, John stops.

"My mother said that the Pack would accept a lone wolf if there was another willing lone wolf." A short cough tightens his face in pain. "She told my father," he says. His skin is graying, and the circles beneath his eyes are so dark. "Before she died. She told my father."

There is some truth in what the Shifter says. *Some*. Unfortunately, none of us has the paper, the pencil, the voices, or the hands to sit him down and explain the complexities.

John motions me toward him and rests his head on my shoulders. He's so huge and comforting. His smell is the smell of home, and I can't imagine not being surrounded by him. He represents protection from the outside and order at home.

He butts me lightly with his nose. The stranger doesn't know the complexities, but I certainly do. The choice is mine. If I return with my Pack, the stranger will die and I will be a *nidling*. As low as it is, I will have my place within the Pack.

But if I stay...

Then I am gambling that this Shifter and I are strong enough to fight for—and win—a *full* place in the Pack. It is a gamble, though, because if we can't, both of us are exiled. He will be no worse off, but I will careen from bad decision to bad decision, ending up in the same damn puddle of blood and/or vomit as Ronan.

The enormous Shifter weaves in our midst. I run back

and sniff at him. He's lost a lot of blood, but he looks really strong, and with a little help, he should make it. He lifts his head, and for the first time, I see his face. He's darker than John's mate, Evie, but where her eyes are pure black, his are black shot through with shards of gold.

He whispers something that even my sensitive ears must strain to catch.

"Runt?" he murmurs. "I don't want to die." Then he collapses into the grass.

The Pack is already filtering out of the Clearing. Demos gives a curious sniff of the prone body and snarls. He swings his fat head, hitting my backside, telling me to get a move on.

Maybe if he hadn't done that, I'd have crouched down and followed. This is my world, and the Pack is my life, but I haven't put this much work into surviving only to spend the rest of my life obeying every snarky whim of a thuggish half-wit like Eudemos.

I nip at his ear, the universally understood signal—at least among Pack, it's universally understood—to go fuck yourself. I shake out my back and straighten my tail and walk as tall as I can back to the Shifter. I lay my head across his shoulder.

John takes one look along his flank and starts to run. The Pack follows quickly until they are nothing but the occasional flicker of fur among the spruce.

Except for the low, slow plaintive cry of the loon on Clear Pond, it is silent. Then comes the reverberating howl signaling that John is home. The wolves stationed at the perimeter take up the howl.

"We are," they say.

I'd cry if I could, but I can't. I'd howl if I could, just to say *Me too*, but I can't.

All I can do is nudge the huge mound collapsed in a damp hollow of the Clearing. Early fall nights in the Adirondacks are too cold for humans, especially lightly clothed, partially eviscerated ones. It takes a few nips to find a good purchase on his jacket, then I lock it between my jaws. I don't like the plastic taste, but I pull anyway. In fits and starts, I move his inert bulk to a slight rise where it's not so damp, but there's no way that either the jacket or I are going to be able to make it much farther.

After pulling on the jacket to cover as much of his body as possible, I curl around him, giving him the warmth of my body.

The moon shines down on the Clearing. This is a place for a Pack, not for a single wolf on her own, and it feels exposed and huge and empty. Not to mention damp.

A coyote creeps closer, picked out by the moon. I jump up, straddling the body with my shoulders hunched and my fur bristling so I look larger. I growl in the way John would—or Tara or Evie or Solveig or any of dominant wolves would—and hope.

The coyote hesitates and then retreats. I settle back, covering more of this man's big body with my smaller one. As I drop my head to his broad chest, a warm sigh ripples through my fur.

I wish the loon would shut up.

Terms used in the Legend of All Wolves

***Æcewulf*:** Forever wolf. Real wolf. The Iron Moon moves Pack along the spectrum of their wildness. Pack who are already wild at the beginning of the Iron Moon are pushed farther along and become *æcewulfs*. There is no changing back.

bedfellow: A kind of mate-in-training. Since Pack couplings are based on strength, bedfellows must be prepared to fight challengers for rights to their bedfellow's body: *cunnan-riht*.

***Bredung*:** The ceremony by which two Pack are mated. It comes from the Old Tongue word for *braiding* and symbolizes the commitment of an individual to mate, and to land, and to Pack. The commitment is iron-clad.

***Cunnan-riht*:** Mounting rights.

***Dæling*:** The ceremony that determines both the initial hierarchy and pairings of an echelon. Since challenges are a fact of Pack life, the hierarchy established at a *Dæling* may change over time.

***Eardwrecca*:** Banished. Packs are intensely social and exiles rarely survive.

echelon: An age group, typically of Pack born within five or six years of one another. Each echelon has its own hierarchy. Its Alpha is responsible to the Alpha of the whole pack.

***Gemyndestow*:** The memory place. A circle of stones with the names of dead wolves and the dates of their last hunts.

Gran: An elder. The word does not imply blood relationship, as family ties are relatively inconsequential in the face of the stronger ties of Pack.

Iron Moon: The day of the full moon and the two days surrounding it. During these three days, the Pack is wild and must be in wolf form.

lying-in: Pack's mutable chromosomes mean that pregnancy is rare. When it does happen, the last month is fraught as pups change into babies and back again. The mother must change with them before her body rejects them. It is exhausting.

***nidling*:** A lone wolf at the bottom of an echelon's hierarchy. Because lone wolves are considered disruptive, the *nidling* is forced into a kind of indentured servitude to his or her Alpha pair. They rarely last long.

Offland: Anywhere that is not Homelands, the Great North's territory in the Adirondacks. Offlanders return to Homelands only for the Iron Moon and the occasional holiday.

Pack: What humans would call werewolves. Pack can turn into wolves at any time and often choose to be in wolf form, but during the Iron Moon, they *must* be wild. These three days are both their greatest weakness and, because it binds them together, their greatest strength.

***schildere*:** A shielder is a protector, the lowest degree of wolf pairing. From the Old Tongue. In the youngest Pack, shielders protect one another from being eaten by coyotes.

seax: The dagger worn by all full-fledged adult Pack when at Homelands.

***Slitung*:** Flesh-tearing. The ultimate punishment. Every wolf participates so that the whole Pack bears responsibility for the life they have failed.

Shifter: Shifters are not bound by the Iron Moon, and since humans are dominant, Shifters see no advantage in turning into something as vulnerable as a wolf. Unfortunately, they have adopted many of humans' less-desirable traits, while retaining the strength and stronger senses of a wolf-changer—the worst of both worlds for Pack. In the Old Tongue, they are called *Hwerflic*, meaning changeable, shifty.

***Wulfbyrgenna*:** The wolf tombs. It is what the Pack calls the coyotes who eat their remains.

Year of First Shoes: This is the first year during which pups start changing into skin and, as the name implies, the year they start wearing shoes and clothes. It marks their transition from pups to juveniles.

Acknowledgments

As this project has gone on, I find myself with more people to thank. People like Jeaniene Frost and Terry Spear and Amanda Bouchet, truly great writers who lent their enthusiasm to an unknown writer. Of course, I am enduringly grateful to the women of Sourcebooks—Susie Benton, Heather Hall, Laura Costello, and Beth Sochacki—who have always been kind and patient and there when I needed them. A special shout-out to Stefani Sloma, whose unflagging support for these books has left me speechless, though still capable of sending bullet point emails. To Dawn Adams, who threaded a camel through the eye of the needle and came up with the most perfect covers for the series. To my fantastic editor, Deb Werksman, who has been endlessly patient and encouraging. And, of course, to my perfect agent, Heather Jackson, who believed.

Thank you.

About the Author

Maria Vale is a logophile and a bibliovore and a worrier about the world. Trained as a medievalist, she tries to shoehorn the language of Beowulf into things that don't really need it. She currently lives in New York with her husband, two sons, and a long line of dead plants. No one will let her have a pet.